REQUIEM FOR IDOLS
and
YOU'RE BEST ALONE

Also by Norah Lofts

With Margery Weiner:

Norah Lofts

REQUIEM FOR IDOLS

and

YOU'RE BEST ALONE

1981
Doubleday & Company, Inc.
Garden City, New York

ISBN: 0-385-01768-5
Library of Congress Catalog Card Number 78–22817

REQUIEM FOR IDOLS originally published in Great Britain
by Methuen & Co. Ltd., 1938.
YOU'RE BEST ALONE originally published in Great Britain
in 1943 by Macdonald & Co., Ltd.
This volume is fully protected under the terms
of the International Copyright Union.

CONTENTS

REQUIEM FOR IDOLS

CONTENTS

Part I

COMING

I came back to London in the third week of August at the tail end of a heat-wave. London was empty and smelt of dust and petrol. I realised how clever it was of Dahlia to delay her return for a week or two. I telephoned four people, one ofter the other. Three were away, and the fourth was just leaving for Denmark. "Come too," he said—he was a kind person—"there's a good party of us, and it's God's chosen country at the moment." I said, "Thanks, but I'm only this minute back. I've got a lot to do. I'll be all right. I'll look into Monty's tonight, there'll surely be somebody there."

But Monty's was empty, too, except for a few people up from the country. Not a soul I knew. And the coffee wasn't fit to drink. I went back to my hotel. The light was wrongly placed for reading in bed, and the chambermaid hadn't given me the third pillow I'd asked her for; and it was then, at that moment, that I made up my mind to get back to my flat, or failing that another —anything, anywhere so that I could be on my own.

And then next morning I went down Regent Street. It was a bright morning, though not so hot, and over the grey curve of stone there was the blue curve of the sky. I walked along looking at it, and quite suddenly nostalgia had me by the throat and I was madly planning a thing I should have scoffed at forty-eight hours before. I was going to have a house of my own, and it wasn't going to be in London.

I bought a paper and took it into the park, meaning to work straight through the lists of houses for sale. And then the miracle happened. From the place where it was humbly tucked away the name of the house leaped up at me, the first words I read on the whole of that page. And although it set my heart racing it left my mind untouched by anything but scorn for my own credulity. Even as my eyes flew over the rest of the advertisement I thought, after all, the pedlars covered England in their journeys, and every village had a green, so there must be hundreds of Pedlar's Greens up and down the country. But by that time I had read the remaining lines and knew that this Pedlar's Green was indeed the one. "Well, hell!" I said, and in my astonishment spoke aloud, for the woman at the other end of the seat looked at me sharply.

I folded the paper and tucked it under my arm and started up the path at a trot. In the street I waved frantically to a taxi-driver and gave him the house agent's address in a voice that shook. It isn't every day that you come up against a coincidence so startling as to seem miraculous. Within an hour I had made up my mind to buy a house in the country and been offered the one house of all others that I would have chosen, the house that I had left, blind with crying, eighteen years ago. I shouldn't have believed it if it had happened to any one else: I couldn't believe that it had happened to me.

Either my excitement or recent experience in America made the taxi seem dreadfully slow, and when at last I reached the place and explained my business the people seemed worse than slow, suspicious. They seemed to think that I ought to want to see it first and then proceed gently, step by step, to the business of buying. They were probably right. I hadn't seen the place for eighteen years; God knew what innovations had been made, what dilapidations had taken place in that time. But I wanted it to belong to me at once. I'm like that. If I want a thing I want it then and there. That is why I am so invariably badly dressed. I get up on a bright morning and think I want a thin frock. I go to a likely shop. There isn't one the colour I want; but the frock I like, and that fits me, can be made in that colour and delivered in a week. Hell, I think, and buy the right frock in the wrong colour. And since I do the same with shoes and hats and handbags, it's easy to see why I never have, and never shall have, anything approaching what they call an *ensemble*.

Anyway, I'd never bought a house before and wasn't familiar with the formalities.

"I'll give you a cheque now," I told the man, "and then I can start moving in today."

He didn't seem to like the idea at all, and it occurred to me that perhaps he suspected my cheque.

"Would you like me to go and get the cash?"

He didn't jump at that either. By that time I was furious.

"Do you want to sell this house?" I asked him.

"Of course. Naturally."

"Have you any reason for not wanting me to have it?"

"Of course not."

"Then take this cheque and give me the keys."

"But," he said with the air of explaining something to a fractious child, "the keys are not here. They're down at Little Swything—at the post office. Now if I give you an order to view . . ."

"All right," I said, "have it your own way. Only remember it's my house from now on. Nobody else is to step in and buy it while I'm trotting about viewing it."

An acid smile came across his face.

"I don't *think* that there's any danger. Pedlar's Green has been for sale for over four years. That's why it's so cheap."

I rushed around to the garage where, before I went away, I had left my car with instructions that it was to be kept in order and that Madge or Benny could use it as they wished. Both Madge and Benny were away—I knew that from my telephoning—so it would be there, and if it wasn't all ready for the road somebody was going to hear something. But it was; it was even clean. Benny always distrusts garages and says that garage men are the spiritual heirs of the horse-copers of an older day. But I have never found it so.

It was grand to order "petrol" and to be understood. It was grand to have the familiar wheel in my hands. It was grand to go slipping along Hendon Way and to obey the sign that said, "Fork right for St. Albans and the North." Dear Suffolk, I haven't seen you in eighteen years and the harvest will be in your fields.

It was only August, and the sun was shining from a sky the colour of harebells, but the year was already menaced. There was no brightness in the green of the heavy foliage and the hard purple knapweeds were all that were left of the summer's wealth of flowers. But the passing of summer never saddened me, because I like the autumn.

I like the flare of colour in the trees, the asters and dahlias and sturdy zinnias on the barrows, and the autumn clothes in the shops. I like winter, too. It's a good season if you're properly fed and clothed and aren't hag-ridden as Penelope is, by the thought of people who are less fortunate.

Penelope is just a little mad. You often hear people say in praise of someone, "He'd give you the coat off his back," but Pen is the only person I've ever known literally to do it. She'd come up to London on business one bitterly cold day and we met and went to a matinée in the afternoon. She had a new coat for the occasion, the nicest coat she'd ever had, black, with some fur on the collar and down the front. When we came out of the theatre a woman who was selling heather or something like that appealed to us. I'd got used to passing such people without much thought in the days when every penny was important to me, but that afternoon I was in funds and feeling cheerful because of having had Pen to myself for a little while, so I fished out a half-crown, and knowing that Pen wouldn't have any money to spare, said out of the corner of my mouth, "That's all right." But Pen wouldn't come away. She put her hand in her pocket and brought out a return half-ticket, four stamps, and a shilling. She made a little face at them and then held them out to me. "Hang on to these," she said, and then and there, in the middle of the crowd coming out of the theatre, she took off the new coat and hung it over the woman's shoulders. Then she dashed away up the street with me behind her. The icy wind pressed the sleeves of her shabby blouse against her arms. "You are a mad fool," I said when I'd caught her. "There was no need to do that. She'll only sell it; your nice new coat."

"I don't give a damn what she does with it," said Pen through her chattering teeth. "She was *blue*."

It was quite true. The woman was blue, and Pen wasn't far off being. I shoved her into a taxi and gave her a coat to go home in. I scolded a bit, too, until she shut me up by saying something that showed me a little of what went on inside her.

"It was cowardice, really, Polly. I'd so far rather be cold myself than have the agony of imagining what it must feel like to be so cold."

"I see," I said. "But I'd a damn sight sooner have given her the one you have now and saved that new one."

"You couldn't have been sure of finding her again," Pen said simply.

I remembered that little episode, and thought, as I saw signs of summer's ending that day, that winter in the North, in a distressed area, must be pretty average hell for Penelope.

The car is a good one, not showy or streamlined; just a heavy powerful two-seater with its value in the engine, and when at last I turned off the road to the North there was plenty of room where she could stretch herself. It was still early in the afternoon when I slowed down to pass through Stoney Market, the ancient little gathering of houses and shops and schools that had always been "town" to us. It looked very much the same, though there were traffic signals where the Haymarket crossed the Tollgate; and a new cinema, very smart in black stone and chromium, seemed to challenge the old Market Cross in the Square. I caught a glimpse of Mr. Woolworth's peculiar brand of scarlet, too, as I drove past the end of the Pinnery.

Once out of Stoney I was in my own country, flat and fertile, with low hawthorn hedges and great elm trees. The last of the corn was being carted and some of the trees by the roadside were hung with strands of wheat and barley that had brushed off as the loaded wagons passed beneath. My heart really raced with excitement. It was far more thrilling than seeing a pre-view of a picture that I'd had a hand in. When I caught sight of the square tower of Little Swything church peeping over the trees, I had trouble with my breathing.

I drew up at the post office and went into the little dark place that smelt of bacon and soap and tobacco and the leather of the heavy boots that hung in bunches like fruit awaiting the needs of a farm-labourer who still shopped at home.

"I believe," I said to the fat woman, who moved with some difficulty in the narrow space behind the counter, "that you have the keys to Pedlar's Green."

"Well," she said in a comfortably oiled voice, "I did have. But it's so long since anybody asked for them. . . . I don't quite know . . . I'll see."

She fumbled about, rooting behind boxes and bottles and under papers. As the hunt grew more desperate she breathed harder and harder. I thought of an amiable pig in search of an edible root. But this waste of time did not, for some reason, annoy me like the house agent's hesitation had done. At last she said, unnecessarily, "I don't seem to be able to lay my hands on them. I must think."

She retired behind the post office end of the counter and held a meeting with herself. Very effective. Suddenly she said in a most relieved tone, "I got it. They was the ones I put down our Fred's back time he had the nose bleed." She disappeared through the doorway, and in a comparatively short time came back triumphant, and the cold iron met my impatient palm.

Front door, back door, side door. Familiar to me as my face: labelled in typed letters on dirty labels bearing the house agent's names. My God, anybody could have had them—our keys! Every night father had gone round and turned them in the locks. Or, if Penelope or Megan were going to be late (I was never late, being only a child then) the front-door key was laid in the candlestick on the chest in the hall to remind the late-comer to use it. You couldn't have carried it up in the candlestick, however absent-minded you might be; it was too heavy, a jailer's key almost. My key!

I thanked her quickly. Neither of us mentioned orders to view or anything about returning the keys. I ran out to the car and in a palsy of impatience turned into the lane that led to Pedlar's

Green. Within five minutes I came to a standstill on the wide rough grass border that lay between its gate and the rutty lane.

I sat still for a moment, just looking at it. It was just like my memory of it but smaller, as things are to the adult eye. It was much overgrown, rather like the castle where the enchanted beauty had slept for a hundred years. The shrubbery had thickened enormously; I could see by the pallor of the leaves that the laurels hadn't been cut back for years, yet even now it looked far smaller and lighter than it had done in the old days when it had been my mental concept of a forest and I had imagined all sorts of terrors in its dusty depths. The eight poplars, four on either side the gate, still rose straight and slim, their heart-shaped leaves quivered so that as the undersides turned to expose their grey the whole tree seemed to change colour.

Beyond the poplars and the stretch of neglected garden stood the low house. The windows were almost completely overgrown with creeper just about to change colour, or with climbing rose sprays where the last frail buds were growing side by side with the withered remains of the flowers that had bloomed earlier in the year. There was moss on the thatch, that was itself riddled with sparrows' holes. Could anybody thatch in these days, I wondered; and to what extent had the neglect, so apparent from the outside, crept within?

I stepped out on to the overgrown grass border of the lane and laid my hand on the gate. It had once been painted white, but it was chipped and stained now, and the suns of several summers had raised blisters which had peeled off, leaving the naked wood exposed. I took out my little notebook and scribbled "Paint"; that was the first thing. Gallons and gallons of paint, white wherever possible, and not too shiny. So I wrote it down. I intended to be very methodical. Method is a virtue that I admire very much because it makes life easier. Every New Year I made a resolution to be methodical, but the numerous muddles into which I floundered proved to me, repeatedly and clearly, that I hadn't yet attained the art. However, over each new piece of work I resolve again; so now, book in hand, I set out to survey my kingdom. Almost immediately I added, "Catch to front gate," for the catch and the mouldered wood that had held it had come off in my hand. The hinges weren't so good either, I reflected, for the gate had sunk, and as I pushed it inwards it scraped up a long velvety fold of moss that had gathered on the gravel. Amongst the tangled undergrowth of the garden there were a few vivid marigolds that had seeded themselves and looked as tough and wild as weeds.

I stepped on to the damp-greened doorstep and fitted the great key into the lock. It turned with a screech, the door stuck for a moment and then yielded. The musty scent of an old tree-surrounded house, long empty, met me. I sniffed at it. I found it neither disturbing nor depressing. It was indeed the right smell, the smell that there had always been in the cupboard under the stairs where we had kept our rubber boots and hoops and skates, and, later on, our hockey sticks. Racquets were never kept there because the damp rotted the gut. I remembered that the word "gut" was only used once with reference to rackets—Mother objected to it strongly and always spoke of "string."

The house had altered very little. Somebody had put in electric light from the grid that crossed the fields at the back of the house, and some of the papers had been changed—not greatly for the better, I thought; but in eighteen years some of the back premises had not even received a coat of whitewash, and in the attic where we had sometimes played on wet days there were our heights marked on the wall and labelled with our names and the date: Penelope Millican Field, Megan Millican Field, Phyllis Millican Field. The pompous young signatures of Pen, Meg, and Polly. I looked at them with amusement. And the amusement surprised me a little. I had expected to feel—what? Sentiment? A wistfulness over the forgotten years? A yearning for the old family days? I don't know. Anyway, I felt none of them. I went around, filling my notebook and recognising things with pleasure and a certain feeling of excitement. I could imagine Madge saying, as she so often had done, "Polly, you're so *hard*." And my reply, "You have to be, in this hard world." And since no amount of yearning would bring back those days, since nothing will in Lamb's words "ring the bells backward," I surveyed the house with eyes on the future, what I would make of it, how to decorate and furnish, how gladly occupy it.

I opened every window, peeped into every cupboard, jumped on every squeaky board. Finally I climbed through the trapdoor to inspect the tank that supplied the bath. Then, warm and grimy, full of plans and utterly content, I sat down on the window-seat in the hall to smoke a cigarette and do a few sums in my head. In eighteen years I had had no place that I could rightly call "home." Other people's houses, grim lodgings, hotels of varying kinds, and a half share of a flat full of mirror glass, chromium plate, and scarlet leather, that was my record. God! What wouldn't I have here! Whiteness and space, dull surfaced walls and shiny wood, silver, thin china and fine linen, mirrors, cunningly placed, not just for show. The low, square, spacious rooms deserved all these, and so, I thought, did I.

I closed the windows again and locked the doors. Then I took the road to Stoney Market through the mellow afternoon, singing at the top of my untuneful voice. And that part of the day wasn't wasted either, for although only one person alive could have heard anything but noise in my singing, the tune was there and so were the words, and at night in the funny dark room at the pub I had chosen, before even I washed my hands, I scribbled the words and some marks that stood for accents on a piece of paper and set it aside for Dahlia.

II

Perhaps I ought to explain about Dahlia straight away. In fact I owe her that, for if there had been no Dahlia I should never have owned Pedlar's Green, or a roadster, or a reliable watch, or, in fact, any of the things that I do. When I met Dahlia we were both utterly down and out. I had three pound notes and some loose silver, so I was better off than she was, though when you're out of a job and have no immediate prospects of anything but scullery work in front of you, there isn't much difference between three pounds odd and a half-crown, which was all she had. I had just bought a paper, intending to look for some kind of work; and as it was a sleety, windy day, I couldn't study it in the street, and, besides, I'd had no breakfast, so I turned into a grub-shop place that looked dim and dirty and cheap.

There wasn't a spare table—there never is in a really cheap place—so the waitress pushed me into a chair at a table where a girl was already sitting. She'd got a pot of tea in front of her, but she hadn't poured any out yet. She sat there staring at the streaming windows and she had the most desolate expression that I've ever seen on any face. I looked at her at first with that guarded kind of hostility that English people show to strangers with whom they have to share feeding or travelling arrangements; and then I saw her misery and the fact that she was a half-caste, or a quadroon, or something of that kind, and my interest quickened.

I don't know why, but any suggestion of a trace of exotic blood in anybody fascinates me straight away, so while I waited for my coffee to cool I watched her from behind my paper. I'd forgotten all about looking for a job—which perhaps explains my character. Father, who was very familiar with his Bible, once said that I would have been a good Athenian, always running after "some new thing."

This girl looked awfully cold, as well she might, for she was wearing a little black suit, which, though it had been good and was well cut, was completely inadequate for wearing on such a day. Her face was small, and to my eyes extremely attractive, thin, hollow, unhappy, and the colour of very milky coffee. Her eyebrows were narrow, very black, silky; and under them the great dark eyes with curiously blue-tinted whites stared out unseeing, oblivious even of me and my badly concealed interest. Except for an untidy strand or two her hair was pushed away out of sight beneath an ugly old felt hat. She had no handbag, and when at last she drew herself together and went to pick up the teapot that stood in front of her, I saw her loosen the clenched fingers of one bony little hand and move what she was holding into the other. A half-crown and a small dark bottle.

She took a sip of the unsweetened, milkless tea, gave a little shudder, and reached for the sugar basin. I counted the lumps. Six, and then another was seven. Very swiftly and slyly she pulled the cork out of the bottle and tipped the contents into the syrupy tea.

I think I am the least psychic person in the world. I seldom dream, never have premonitions or anything like that, but as the cork came with a squeak out of the neck of that bottle a cold trickle went down my back. I shrugged my shoulders to get rid of the feeling. Hell, I thought, am I getting so jumpy that the sight of a girl taking a tonic or any other dope she happens to fancy is going to set me imagining things? Not likely. But all the time I knew. Something far deeper and wiser than my shoulder-shrugging reason knew quite positively that she was up to no good. Her clothes, her face, that one coin in her hand, her furtiveness, were all assurances that I didn't really need. Just as she reached her hand out to lift the cup I swept my paper over the table. The milk jug went over, the cup tilted, seemed to rock for an instant, and then fell to the floor with a crash.

The girl drew in her breath with a hissing sound and looked at me with the whites of her eyes showing like those of a frightened horse. People at nearby tables looked up and a waitress with an air of poisonous patience came hurrying with a dirty cloth.

"I'm awfully sorry," I said. "Just like my clumsiness. You'll let me order you some more, won't you?"

She shook her head.

"I don't want any more, now," she said; and her voice went to my heart. Deep it was, and velvety, with a sort of sob in it, just like the low note on a mellow violin. It was then, and is now, the loveliest voice I have ever had the fortune of hearing.

She put down the half-crown on the wet cloth and in one movement, it seemed, was out of her chair and at the shop door. I fumbled for a sixpence, threw it down, and followed her. The waitress yelped, "Your ticket, miss. Pay at the desk," but I waved my hand towards the table and rushed into the street. I caught hold of the girl by the elbow.

"Look here," I said breathlessly, "I dare say you think I'm clumsy and pushing, but I just couldn't help myself. I had to do it and I had to follow you."

She jerked her elbow and stalked on without answering. In a minute we were in the crush of the Strand. Feeling more of a fool every second, I renewed my grip of her sharp elbow and managed to keep beside her at the cost of a few black looks from the people that our ill-directed progress jostled. Then I saw a few interested glances and realised that the girl was crying. We were just at the mouth of a little quiet street, almost a cul-de-sac, and I braced my feet on the pavement and swung her out of the crowd. Just ahead of us a man came through the swing door of a public-house and inside I could see, before the door closed on it, the glow of a red roaring fire.

"Do stop crying for a moment," I said, holding out my handkerchief. "Whatever it is, short of the police being after you, I can cope with, if you'll let me. Now come in here and let's have a drink and get warm."

I'd completely forgotten that I was broke to the wide myself.

Compared with this thin, sobbing, little Negro girl I felt big and
solid and capable. I pushed the door with my shoulder and pulled
her inside.

We were very lucky. All the men in the place but one were
standing or perching on stools at the counter. The one who was
warming his behind at the fire moved away when we sat down on
the padded seat that ran along the wall by the fireplace. I pushed
her along so that she was in the range of the outflung heat, and
then I went to the counter and bought two double whiskies.

"Here you are, drink this," I said; "it's better than tea the way
you make it, so now I don't owe you anything and you can snap
out of it and tell me why you've spoilt my morning."

"It was nothing to do with you."

"True," I said with a grin of embarrassment, "but I didn't like
the look of your medicine. Tell me, was it medicine?"

"Only in the sense that somebody said the axe was—a cure for
all diseases."

"I thought so. And what on earth do you want to do *that* for?"

"I can't see what it is to do with you," she said stubbornly.

"Oh, nothing," I said. "Only you're young—and far too pretty
to go out that way."

She looked at me oddly.

"Women don't generally think other women pretty . . . or
bother about them if they are."

I laughed.

"Wrong again," I said. "I'm not that sort. I interfered, I'll
admit, and in return I'll do what I can to help you. God knows it
mayn't be much, but we may as well try. Drink your dope and
then tell me."

She poured down the whisky as though it were water, and she
thawed visibly in the heat of that wonderful fire, but it was a long
time before she would talk. However, I stuck at her and by alternate coaxing and bullying managed to get the gist of it, at least.
She'd been a singer—a good one, she said, and from hearing her
speak I could believe it. She'd been brought over from Kingston
by an agent of Joe Tolly, whose boast is, as you know, that he
rakes the world for talent. She'd starred in three shows, none of
which I'd seen, of course, and then she'd caught diptheria.

They'd had to perform tracheotomy to save her life, and when she was well again her singing voice was gone. She'd saved a little, not much, but something, and instead of hopping off home she'd hung about looking for work, which, as I knew, was scarce enough when you were white and had references and things. Down to rock bottom at last, and turned out of her room, she had been all ready to cash in when I knocked her cup over.

"Hell," I said, when I'd mastered the story. "Why kill yourself? Plenty of people waiting to do that for you. Big buses and things. What you've got to do, with little encouragement and in the face of opposition, is to keep yourself alive. I'd go on the streets before I'd kill myself."

Dahlia (she'd told me her name) shuddered. "I couldn't do that," she said.

"Well, I haven't any great fancy for it myself. I've done all kinds of things, but not that, yet. As a matter of fact I was just going to look up advertisements for parlourmaids and cook-housekeepers, though I cook like the devil. I don't think you'd quite do for that kind of thing, you're too decorative. What can you do?"

"Nothing, except with music. Once I got a job playing at a cinema. But they got a gramophone thing and didn't want us any more. Always it's like that. Not wanted."

She looked at me with those great tragic eyes, and suddenly, just like that, my brilliant idea took birth.

"Look here," I said, "how musical *are* you?"

"Very musical," she said simply.

"Can you write it?" She nodded. "I mean can you put down on that lined paper stuff notes that you've never seen, only heard?"

"Of course."

"Almighty God!" I said. Then I dropped my head in my hands and stared at the red cave of fire and I thought—if only it worked! God!

I made songs, you see. I'd been making songs since before I left school. The words would come into my head and I could hear the tune that came with them. It was there, whole and fitting, but I might just as well have tried to show somebody my left lung as to try to make another person know what the tune was. I just couldn't understand music, read it, or write it or even sing properly. And so there I was with a thousand songs in me, doomed to eternal silence so far as I could ever see. But now . . .

I tore the woolly scarf from my neck and wrapped it twice round Dahlia's, tucking the ends down like a bib inside her flimsy coat.

"Come on," I said. "I once heard a joke about Mr. Derry meeting with his Tom, but that is nothing to this meeting if you're as good as I think I am."

I stopped at three shops. At one I bought the smallest quantity of lined paper that they would sell me; at the next, four of the largest ham sandwiches they could cut; at the third, a packet of cigarettes and some matches. I'd given up smoking weeks before, but now I felt that inspiration must have its incense. Then I found a piano shop that let off rooms for practise, and hired one till six, when the shop shut. At ten minutes to six we staggered out of the place, blind and almost dumb with concentrated effort. The paper was full of the funny little squiggles that Dahlia had made with my fountain-pen: seven songs of the best.

It was still sleeting, and, Lord! I felt I wanted to pick her up and carry her to my room, she was so precious—wizard means nothing; genius doesn't touch it. I'd just sit down and say, "Now this song is called 'The World Is Too Much for Me.' It's kind of half mocking and half serious, if you can understand that, and it goes like this."

Then, in my quite tuneless voice, I'd chant it to her, bringing out the words clearly and emphasising the beat as I could hear it. And she'd fiddle about and strike odd notes with her head on one side as though she were listening to something that I couldn't hear. Then, presently, she'd play it through and I'd say, "Faster," or "Slower," or "A shade higher there." And suddenly it was all complete—just as it had always been in my dumb head. When she said at last, "I only wish I could sing some of these. I never had a song half so good," I was almost choked with excitement. So, humming and tinkling and scribbling, we got down seven songs before the shop closed; and then I took Dahlia home with me.

That evening I sent the manuscripts off. I knew exactly what to do with them, because I'd so often thought about what I would do if ever I learned to understand and write music. Only, of course, I never could have learned.

And now that I had cast upon the waters some bread that might conceivably return to me buttered, I gathered enough courage, or rather face, to write to Penelope, to ask her for a loan. She sent me ten pounds like a lamb, though heaven alone knew how she raised it, kept the room for us and bought us bread and coffee until somebody realised that the stuff was good, and after that it was just like a fairy-tale.

A successful song can bring in the money quicker than almost anything. It has so many angles. And I'd been making songs for so long that I had a great stock. Besides, now that the dumbness had lifted I could see a song in the slightest incident. They came flocking. I happened, for instance, to say to Dahlia, "You're my mascot. You're what I've been wanting all my life." And there it was, the germ of the biggest song hit of a decade. As easy as that.

My name being Phyllis and Dahlia's being what it is, we put the two together and called ourselves "Phyllida"; and if you will notice the window of any music-shop, or study a list of records of popular songs, and remember that we did all the songs for *Yesterday Calling* and *Sigh No More*, and had got our hooks into the film-song world as well, you will understand why I could buy Pedlar's Green and have it fit to live in in three weeks.

You will understand, too, perhaps, why I have given Dahlia the first place here.

III

For three weeks the house was full of men—plumbers and electricians, plasterers and painters. It was like a human ant-heap, and in the middle of the proceedings the whole thing looked such a muddle that I was seized with despair. I wandered about with no place to sit, I trod on wires and tripped over paint-tins—obviously a nuisance whose sole purpose was to make and serve out gallons of tea from water heated on an ill-disposed oil-stove. I removed myself at last and set out in search of furniture.

And it wasn't until then that I had any idea at all of reconstructing my home as I had known it. I ought to make quite clear —indeed, to emphasise that point—the past was finished, so far as I was concerned. I'd been happy there in the way that children are happy. I'd had enough to eat and wear, I had liked both my sisters and loved one. Mother's intimidating manner had not distressed, nor Father's other-world inefficiency irritated me as they would have done had I met with them later in life. But I didn't in the least mind altering the house or cutting down a tree or two in the overgrown garden. And I meant to buy all new furniture. Not chromium plate and scarlet leather. I'd had enough of that; but new stuff, solid and comfortable.

I went to shop after shop. I bought china and glass and cutlery. I "considered" dozens of different tables and chairs and beds. None pleased me. One day I drifted, almost by accident, into a

second-hand and antique furniture shop, and there suddenly I
was at home. A black old dresser, a bow-fronted chest, a rosewood
dining-table with thin brass splints to strengthen its corners, a
grandfather clock, made in Colchester in 1692, two dower chests,
a pew-like seat that might have been torn from church or inn—
these took more money than I had expected to spend on all my
stuff. But I had to have them, and when I found a work-table
with a faded green silk bag hanging down like a dropped stomach
and claimed that for my own, I realised that these were all things
whose very close relations, at least, had stood in the rooms when I
was a child. The hunt was on.

Every day I went out with unabated greed, and my store in the
barn grew daily, as though every day a fresh grandmother had
died and left me all her household goods. I avoided, I hope, the
obvious and the ugly, though I did admit a reproduction if it
were made with care and skill. I enjoyed that shopping. I met
some curious people, too: old men mostly, with odd interesting
bits of historical knowledge tucked away in their unprepossessing
and often rather dirty heads.

When I gave my attention to the house again it was miraculously clear and calm. The lights and the stoves and the handles
worked, the doors and windows opened easily and closed securely,
the white paint shone, the rough white paper was ready to be an
unobtrusive and flattering background for my findings, the dark
stain lay ready for my coloured rugs. Help, that was the next
thing.

The last maid we had had there, the one who had been trained
by Mother and had remained to look after Father and me, had
been a girl named Agnes, a big, fresh-coloured youngster with a
crop of freckles and carroty hair. Her home was in the village, and
I thought that I would begin by calling there and asking Mrs.
Porter, Agnes's mother, if she knew any one who would at least
help me move in.

Mrs. Porter, whom I dimly remembered, came, as I thought, to
the door. It was ridiculous, of course, but I had forgotten those
eighteen years.

I addressed the woman as Mrs. Porter. I was aware of a certain
stiffening, and she said coldly:

"I'm Mrs. Turner. My mother, as was Mrs. Porter, has been dead five years."

I looked rather more closely, and then, greatly daring, said, "Agnes. I don't suppose you remember me, do you? Phyllis Field. I used to live at Pedlar's Green, and I've come back."

"No, I shouldn't have known you."

"You've altered, too," I said foolishly.

There was an awkward kind of silence. A bit haltingly, in the face of Agnes's unmoving expression, I explained what I had come for.

"Only for the move?"

"Well, really, I want somebody who can cook a bit. There'll only be myself, most of the time, anyway."

"I'll come," said Agnes, still without a glimmer of expression. "I'm looking for a job—only, there's the boy; most people 'on't have him."

"Your little boy?"

Agnes nodded. "He ain't so little, he's five and he's quiet, only people 'on't believe it."

"I don't mind a bit. And he needn't be so quiet, there's plenty of room there, as you know."

"Answer to prayer, this is," said Agnes, without joy. "Cissie and me had a set-to this morning. She don't want me here, and I don't want to be here. Shall we come now?"

I looked at my watch. It was almost noon.

"Yes," I said, "we can get the beds set up and so on. I've got a couple of men moving stuff in now. Shall I wait and drive you up?"

"Yes," said Agnes. She turned into the house, leaving the door open, and I went to sit in the car. Voices reached me. ". . . going now this minute. Told you I would."

"Taking your bastard with you, I hope."

A tumult of shouts. Cissie? The younger sister who used to carry washing. Bastard? Only by courtesy "Mrs. Turner" then. Dear, dear Agnes! And how awful for the little boy, who would soon notice what names he was called. A crude people. In a surprisingly short time Agnes reappeared, a bulging wicker dress-basket with a strap round its middle in one hand, with the other dragging a small, doleful-looking little boy with a cropped head of almost white hair, and prominent teeth.

"Tommy," said Agnes, by way of introduction.

I smiled at him and said, "Hullo, Tommy," but no answering smile appeared on the small face. He looked at me stonily and allowed himself to be seated upon his mother's rather inhospitable-looking lap. A pathetic, unwanted scrap of humanity, I thought, wronging Agnes, who, I later discovered, loved him with a fierce if rather uncomfortable love.

Agnes only volunteered one remark to me in the course of the hours that we worked together. The improvements that I pointed out to her with rather childish pride elicited no more than a grunt, whether of approval or the reverse I couldn't have said; but when I came across from the barn with the work-table clutched to my stomach the stony expression of her face just cracked a trifle, as she said, "That always stood in your ma's bedroom." I did not tell her that it was not, to my knowledge, the same. It might have been.

I brooded a little over Agnes as I ate my supper of eggs and bacon, cooked on my own stove, at my own table. What had happened to turn that big, cheerful, raucous, grinning girl into this dumb and doleful woman? Was it simply what the village would call "her trouble," or was it natural development? I thought of the number of times that Mother had had to rebuke her for singing so loudly in the kitchen that the whole house was disturbed, and sighed a little. Mother would so much have preferred "Mrs. Turner," and I would rather have had Agnes.

It was a mild evening, so mild that one was acutely conscious of the early darkening. I wandered out into the garden, the spark of my lighted cigarette going before me, and I thought of bulbs in hundreds, and of flowering shrubs that would bloom, one after the other, from March to August. Daphne first, flowering before the first leaf unfolded, pink almond, prunus, lilac, laburnum, syringa, hydrangea, fuchsia, and buddleia. Roses in the June twilights opening their hearts. I think I touched the peak of existence that night. The freshness and the accomplishment of beauty within awaiting me, and the promise without.

And I was young—though I didn't think consciously of that at that moment, and I'd been very lucky. My windows, lighted and uncurtained, shone for me. I thought, "I have lighted a hearth." I hadn't exactly, but I thought of it. And I twisted other words round the thought. It would make a song. Only, of course, it would have to be "*We* have lighted a hearth," and then it would appeal to all the couples who *had* got some sort of a home of their own, and it would wring the hearts of all the people who wanted one. In short, it would be a popular song. Toying with it, I went in at the kitchen way.

"Tommy asleep?" I asked conversationally.

"Yes. He go to bed early," said Agnes.

"Well, I hope you'll both be happy here."

"I hope so."

Not a spark, not a spark. Agnes didn't like me. I thought, but dismissed the idea as imagination, that her eye fell disapprovingly on my cigarette. A few days later when Agnes broke silence to mention Mother, and ended, "She was a lady, your ma was," I understood it all. I had fallen short of the standard that Mrs. Field's daughter should have measured to. I smoked, I drank, I swore, I wore pyjamas. *O tempora, O mores!*

Except for Agnes, whom I could have wished more cheerful, but who was an excellent cook (gloomy people often are, most surprisingly) and a willing servant, I was perfectly, almost idiotically, happy at Pedlar's Green for a whole month. There were still things to buy. I bought four dogs. After eighteen years of frustration I could indulge my passion for dogs. Method failed me again there. I meant to buy only recognised kinds, and began with a Scotch terrier, called Block, and a little smooth dachshund with an unpronounceable name which I altered to Velvet. Then one day, going through the market at Stoney, I saw two little pups in a cage. It was a warm day, one of those that come suddenly in September to remind one of Keats' "Ode to Autumn." Their tongues were hanging out; they had no water in the cage; and some children were trying to poke them out of their lethargy with sticks. I bought the pair for seven and sixpence. They were both mongrels, but I didn't really mind, because it was so fascinating to see a collie tail wave from a whippet hindquarters, and a spaniel's curly ears frame a long greyhound face. One was a bitch, and I did have some misgivings about what the third and fourth generations would look like after the two pedigree gentlemen had added their quota, but the time for bothering about that hadn't yet arrived. They were all very happy, and so was I.

It was lovely to wake in the white-walled, beamed bedroom and lie looking at the dark edges of the copper beech against the pale sky, waiting for Agnes to come up with the tea. She would open the door, and a flood, it seemed, of dogs would come pouring in, all bright eyes and wet noses and waving tails. I would give them biscuits out of the tin that I kept on a shelf near by. I drank my tea, bathed, and dressed in easy stages, playing with the dogs, looking out of the window, reading an odd page of my book, jotting down a line for a song. After breakfast I took the dogs out into the fields. The blackberries were ripe and shone richly black against their reddening leaves. Block would sometimes sight a rabbit and set off after it, looking like a cut-down rocking-horse in motion. The others followed. They never caught anything. After that I got the car out and went into the town, or drove idly through little-used country lanes.

Evening came all too soon, and at that season there was a bloom on it as there is on a grape. Sometimes after dinner I walked again, or saw a picture at the little cinema in Stoney. I like pictures, even bad ones offer you something. Sometimes I stayed in and read or played my gramophone.

It sounds a dull life, but to me it was delightful. To be able to do just what I liked, when I liked; to be able to have the kind of food I wanted, not the sort that some one else had chosen; to be able to arrange my own flowers even—to me these were all poignant pleasures. I fed fat my ancient grudge against penury and exile.

But there came an evening, the kind that every recluse must know, when I yearned for some one to talk to. It was a coldish evening and I held a match to the fire and drew the curtains. There was a nagging wind, too, that flung handfuls of brittle leaves against the windows. I thought, tonight I will indulge my shameful taste for hackneyed music. I opened my gramophone, and then, ignoring my new records, went upstairs for my old ones.

I fished out "Valse Triste," "Finlandia," and "The Lute Player," my old, and much begibed favourites.

Every single one was cracked. I swore. I felt just like a hungry person who has been offered a savoury dish, tasted it in anticipation, and had it snatched away. "Finlandia" had the slightest crack, and I put it on, determined to ignore the little recurrent click. Music without words to me is a dead thing, and though I had fitted some of my own to "Valse Triste," I had chosen Humbert Wolfe's "You, too, at midnight, suddenly awakening," for "Finlandia." "The Lute Player" had its own.

An orgy, deliberate and self-imposed, of sentiment.

> You, too, at midnight, suddenly awakening,
> May wonder, if you hear a step outside,
> Until your heart replies, what set it aching;
> And listen knowing that your heart has lied.

I was just thinking, my God, this is a mistake. I haven't gone through this since . . . when the lid of the gramophone, insecurely poised, crashed down. Bits of poor "Finlandia" spattered out over the floor and the rest grated together as the table of the machine went on revolving.

I said "Hell!" and burst out laughing. It served me right. It was the best thing that could have happened. God bless that gramophone! I picked up the pieces and dropped them into the wastepaper basket. I held "The Lute Player" and "Valse Triste," one in either hand, and smote them together so that their fragments followed the others. So perish all traitors!

A good absorbing job, I told myself, is what you want. And there was one to hand. I had not yet written to either of my sisters to tell them the news about the house. I replenished the fire, filled my fountain-pen, hunted out the last letters I had received from them, sent actually for my birthday, and settled down to strengthen family ties and issue invitations.

They had always been known as "the girls." "The girls are coming home tomorrow," "The girls want half a crown each for a subscription," "The girls send their love to you, Polly." Pen was a little over eight when I was born, and Megan was nearly seven.

They were, quite literally, gods to me, Penelope especially. How far that was due to premature insight into a really sterling character, and how far due to the fact that even Mother seldom found fault with Pen, I cannot say. Now that we were all grown up, and past our first youth at that, the eight and seven years between us made little difference, but when we were children the gulf was wide and deep. They were always very good to me, and in many ways I profited in the early years by being the last of the family. Privileges that had cost them bitter struggles to attain, our mother being very old-fashioned, fell to me by right of custom; and I inherited their outgrown clothes and sports gear without having the cost thrown up at me as they had.

Penelope was clever: one of my earliest recollections is of being taken, all tortured curls and starch, into the town to the school's annual prize-giving, and seeing her, with her black legs quivering and her long plaits slapping her thin back, mount the platform to receive a pile of books in their shining presentation covers. Not until I was older did I appreciate the sheer drive and force that carried her, in those pre-war days, from a small remote farm to a university degree. And until one had appreciated the cost of her progress it was impossible to gauge the force of conviction that had made her throw it all away and give her life to the service of the Mary Montague Settlement in that grim northern town. How Mother would have grumbled about waste and folly had she ever known of it: but Mother was dead by then. Not, of course, that even Mother could have deterred Pen from doing what she wanted.

From a distance I had adored her, but since the break-up of our home I had seen remarkably little of her. She had come home from Oxford for Father's funeral with her face in bandages and hands that shook when she tried to pick up or reach out for anything. There was a mystery that I was not allowed to share, I knew that. I'd heard talk of an accident, and of an inquest, but my aunt who was my father's sister, and our only living relative and who had come to Pedlar's Green when he was taken fatally ill, had hidden the paper from me for over a week and had snubbed me brutally when I asked what kind of accident it had been. I meant to ask Pen, but my aunt asked first, and Pen had said in such a final way, "I prefer not to talk about it," that my own question was never asked.

After the funeral she and my aunt had had a long talk, to which I had listened from outside the door, since I knew that it was about me and I was anxious to know my fate. Pen had offered to leave Oxford, find a job and keep me. I stood outside the door and breathlessly prayed that she would be allowed to carry out this plan. I was only twelve and didn't realise what the offer meant in the way of sacrifice. And I hated my aunt. The month or so that she had spent at Pedlar's Green had been enough to assure me that we were never intended to live together. But Father, it appeared, had made other arrangements, almost the only ones he had ever made in his life, I should think. He had left enough for Pen to finish at college, and the rest, together with what the farm and the things on it fetched, was to go to my aunt to support me until I was sixteen and could, presumably, fend for myself. And since the will of the dead is sacred, however ineffectual the living person has been, Pen was overridden. Incidentally, Aunt Ada had taken a very bad bargain about which I did not fail to hear; I was glad enough of my first job when I was fourteen. And that had set me at a further disadvantage with Penelope, for, compared with her, I always felt ill-educated, raw and crude, as well as a defective character. And I knew only too well that if I had had a degree I wouldn't have spent my time in working for a pittance in the name of charity; I'd have been looking out for Polly Field.

I never wrote in my letters to Pen of how much I hated the feeling of dependence upon Aunt Ada, and of having to be meek and polite in the face of insult because of that dependence. And since I couldn't write about the things that were in the forefront of my young mind I had written very little to Pen at all. I had worked and drifted, and fallen down and got up again on my own. The ten pounds on the day I met Dahlia was the only thing I'd ever asked her for in my life. Since then we had met once or twice in London, and we exchanged letters at long and irregular intervals.

Megan, my other sister, was as different from Pen as possible. Curious tribute to heredity lay somewhere there, for they had been born of the same parents, fed on the same food, slept for years in the same bed, attended the same school. And no two people on the face of the earth were less like one another. Megan was pretty, very pretty, Ever since I could remember she had been referred to as "your pretty sister." Megan had made me beauty-conscious. It used to be such a mystery to me. I used to look at Pen's face, then at Megan's, and then sometimes at my own reflection and think—what *makes* the difference? Two eyes, a nose, a mouth, some skin, features that individually even resembled one another, why was one arrangement so pleasing that every one remarked it, and another so commonplace? They were both fair, but Meg's hair verged on the golden, Pen's on the drab. Mine was plain brown. Meg's hair was prettier, I could see that, because of the colour and the curliness, but Pen's eyes were far more definitely blue. I used to go over them, feature by feature, like that, but the secret always eluded me.

I was about ten then, and ignorant. I didn't understand that quite a lot of Meg's advantage over Pen in appearance was due to her determination to exploit what she had in order to make up for her mental inferiority, or how much, again, her attractiveness lay in her gestures, her grace, her poise, her complete confidence that she was pleasing. Pen could have competed far more if she had ever bothered. But, then, I *did* bother; I tried to copy Megan's looks, just as I tried to imitate Pen's cleverness, and with equal lack of success. Indeed, I laid a pretty foundation for a nice little inferiority complex, had I known about such things then. I used to copy Megan's style of hairdressing, her way of tying a ribbon, the angle at which she held her head when she was asking a favour. Useless. I was so much bigger of bone than either of them, my eyes didn't pretend to be blue, my feet grew so that I couldn't wear the shoes they had outgrown; I was clumsy and I was not clever. What hope had I?

And yet, I thought, brooding over my letters on this late September evening, it was "poor Polly" who had made money with her unclever head and managed to secure a lover or two for her undistinguished body. That line of thought closed abruptly—it was neither seemly nor safe. I thought about Megan instead.

She had married immediately after the war. With some quibbling over her age she'd got into a hospital where her lyrical beauty had probably compensated for her lack of other qualities more usually associated with "good works." Henry her husband was a coffee planter, and they'd been in Kenya since nineteen-twenty. During their visits home I had seen her occasionally, but not much, for with her I had been ashamed of my clothes and general lack of sophistication. She sometimes sent me a cheque for a present in the old days, but I always felt it was Henry's money, and I didn't like Henry much; so if I was in a job I tore up the cheques and Megan never seemed to notice. In that way she was just like Father, who would read a pamphlet when he should have been at market or buy a first edition of some quite worthless book when what he needed was horse pills. Over money, dates, time, and tickets, Megan was as vague as only a beautiful woman can afford to be. Over other things, such as clothes, fashion, make-up, and current funny stories she showed a compensating practicality. I re-read their last letters.

Neither of the letters had reached me on my birthday, though both were written for that. Pen's was two days late and Meg's more than a fortnight. Tonight, reading them together for the first time, I was struck by a similarity between them. Penelope had written her good wishes and explained why she had no present for me, and added in the clear small writing that was so like her clear dry speech:

This is, I'm afraid, a dull letter, and I know it will be late. I was up all last night, and I must admit that sometimes this place and the work here depress me rather. "Depressed" rather than "distressed" area, though God knows it's that, too. Last night we were with a woman, slaving to bring alive into this world that doesn't want it, the eleventh child of an unemployed miner and his consumptive wife. Kay—she's the doctor, and a fine woman—said she was in two minds about smothering it, and honestly it would have been much the kindest thing.

Oh dear, Polly, wouldn't it be grand to be happy kids again at dear old Pedlar's Green? I often think of it. Can you remember it at all? How we used to gather those peach-scented oxlips in Galley Wood, and blackberry in the brakes? And we knew nothing of other people's troubles. You probably wouldn't go back. You've made a success of your life, and you're still young. So here's to another year; may it bring you more success and prolong your youth. . . .

Megan's was quite different, naturally.

How I envy you being only thirty, it's the best, the very best time of a woman's life. Young enough, old enough; just perfect. What wouldn't I give for it back again. Life is very cruel to women, I always think, Polly, and I tell you this so that you can make the most of your time. One wrinkle, a little sagging, a few grey hairs, and you're finished. What was that thing Father used to quote, "Not all your something and your wit can something it back," I often think of that. I wake up looking a fright; and then I long, I can't tell you how much, to be waking up in that back bedroom with Pen, seeing myself in that blurry little glass, tumbled and sleepy-eyed—but not a hag. Where does it go, that youngness?

Perhaps you'll do better; anyway, don't think that you'll be a fright at thirty-seven, this climate is not kind. And you're only thirty, lucky Polly. I hope the songs are doing well; I've almost worn out the record of "Heart, Be Content." It's a lovely thing and I love it. What an egoistic—or should it be egotistic?—anyway, what a beastly letter for your birthday.

Of the two, I think I pitied Megan more. Perhaps I was wrong. But it seemed to me that every day Pen did something to alleviate the conditions that depressed her, whereas Megan, who had relied entirely upon her looks, was helpless in the face of their betrayal.

Anyway, I thought, as I stamped the envelopes of the letters I had written, they could both assuage their nostalgia, not for youth, but for Pedlar's Green. How surprised they'd be when they looked at the address of my handsome paper. They'd be certain to look at the address first; I had changed mine so often. They would know that I had come home.

Walking to the post-box that hung on a telephone post just beyond the mouth of the lane, I was filled with most unusual faintly melancholy abstract thoughts. Home, I thought, what we are all in search of. For Pen it would be a place where things were orderly and fair and just a trifle antiseptic in flavour. Megan would only find hers in a world where beauty lay beyond the hand of time. I, lacking alike ideals and beauty, could lay my hand on my home, tangible possessions, house, food, money, dogs. Without regret I reflected that I had what the Bible called a carnal mind. Outside I did not mind the wind, it seemed to bring the scent of bonfires and fallen apples and just a hint of frost. I dropped in the letters. One would go to the grimy house that was the M.M.'s headquarters, and in the cheerless hall be stuck in the rack under "F." The other would emerge into the sunshine of Africa, and Meg would receive it from a black hand.

I hoped that Pen would come before the colour had all gone from the countryside. Then if Megan took notice of my invitation and came in the spring, so that she missed the African summer, Pen could come again and so get two holidays. We'd all be together, and we could talk a lot and eat a lot, and try on one another's hats, and remember things and sit about munching the apples that had steadily ripened, even while the house was empty, and were now stored in the attic. It would be grand, I thought, to be all together at Pedlar's Green.

Hell, they say, is paved with good intentions. Merry, merry hell.

Pen's letter came within a week.

Dear Polly—Your letter was a surprise. I noticed the postmark at once and thought I was dreaming, then when I saw the address I felt delirious. What a wonderful coincidence, your seeing it like that, and how nice your description of it sounds.

Have you heard or seen anything of Meg? I had a telegram ten days ago saying that she was in London, since then not a word. Henry is not with her. The telegram cost two shillings—isn't that just like her? Two shillings to whet one's curiosity and not a penny-ha'penny to allay it.

It's nice of you to ask me to stay with you. One day I will; perhaps next summer. We're never so busy in the summer. Now we are, terribly. We've just started the children's meals

again at the M.M. and we aren't sure of enough money to carry
on to Christmas even. If people could only see the poor brats'
faces I don't think there'd be a pet dog or a racehorse in England by the New Year. And yet I don't know. They must *know*
and hear about work like this and the necessity for it. Oh,
Lord, here I am, off again: but, having started, I may as well
conclude—drop us a shekel or two if you've got a spare one.
After all, we're very faithful to your "You're My Mascot" song.
At least two people in the settlement can be guaranteed to be
singing it at any one of eighteen hours. Did I say thank you for
asking me? If not, thank you.

                                                        PEN.

She hadn't had a holiday to my knowledge for five years and then
it was a seaside camp with a pack of children. She could have
come if she'd wanted to. That was what her talk of longing for
dear old Pedlar's Green amounted to. It reminded me of a play I
once saw in which some women were always longing to go
somewhere—Moscow, I think it was—and never did a thing
about getting there.

And Megan was somewhere undefined in London while my letter went ramping out to Kenya. Well, hell, I thought, I can do
without either of them. Dahlia had been in London for a month
by that time; she'd be ready for something different. I went out
to send her a telegram. She'd come, if only for free board. Poverty
hadn't taught Dahlia to save her money. She was always very
hard up.

Next morning, guided by the kind fate which looks after idiots
and drunks, I was filled with the idea of getting extra help into
the house. Why I thought of it I don't know; Agnes was perfectly
capable of looking after two people. Perhaps I was afraid to face
her with the news of a possible guest without an offer of help to
soften the blow.

"There'll be another person to cook for," I explained. "Do you
know any one who would come and help with the cleaning?"

"No, I don't know anybody."

"Oh, Agnes, think," I said. "After all, it's for your convenience.
There'll be two of us, and probably more later on" (I could think

of at least eight people who would be glad of a nice quiet time in the country), "and we mustn't entirely overlook Tommy, he has some claim on your attention."

"There ain't no need to mention him. He come last," said Agnes with a bitter note in her voice.

"But he shouldn't," I persisted. "That's what I mean. I don't want you to be driven and bothered. Think of some one who could come in for just an hour or two."

Agnes said nothing. Oh, Agnes, my mind cried, be a little human, try to make life a little happy for yourself. Why make whatever it is worse with all this stubbornness?

"You can't think of any one? Then I must ask at the post office." I got down off the table where I was perching, and Agnes, with a swift look at me, said,

"There's Mrs. Pawsey."

"Mrs. Pawsey? You don't mean our Mrs. Pawsey, the one who used to help Mother sometimes."

"The same."

Mrs. Pawsey had seemed old to me all those years ago. I was surprised to hear that she was still alive.

"She must be very old."

"She's sixty-nine, but she's active," said Agnes reprovingly.

"Do you think she would come?"

"I'd rather have her than anybody," said Agnes, not exactly in answer. I was so much annoyed that I wouldn't even ask if the old lady still lived in the same house. I could find out.

Why Agnes even half approved of Mrs. Pawsey was a mystery, for she was a garrulous old woman, who, in the course of ten minutes' conversation gave me a vivid synopsis of the history of the whole village during the eighteen years I had been absent.

"That Mrs. Pamment now—oh, you must remember Mrs. Pamment—your ma used to give her some of you children's clothes. You don't remember? Well, no matter, makes no difference, but as I was saying, she—" and so on.

Agnes's story came out, of course. "Bad thing that was. Aggie Porter was a decent mawther. An' of course, coming back and calling herself 'Mrs.' didn't do her no good, not with that Cissie's tongue; yelling all over the place, she was, every time her an'

Aggie had a few words. Still, Aggie an' me get along all right. Yes, I'll come in in the morning an' give her a hand. Glad to. You ain't finished while you can stir about, I always say. The pension's killed off more old tough 'uns than work ever did." She laughed heartily at her own wit, and I took advantage of the slackening of the spate to say hastily, "Nine o'clock, then," and beat a retreat.

Dahlia arrived next evening, just as the cyclamen and lilac colours were fading from the sky. I heard the dry skid of a hastily braked car and ran down to the gate, realising as I did so that I was not the only one who had been buying things during this month since our return. Dahlia's car was long and white and carried more chromium plate than a milk-bar. The back seats were piled with suit-cases and hat-boxes shrouded in initialled linen; and flung carelessly beside them was a fur coat which even my untrained sense informed me had cost more than all my dogs would do, though they lived each to be twenty and had pups (those that could) every year. She swung her slim legs out of the car and sat there, sideways, smiling at me. "So I have found it," she said, and held up her face like a child for a welcoming kiss. I put my head down and sniffed. "Ah, Jeunesse Dorée again, isn't it? How nice to see you and smell you again, Dahlia." I walked round the car and got in at the other side. "I don't know how you'll feel about lodging this shining thing in a barn, but there's no choice. I'll come round with you. The gate is just up here on the left; you'll have to go slowly."

By the glitter of its coachwork, no more, the car was steered through the old farm gate that led to the barn, and just at the crucial moment when I was straining my neck to see if we had cleared the posts, something seized and pulled my left ear. I turned round and found myself staring into the solemn face of a little monkey. "Hell," I said, "let go my ear! I suppose this abortion is yours?"

"Not exactly my abortion, my monkey," said Dahlia gravely, breathing carefully as she took the turning into the barn. "I didn't exactly mean to buy a monkey," she continued, "but I bought it from an organ-grinder because it was ill, and, as he had no home he could not look after it properly. It hasn't a very nice nature—yet."

"But you trust that living with you will improve it."

Dahlia showed her glorious teeth in a small controlled smile. "I smack it regularly, now that it's better," she said hopefully. "Merciful Father, what is this? They will eat the monkey and me, too."

All the dogs came streaming round the corner of the house, and ran, barking and sniffing, towards the strange woman who bore something even more strange in her arms. I dispersed them with words, rough or soothing, and a few pushes. Then I said to Dahlia, who was now helpless with laughter, "Let's run into the house. The boy who does the garden will bring your bags in, if he hasn't gone."

We ran over the cobbles to the back door, and as I ran and pushed and shouted, cursing myself for not having thought to tie up the dogs, I saw Agnes looking out of the kitchen window. The window was of old glass and the greenish tinge of it made Agnes look like a fish pressing up to the wall of an aquarium; nevertheless, I could see her expression clearly. Interested at first, in this my first visitor, it slowly changed to a kind of incredulous horror. The reason for this change eluded me.

I opened the door that led to the front of the house and let Dahlia through ahead of me, and then, leaning back so that my voice would carry to the kitchen, I shouted, "Agnes, ask Billy to bring the bags in, they're in the car. Or if he's gone get them in yourself, will you?" I took Dahlia up to her room, which I had filled with her name-flowers in lemon and apricot colours, and I sat on her bed and tried to hold the monkey while she took off her hat and smoothed her hair with her fingers. She had the loveliest head, small and oval and rather pressed in at the temples as though it had been moulded carefully between a craftsman's hands, and her hair clung to it, black and silky and smooth, except over the eyes where a few tiny flat C-shaped curls fell over her forehead.

"You are thin," I said, watching her; "thinner than ever. I'm going to stuff you up with soup and milk and things. How long can you stay?"

"Oh, a long time," she said vaguely. "I'm sick of London, anyway, and November is coming. If I like it here I think I'll 'build a willow cabin at your gate.' Would you mind?"

"Mind, I should love it. But why build? There's plenty of room here and you're welcome for ever."

"I wish everybody was as nice as you."

"Everybody doesn't owe you what I do."

Dahlia gave me a brief smile that hadn't much heart in it. "Show me the garden while it's still light enough," she said.

"There's not much to see now, but wait till next year. What are you going to do with that?" I asked, nodding towards the monkey.

"I'll slip its chain under the leg of the bed," said Dahlia, doing so as she spoke. "It's a good little thing, really. It'll lie on the bed quite quietly. Poor scrap. Why are they so pathetic, Polly? Is it because they're so like us. Look at its nails."

She lifted the tiny paw and I looked at it. The nails were really rather amazing.

It clung to her hand for a moment, uttering little squeaky noises, and then settled itself with an oddly resigned gesture on the end of the eiderdown.

We went down and walked slowly round the darkening garden that was full of the cool earthy scent of raked soil and chrysanthemums. The mist was gathering so quickly that before we had completed the circuit the smoke from our cigarettes was lost in it.

Indoors again I held a match to the fire, and the fact that the flames leaped up bravely and bit into the sticks with a crackle seemed to fit the enchantment of the evening, and the company, and the pleasant feeling that had shot through me when I had said, at the sight of the gathering mist, "It'll be another nice day tomorrow." It was grand to think that tomorrow would find me here, and Dahlia here, and everything just the same.

Dahlia went upstairs to put on one of the trailing dresses of which she was so fond. Almost at once she was on the stairs, calling in the husky whisper that served her for a shout, "Polly, my things haven't been brought up."

"All right," I called back. "I'll see about them. That boy is a fool."

I went into the kitchen, from which came sounds of animated

conversation. Tommy sat by the glowing range eating his supper of bread and dripping. Mrs. Pawsey was pinning on her ancient hat and talking over her shoulder to Agnes and a woman whom, from her resemblance to Agnes, I judged to be the redoubtable Cissie. The conversation stopped at my entry. Mrs. Pawsey drove home the last of the fierce pins which secured the erection to her top-knot, and with a spatter of "good nights" made her way to the door and was gone.

"Cissie dropped in for a bit of a chat," said Agnes shortly.

Surprising, perhaps, but not unlikely. Rows between the members of such families spring up very suddenly and die down just as quickly.

"Did you tell Billy about the bags?" I began.

"He'd gone," said Agnes.

"Then why didn't you get them in? I asked you to," I said, speaking more abruptly than was my wont because of the look of sharp interest upon Cissie's face.

Agnes put her hands on her hips.

"I have fell low," she said, speaking slowly and with dignity. "I have fell low, but I have not fell so low as that. I'm not going to wait on no Negro."

The import and the insolence of the words staggered me for a second. Then I said, "Blast you! How dare you speak to me like that?"

"I didn't use language, anyway," said Agnes.

"Wouldn't soil her tongue," added Cissie.

God, I was so furious that I thought I would choke.

"Get out of this kitchen," I said in a low, strangled voice. "Get out, now, both of you." I should have loved to have added Cissie's farewell, "And take your bastard with you," but the child in question was sitting there, bread and dripping poised, mouth and eyes wide, drinking in the drama of yet another row.

"Glad to," said Agnes. "And, before I go, let me tell you, Miss Phyllis, that if your mother could see you now, using such language and keeping such company, she'd turn in her grave, poor dear lady, that she would."

"Good for you, Ag," said Cissie.

I was helpless. Furious words certainly formed themselves in my mind, agonising for utterance—but what could the most searing words do against such ignorant, barbarous self-righteousness? What they both wanted was a bloody good smack of the head, and they came damn near getting it, too. "Get your things and be quick," I said to the chief offender, "and you take Tommy and wait outside."

With elaborate insolence Cissie straightened Tommy's hair, pulled his coat straight, and moved slowly with him to the door. I pushed it to after her smartly enough to catch her a bump on her heel and her fat behind.

I stood in the kitchen, listening to Agnes blundering about overhead, until the direction of the noise changed and she came clumping down the stairs with the wicker dress-basket under her arm. She paused at the foot of the back stairs.

"Well, what are you waiting for?"

"My money."

I laughed. That did touch her a little. I saw the aloof, righteously-injured expression break up to admit a glimpse of annoyance. So I went on laughing, long after I could have stopped.

"Don't be funny," I said, at last, still smiling. "You don't get any money. I'm not sure that I shan't sue you for leaving without notice."

"You told me to go."

"Because you defied me and insulted my guest. Now are you going to walk out, or have I got to throw you?"

Agnes made for the door.

Shaking, and struggling against tears of impotent fury, I went out to Dahlia's car and fetched in the luggage. How I wished, weakly, that I had done it myself in the first place and so never set match to the piled tinder of Agnes's strange hatred. But even so, I reflected, she would have struck over something else she was asked to do for Dahlia: and it was far better that she should be gone now, before she had had time or chance to insult Dahlia to her face and so hurt her.

Would any one have believed it? Nineteen thirty-seven, in enlightened England, within seventy miles of the city that is the heart of a multicoloured Empire—"I'm not going to wait on no

Negro." Dahlia, clever, cultured, the loveliest thing that Agnes's little pig eyes had ever rested on, to be dismissed with that one scornful, ignorant word.

God, I was angry. So angry that the inside of my head felt hot and raw. And when, dumping down the last bag in Dahlia's room I caught sight of my own face in the glass, I was glad that on my way upstairs I had prepared a good lie to account for my discomposure.

"My woman's brat has come out full of rash," I said as casually as I could. "It may not be anything, but she thought she'd rather not stay here, and I didn't want her to."

"How awful," said Dahlia. "Has she got anywhere to go?"

"Her home's in the village," I said shortly. "There you are. Now I expect you to prepare for me a perfect vision of beauty, because the boy had gone and I've lost a lot of sweat getting them up."

Not, I thought to myself, that Dahlia would look better in any clothes ever designed than she did at that moment, naked except for a narrow brassiere and a pair of very brief knickers, with every muscle and, it seemed, every bone, visibly and exquisitely sculptured under that warm coffee-coloured skin. I could have yelled with rage over a state of society in which Agnes, large and raw and surly and stupid, could, by virtue of her completely English hide, take up so superior an attitude.

I went down into the deserted kitchen and lifted the lids of the saucepans that were simmering on the stove. Except for boiling eggs and milk on the smelly gas-rings of odious bed-sitting-rooms, I hadn't looked into a saucepan since I had done so, long ago, in this very kitchen, when I used to peep to see how the Christmas puddings were doing, or scooped out a spoonful of green peas, which I much preferred uncooked—and still do.

I identified the bread sauce with a clove-stuck onion like a medieval plague-ball riding in the middle, and the potatoes, the cauliflower and the gravy. Then I opened the oven door and, blinking in the wave of hot air that rushed to meet me, surveyed the chicken and some kind of pudding in a glass pie dish. Baste, I thought, one bastes chickens. I endeavoured to do so, scooping fat from the tin with a kitchen spoon and pouring it over the

browning fowl. Then I burnt my hand on the tin and put the
whole affair back hastily.

I mixed the dogs' dinner in an enormous bowl and doled it out
into separate pans, over which I stood to see that the greedy ones
didn't steal from the others. When they had finished I shut them
in the kitchen, went into the lounge and poured myself a glass of
sherry. Tomorrow, I thought, I must find some one to take
Agnes's place: and would Mrs. Pawsey turn up, or would sedition
have spread? I brooded for a bit over Agnes's reference to
Mother. No doubt she was right. The idea of an exotic half-caste
who had been on the stage, installed with an organ-grinder's monkey in the best spare bedroom, would be enough to make Mother
"turn in her grave."

But so, after all, would a great many things that were insepa-
rable from my mode of life. Mother had been dead for twenty
years and things had changed. She had lived a sheltered life of
the kind that didn't exist any more. She had pleased herself during her chatelaineship and I must do the same.

The fact remained, nagging at me, that Mother could have
quelled rebellion in Agnes, or any one else, with a look. If she had
invited a Chinese juggling troupe to occupy the house Agnes
would have waited on them without a word. I knew that. In some
almost occult way Agnes knew that Mother was strongly rooted
in depths of respectability and moral rectitude, therefore whatever she did was right. I wasn't, therefore whatever I did was
wrong. Probably my unquestioning acceptance of, and attempted
kindness to Tommy, "the bastard," had set Agnes, in some perverse way, against me at the very beginning. To the intolerant, tol-
erance is a most intolerable thing.

Dahlia came down in a dress of silver-grey velvet with the neck
gathered like the calyx of a flower and tied with a thick cord of
coral-coloured silk. A lovely dress, a tasteful dress, a costly dress,
but not the dress for her because, although it emphasised the
vividness of her lips, the brightness of her eyes, the almost
lacquered brilliance of her hair, it threw up distinctly the dusk-
iness of her powdered skin. Sometimes, in brown or black clothing she might have been Italian or Provençal. Tonight there was

no mistaking. A pity. Yet why, after all, deplore the means by which such beauty was attained?

I poured more sherry and sat gloating over the companionship of which I had suddenly felt the need forty-eight hours before.

Presently Dahlia wrinkled her nose, studied the end of her cigarette and then looked round.

"Something is burning," she said. I sniffed, smelt nothing but burning wood and tobacco for a moment, and then my slower senses became aware of the stealthy, acrid scent.

"Oh, blast Agnes," I cried, leaping from my chair.

"Why?"

"For having a brat and letting it get spots," I yelled back and flung myself kitchenwards. Billows of blue smoke were pouring from the oven. The chicken was much browner than it need have been, and the pie dish was full of something very much like coke. I dropped it into the sink and turned the tap.

The rest of the meal was perfect, for the overbrowned skin of the chicken didn't matter, and the flesh had not dried. Dahlia hardly ate any of it. She pushed her food about her plate and pretended, but it was easy to see why she was so thin. I had a sudden, vivid memory of the way in which, on the day of our meeting, we had fallen upon those thick ham sandwiches, munching hungrily, scooping up every crumb.

Dahlia seemed to have outgrown such a simple pleasure, but I was still fond of food. I thought—as I savoured the smoothness of the sauce and crushed the delightful slight brittleness of the cauliflower—that people who are indifferent to food, Penelope for example, miss a great deal of quite harmless and regular pleasure. Love of food, like love of other crude comforts, is a thing that you can take with you along the years and enjoy when you're quite old. You don't have to be clever or pretty or nimble as you have to be for the enjoyment of intellectual, erotic or sporting pleasure. A comfortable chair, a good fire, a hot-water bottle in its season, soft underclothes—we don't give them honour enough. Once, I remember, after the shattering end of a love affair, I went to bed with my hot-water bottle clutched to my chest that felt bursting with the tears I would not shed. I thought, "I've got a bed, and I'm still alive; I can still appreciate the comfort of heat, this isn't the end of everything." And I soon slept.

I said now to Dahlia, "You don't seem to be making much of a meal. Don't you like it?"

"I'm loving it," she said, untruthfully, and pushed it about some more.

Presently I took away the plates and dishes, and, with apologies for burning the pudding, set a bowl of fruit on the table. Dahlia shook her head at it and took a cigarette. There were nectarines in the dish too, and large William pears with all the richness of autumn in their scent, as well as crunchy red apples.

"Well," I said, "if you won't eat we needn't sit here any longer. It's warmer in the lounge. Go across and put some logs on. I'll just make some coffee. It won't take a minute."

I took a pear with me and ate it, with the juice running over my fingers, while I heated the milk. Then I carried the tray along the passage, pushed the door shut with my heel and drew up the little table to the fire. Dahlia lay back in a chair with the firelight on her face, and for just a moment, until she realised that I was looking at her and smiled at me, I saw and recognised upon her face the same expression of despair that had arrested my attention all that time ago in the tea-shop.

It was gone immediately. I returned her smile, poured the coffee, set her cup within reach, lighted a cigarette and sat down. All the time I was wondering what had happened. Nothing much, probably. Dahlia was very easily depressed and just as easily elated. I'd known her to weep because she was disappointed over a hat that she'd liked better in the shop than she did when she got it home; and, anyway, I'd got her under my roof. I'd be tactful, and yet fuss her a little, feed her up if I could, and listen to any complaints she had with patience. After all, I had saved her, in a way, from despair and poverty; and that gave me almost an omnipotent feeling where she was concerned.

That set me off reflecting upon the mystery of personality. How could any one regard it as a static thing? How could any one ever make definite and final remarks about it? With Dahlia I could be maternal and tolerant, kind, and sensible, a trifle domineering—and yet I am not a tolerant, maternal, kind, sensi-

ble or domineering person in other relationships. I roused myself
from these unprofitable reflections and picked up my coffee,
which immediately went slopping into the saucer as my hand
gave a jerk at the sound of a shrill screaming, a growling and
pounding that came from the room immediately overhead—
Dahlia's room.

"The dogs, that monkey!" I cried, and took the stairs two at a
time. They had got it. Block and Velvet and the mongrels united
for once in an act of destruction, like the incongruous allies that a
war will make anywhere. Agnes, I remembered, had left the door
of the back stairs open and they had slunk out of the kitchen and
up that way.

The shoes Dahlia had taken off stood near. I took one in either
hand and drove them off. It was too late. The monkey was literally torn to pieces and the little red collar and the silver chain
that had prevented it from escaping were still swinging, blood-
bespattered, from the foot of the bed. Block was still growling
and slavering, so I gave him another blow for good measure, and
was going, in strict justice, to deal three more for the others,
when Dahlia's voice said, "Don't hit them, hit me." She was
hanging on the door and her face was the colour of dirty ashes.
Instinctively I moved so that I stood between her and the
remains.

"It's dead," I said, "but it died quickly."

"It's all my fault. I tied it there and then didn't shut the door
properly. That monkey was fond of me."

"I'm most awfully sorry," I said. And at the sound of my voice
speaking soothingly the four dropped tails began to wag, fe-
verishly apologetic.

"Go downstairs, blast you, you horrible brutes," I cried. I
pointed the way, shoe in hand, and they dropped their tails again
and trailed out, one behind the other. "You go down, too, and sit
on something, Dahlia, please. I'll clear this away, and bury it
decently. I can't tell you how sorry—but do go on down now, and
get a drink or something, and don't fling a faint on me into the
bargain."

"I should apologise to you," said Dahlia with a gulp. I pushed
the door on her, and holding back a shuddering nausea with an

effort that was only just sufficient I gathered up the bits into a box and scrubbed the carpet. A damn fine beginning to a visit, I thought, as I tugged the bed forward to hide the wet patch. And so exactly like Dahlia, my mind went on while I was washing my hands, to bring a monkey into a houseful of dogs and then not shut the door securely. If it had been the action of any one else in the world I should have said, "Serve you right," but with Dahlia in it the miserable little drama had the pathos of an orphan child losing its rag doll. I hurried down to her.

"Forget it, if you can," I said awkwardly, for even with her tenderness is not my *métier*. "It didn't suffer."

Dahlia mustered her meaningless smile.

"Poor Polly, don't bother about it any more. You can't expect dogs to be wiser than people who distrust anything that's a trifle different and would destroy it if they could. Let's forget it. But I'm grateful to you for coping with it."

I looked round the room and then said briskly, "Do you see that piano? That's been put there specially for you. If you're not too tired you might try it."

"I'm not tired at all. In fact, I'd rather work than just tinkle. Isn't there something nice and new and a bit hard we could tackle?"

"Well," I said, with the senseless diffidence that always comes over me when I have to produce some untried stuff, "I had a bit of an idea for that old woman's song in *Slave's Saga*. A moaning kind of thing, with a good strong beat in it. Like this . . ."

I gave her my version of my latest creation.

"Got it written? Let's have a look at it."

I found the words, scribbled on the back of a bill, and gave them to her, together with a good sharp pencil and a sheet or two of lined paper.

"Oh, good title, Polly. 'Lawd, Turn Your Face to Me.' Just right." She read out the words in the pseudo-negro pronunciation that had been insisted upon.

"*Ah'm singin'*
Though Ah'm low as Ah cin be.
Ah'm singin',

Though de Lawd has turned His back on me.
Ah'm waitin' till de sun breaks through,
An' Ah'm singin' cause there's nothin' else to do.

"*No sun in Heav'n.*
No blue overhead.
Ah'm poor an' Ah'm lonely
An' soon Ah'll be dead.
But Ah'm singin' in the shadows, an' Ah'm singin' in the rain,
Dear Lawd, hear me, turn your face again.

"*Ah'm singin'*
Though Ah feel that Ah could cry.
Ah'm singin'
Though the days go slippin' by.
Dear Lawd, watch me, brave as Ah cin be.
Hear me singin': turn your face to me."

"That's splendid, Polly. Just what's wanted, and with that nice bit of variation in the second verse. Mutter it through again. I hope I'll catch it."

So we began our humming, banging, one-note-striking perform-ance that would have convinced any observer that we were a cou-ple of lunatics, but which did result, at the end of an hour, in a song that was exactly as I had imagined it: a rhythmical thing with a catching tune and with that undernote of patient yearning that would just suit the old woman in *Slave's Saga*.

When Dahlia had finished making squiggly marks, and tucked the pencil, as usual, behind her ear and then played it through, singing in what remained of her voice, I knew it was good. I wasn't conscious, as I had been, of the foolishness of the words or the wealth of repetition. Once again I wanted to hug Dahlia. I knew just how fathers feel towards the mothers of their children, who have taken something shapeless, and in itself useless, and transformed it into something real and living.

I reached out and took hold of one of her thin little hands. It was cold as a leaf.

"You're a marvel," I said. "Come over to the fire now and get warm." But the hand slipped through mine.

"Just a minute. Playing like that has made me want to." She fingered the notes uncertainly for a moment, and then broke into the song that she knew was one of my favourites, "The Lute Player." I sat there by the fire with my arms round my knees, while against the background that was an odd mixture of pictures of Carcassonne and fairy-tale illustrations I watched the story unfold for the hundredth time.

> *"There was a lady, great and splendid,*
> *I was a minstrel in her halls . . ."*

She brought out the strong chord at "immortal," and then whispered the end, "immortal, by virtue of my hate—and love." I said, "Thank you. You know you can still sing, Dahlia."

"At a range of six yards; no more."

"And now that I've heard it once again, perfectly, I never want to hear it again. Will you remember that?" I told her about my other records.

"I suppose," said Dahlia, eyeing me with her head on one side, "that you have a private life that none of us know anything about?"

"Everyone has," I said.

"Listen to this. See what you think of it. I made it all myself after the style of those little tinkling songs—Elizabethan, aren't they?"

She fingered the notes again, and then, very softly, and it seemed, inconsequently, voice and notes ran together.

"My body goes a-whoring
After strange men
Who hold her and ravish her and leave her and then
My soul goes in search and brings her home again.

"My body, like a greedy sheep
Must go astray
In the strange fields and the new pastures all through the day
But my soul always chides her home your way.

"The strange men are forgotten,
The new spells fade.

And after all the mouths have met and the hunger's allayed
My soul like a sheep-dog chases home the jade."

The little tinkling notes, so light that it might have been the virginal beneath her fingers, fainted on the air. I was silent for a moment, then I said,

"Hell, if you made that all yourself you'll soon be able to do without me. I'm very jealous."

"You needn't be. You see, I borrowed most of the words. And, anyway, it's *verboten* to mention the soul, these days."

"Well, come over here then, and have a drink and cherish the body for a bit."

"In half a minute." She played a short tune through twice and then, just strumming softly, threw her voice at me over the sound. "Polly, tell me, how black am I?"

My heart, that usually well-controlled organ, gave a leap, as if I had been faced suddenly with a dreadful, personal danger. My breath went, and even if I had had an answer ready I couldn't have spoken for a moment. But my mind, so far as an answer was concerned, was a blank. Colour was a thing that had never been mentioned between us . . . and I realised then, for the first time, that we had accorded it the silence that one accords an affliction, fits, a clubfoot, a harelip. What could one say? It was like being faced by an insane person asking, "How mad am I?"

Crazy answers formed themselves. "Why ask me?" "You should know." I couldn't say that kind of thing, of course. I couldn't say anything.

At last I forced myself to look at her. Her eyes were fixed on my face. It was as though her soul were drowning and clinging by means of her eyes to me, sole hope of safety. A silly simile. Souls don't drown and eyes can't cling. But it felt like that. There was nothing about her but those searching eyes, and the fingers that went on drawing sound from a box of wood and wire. I quibbled.

"I don't quite get your meaning," I said slowly. "You aren't *black at all.*"

"How white am I, then?"

"Very white," I said foolishly. "More than half . . ."

"When you first saw me, Polly, that day at the table, did you know at once?"

"Know what?" I asked, fighting for time.

"That I wasn't white." Her voice was relentless. I gave up the struggle.

"Dahlia," I said, "I don't know whether you appreciate what hellish awkward questions you're asking me; but I suppose you want an answer and I suppose you want the truth. Yes, I did."

Ought I to have said that? If it wasn't plain from her mirror, and Heaven knew she looked in it enough, ought I to have told her? Why not? It was the truth, and though I frequently lie in the way of business, and occasionally in my personal dealings, I avoid it when possible if the matter seems important, or if I like the person to whom I am talking. But even when I had taken that fence I wasn't safely on the level. Dahlia was working towards something, of what I had no idea. She said, quite calmly, "Of course, I knew that really. It sticks out a mile. And even if the Haiti miracle worked for me there'd still be my hands, my feet, something in the way I walk. Wouldn't there?"

I nodded, and then partly to sidetrack the issue and partly from curiosity, I said, "The Haiti miracle. What's that? And do for the love of God stop that fiddling. You're getting on my nerves."

"Sorry," she said, and got up and, coming over to the hearth, threw herself down in one smooth movement so that she was sitting at my feet and the faint perfume of the Jeunesse Dorée rose to meet me.

"They say," she began, "that in Haiti there grows a seed that will turn even a full-blooded Negro white, if it doesn't kill him. Some slaves discovered it, many years ago, and some died, but those that didn't were made white. So many tried after that, as the legend grew and strengthened, and so many died of it, that the white men went about destroying the plant that grew it. But it is still found in places and it's still believed in. You'd have to be very brave to try it, I suppose."

She broke off and looked into the fire, and I hoped that the discussion would end there.

"But, Polly, does it matter?"

"Does what matter?"

"Colour."

"In what way? And to whom?"

"To you, for instance."

"Not a scrap . . . if you mean do I mind it. Actually, it gives you something, I think, a decorative quality, and, quite possibly, a talent that you wouldn't otherwise have."

I was conscious a trifle too late of the shallow selfishness of that speech. It was as though I had said, "I don't mind your being off-white so long as you're good to look at and have a talent that can serve me." So I added an amendment, quite genuine, too. And in a sense it was an insurance against anything more that she might ask.

"Besides that, Dahlia, I like *you*. If you suddenly lost your looks and went stone deaf, you'd still be there, with all the things that make you *you*. Do you see? So what colour you are can't matter."

"It matters to some people," said Dahlia heavily. "You're an exceptional person, Polly . . . and you're a girl."

I knew then that we had reached the heart of the problem. I knew then that Dahlia was in love with somebody who was white, and who minded her not being.

"Have a drink," I said. Dahlia nodded. I went across to the built-in cupboard in the white-panelled wall, against which the tall branches of Michaelmas daisies cast slender shadows that danced in the leaping firelight. It used to be called "the jam cupboard," I remembered, and I used to stand there in the days of my greedy childhood gloating over the shapes of the whole strawberries pressing against the jars. I took out the whisky and the siphon and the glasses, and thought as I poured hers that I'd make it strong. Then if she wanted to tell me it'd help her, and if she wanted to forget it, it'd help her do that, too. As for me, I needed a drink darn badly.

I suppose I might have guessed that this was what would happen to Dahlia, sooner or later; but now that it had happened I was taken aback. Heaps of people suffer from unrequited love, it's as common a trouble as a cold in the head, and as unpleasant to watch. But those people can mostly snap out of it and look elsewhere, and usually do. But Dahlia's problem wasn't quite so simple. After all, if people with cross-eyes could only marry cross-eyed people, you'd be a little sorry for them, wouldn't you? And it seemed to me that Dahlia's field was more constricted than cross-eyes could make it. She ought to fall in love with somebody just as much white and just as much black as she was. And where would you find him?

She stretched up her hand for the glass and I caught a sight of her face as she turned. I thought, she wants to tell me about it, that's why she's looking at me like that—a dog wanting a bone and not daring to ask.

I said, as gently as I could, feeling horribly self-conscious, "Would you like to tell me about it? Who is it?"

"Roger Hayward," she said, with a promptitude that justified my question.

I lifted my glass, just to give me a moment in which I need neither speak nor look at her. But it was no good. The glass banged against my teeth and a thin stream of liquid dribbled out of the corner of my mouth and began to run over my chin. I caught it with a flick of my tongue and swallowed before I said, "Poor Dahlia."

"Poor bloody fool?"

"Yes, poor bloody fool."

"Two nights ago," said Dahlia, thoughtfully, "he said the cruellest thing to me."

"I believe you. He has a gift for it."

"Do you know him well?"

"Pretty well. And you?"

"I've slept with him," said Dahlia simply.

That time I managed a good long drink.

"Go on, tell me about it if you want to."

So I sat there and listened to the story, the oldest story; the story that Eve's daughters—if she had any—got together and told in the evenings, the story that Eve—if she overheard it—would recognise as the curse beginning to work out. They'd met at a party, Maisie's or somebody's.

"He sort of hung around and looked at me," said Dahlia, and my heart skipped another beat, remembering, as it did, that look.

"There's something," said Dahlia, to the fire, "about that look.

It's like a compliment, or a bouquet, or a sonnet being laid at your feet by an Elizabethan courtier. It transports you, translates, just a look. You know?"

I nodded. I knew.

"It began there. I can't tell you how it went on. We danced. He said the most impossibly flattering things—things that you might read, or perhaps imagine, but never expect to hear spoken, and all in that matter-of-fact voice of his, as though he were talking about the weather. I hadn't any will left, or any sense. There was nothing left but my body and that was gaining a consciousness of itself that it had never had before."

"I know," I said. "That's the effect of the tremendous animal magnetism, vitality, sex-appeal, call it what you like, which is the *only* thing, the absolutely *only* thing that he has in any unusual quantity."

Dahlia twisted round and looked up at me.

"You know a lot about him, don't you, Polly?"

"Yes," I parried, "I know a lot about him." More than you, probably, I thought; I'm more critical. "Go on."

"There isn't much to tell—especially since you understand. It just went on. He came to the flat and stayed sometimes. I was mad, of course, to get into such a tangle of feeling. To let it be heaven when he was there and hell other times. We didn't go out much—only to meals at quiet places, or in the car, or to places like Maisie's. Two nights ago I just happened to suggest going some place to dance—Greegi's, and he said . . ." I waited through the pause, knowing what was coming. "And he said, 'My dear Dahlia, I know a great many people in London; some of them rich, many of them useful, if somewhat reactionary in their views. I can't afford to be seen in a place like Greegi's with a coloured song writer.' I," Dahlia added unnecessarily, "am the coloured song writer."

"What did you do?"

"I laughed. God be praised, I laughed and I laughed. It was the sheerest hysteria, but he didn't know that. I said, 'Frank must be your middle name.' Then he laughed and said, 'I'll take you to Marc's.' I said, 'You'll take me to hell!' And he didn't know how true that was either. Then we had some drinks and he wanted to stay the night. But I proffered the unsurmountable and he went away. In the morning he rang up, but I put on a voice and said that Miss Whitman had gone out of town and had let the flat. Then your letter came. So here I am. Miserable as the devil, no kind of a guest, Polly."

"You'll do," I said. "And you'll get over it. One does, you know."

"But it's so unfair. Just this miserable colour, which I can't help. And which doesn't make any difference. I'm not savage or anything like that. Of course, I might have quite black babies."

"Might you, really?"

"So I have heard. It's a law of nature or something. But I don't see why a possible some one who isn't born should be considered before a person who is already here. Do you?"

"Well, put like that it sounds silly," I admitted, but there was a grain of doubt in my mind, and my voice must have shown it, for Dahlia said in a voice like a pounce,

"Tell me honestly . . . suppose you really liked a man as much coloured as I am, would you marry him?"

I fended off that question.

"Marry? Did you expect to marry Roger Hayward?"

"Nothing less would be of any use to me."

"Heaven send you sense. Roger couldn't marry you if you were the Lily Maid of Astolat. He's got a wife in Paris. He goes back to her with astounding regularity after each of his major affairs. He's probably with her now—I hand you that as a compliment."

Dahlia had scrambled to her feet and stood breathing like an overdriven horse.

"Is that true? Oh, Polly, how did you know? Tell me, tell me everything else you know. Polly, please . . ."

I was fumbling about in my harassed mind to know what to say without betraying myself—for I hadn't yet made up my mind how much I would tell her (if I'd been sure it would help I'd have spilled the whole story, gladly; but I wasn't), and while I was still hesitating Dahlia raised her head in a way that made one think of a deer in some fabulous forest, and said, "There's some one outside." At the same time I heard Velvet's fussy bark from the kitchen, followed instantly by Block's more menacing note.

Agnes come back, full of apologies, I thought. So I closed the
door carefully behind me lest some incautious word should reach
Dahlia. I opened the door and saw some little lights shining. I
switched on the globe over the porch and waited on the step
while a decrepit little Austin sighed itself to a standstill and the
battered doors of it opened and two figures unfolded themselves
on to the gravel. Penelope and Megan, my sisters.

IV

On how many Friday evenings had I rushed out like this to meet them after a long fidgety wait at the window with my nose pressed white and flat to the cold pane? From Monday morning to Friday evening they lodged in Stoney in order to be near their school. Father drove them in on Monday—and it was typical of Father that though Pen harnessed the pony and brought the trap round while Megan raided the pantry for tuck and Mother fetched Father's boots and muffler and pressed the grocer's list into his hand, there was always at least fifteen minutes of impatience and quietly blasphemous waiting before they could set off. "How I wish," Pen would mutter, twisting the reins in her hands, "that Flip could come home by himself. Then Father needn't come. Every Monday of our lives we're late."

"I miss some beastly algebra," Megan would say gloatingly. And then, after a careful glance around to see whether Mother had yet emerged from the house, she would unwrap and display some unusual spoil that the raid had afforded.

"You'll never get it there: it's coming through the paper already," Pen would say. Then Megan would laugh again and say, "Don't be so superior. You'll be glad enough to eat it, paper and all, after you've seen what Mother Craske has been hatching up for you this week-end."

I used to hang about and listen and envy them. Their life at

Stoney, bounded by the school and Mrs. Craske's lodgings, had
for me the charm of the unknown. When, years after I explored
and knew it, it was very dull. Pen and Megan had left it, of
course; the teachers whom I knew by report were gone; and Mrs.
Craske's were just the first of my dreary lodgings. Also, the war
was on and no pantry was worth raiding, even if I had bothered
to try.

At last Father would come out, grumbling about being late. He
would offer to take the reins; Pen would refuse to relinquish her
one hope of speeding up the belated journey; with some relief Father would sink back and with waves and back-called good-byes
the girls would go out of my life until Friday evening when the
carrier brought them home in company with crates of ducks and
hens, netted pigs, or a roped calf.

In summer I met the wagonette on the Green and very proudly
carried Pen's satchel of books home for her. In the dark evenings
I was far too frightened of the empty road to venture out, even if
Mother had allowed it As a child I was nervous, and there was always a certain relief in the pleasure with which I greeted them on
winter Fridays. For three nights the long passages and the big
shadowy bedroom held no terrors for me. Penelope had courage,
she would face any dark silence. She always went first on our trips
to the attic for apples and walnuts. Megan, though more given to
carrying candles, was not so nervous as I, and her cheerful loud
voice and way of banging doors were as comforting to me as Pen's
quieter confidence.

They would come in, blinking at the light, red-nosed and cold-
fingered from the slow chilly journey. We always waited tea on
Fridays and sat down together to a meal that was neither tea nor
supper—stacks of hot toast, a pie of some kind, cheese cakes, and
sodden brown farm-house cake, rich with eggs and butter. The
week's news was exchanged. "Pen had top marks in her form
again," Megan would say with generous pride.

Father would say, "Good girl," and Mother, "Mind you keep it
up."

Nobody made any inquiry or volunteered any statement about
the progress of Megan's studies, but there were often other things

to report. Whispered conversations took place on the stairs or in the hall.

"Would now be a good time, do you think?"

"I think so. They're both in a good mood."

"Support me, Pen." Pleading, irresistible voice—almost weeping and yet almost as ready to burst into laughter over the whole ridiculous affair.

"With my life, fool. Come on."

A strained sort of entry, and then Pen saying in an apologetic way, a trifle casual, none the less:

"Oh, Mother, Mrs. Craske sent you a note." Good, stiff notepaper, supporting Mrs. Craske's reputation as a distressed gentlewoman, written all over at odd angles so that Mother, legitimately angry, could turn the pages about with a sharp thwacking noise. It was always a note of complaint, and with one exception, always about Megan. She had complained about her food and refused to eat it. She had left the light burning all night in the corridor after visiting another room—in itself an offence. She had leaned from her bedroom window and talked to some boys. She had consumed some contraband provisions of a sticky nature in her bed and smeared the counterpane. There was no end to her sins. Mother, true to her Victorian upbringing, would pass the letter across to Father, who, putting down his book or paper unwillingly, would say mildly, "I'm sorry to hear this, Meg." Mother never said she was sorry. She took care that the sorrow should be Megan's—and incidentally Penelope's and mine. "There will be no new hats for the summer now. Why should I strain every nerve to provide things for people who have no idea of good manners? You will kindly refrain, both of you, from taking anything out of the pantry, since you make gluttons of yourselves *in bed*. Of all places to eat!" Worst threat of all. "I shall simply give up all idea of trying to have you properly educated. Learning is wasted upon young hussies whose one idea is to converse with errand boys."

Pen never made any attempt to dissociate herself from the real criminal. Megan was always very repentant, tearful, profuse in apologies, excuses, good resolutions; and then, finally, smiling through her tears, she would produce some ridiculous aspect of

her crime, or of Mrs. Craske's fury and offer it for Mother's unsympathetic inspection. Penelope would say, elaborately casual, "I
think Mrs. Craske has exaggerated a little, Mother." Father
would smile. I would laugh. And though Mother would retain her
hurt and aggrieved aspect all over the week-end, when Monday
came and the girls were ready and Megan came up uncertainly,
wondering whether she would be kissed or not, Mother always
unbent at the last minute and would kiss her and bid her try to
be a better girl. And none of the threats really became realities.

If Megan's resolves—or her luck—had held, Fridays were delightful. Warm and comfortable, with the long hours of the week-
end (and how long they seemed then!) stretching peacefully
ahead, we would troop off to bed, where we ate apples and talked.
Megan would imitate Mrs. Craske, the staff at the school, and
sometimes even Mother, for our entertainment. I would lie longing for the day when I, too, should move and have my being in
that strange, exciting world. I think their stories wove the spell
for me that other children find in books about impossible schools.
I can only remember one complaint that came home about Pen.
She had, Mrs. Craske wrote, been most dreadfully insulting and
offensive at the breakfast table.

"Well, Penelope, if it has come to this! If I can't trust *you!*
What happened? And I want the truth, mind." Mother always
said that, though to me both Pen and Megan seemed paragons of
honesty. I should have thrown the notes in fragments over the
hedge.

"I simply said, 'If this is coffee, bring me tea, and if it is tea,
bring me coffee.' That's all. One day, before I leave, I will insult
the old faggot properly, so that she knows what an insult is."

Father laughed. Mother looked puzzled. "It's a quotation,
Mother," said Pen kindly.

"But which *was* it?" Mother asked, shocked. "Couldn't you
tell?"

"You never can," said Megan eagerly; "she uses the same urn
for both."

"Then *I* shall write Mrs. Craske a note," said Mother firmly.
And did. After that Mrs. Craske's complaints lost a little of their
power to disturb. Mother's faith was shaken. She did add, how-

ever, "Penelope, I don't care for the word 'faggot' used in that connection. You don't have an expensive education in order to pick up slang."

How long ago! And here was I running down the selfsame steps to meet them with the old excitement, mocking the twenty years or more between.

"Hullo," I cried. "Hullo. How lovely of you to come! How marvellous to see you! Both together, too. Oh, joy!"

"God, I'm stiff!" said Pen, stretching her arms wide with a cracking of elbows and wrists and shoulders.

"And I haven't an unbroken bone," said Meg; "two hundred mortal miles! Hullo, Polly, you dear thing. Let's have a look at you. And at the house. Just the same, both of you—or should I say improved? Oh, I am glad to see you. Do you mind us coming like this, all unannounced?"

"You said you had plenty of room, didn't you?" Pen paused in her dragging of bags from the dark interior of the little car. "Or perhaps you've got the house full of people. We hadn't thought of that, Meg."

"All the better, a crowd is a treat to me. Come on, I can't wait to get inside. I *made* Pen come; I simply *made* her. I couldn't bear to stay away another minute once I knew. Oh, Polly, what an improvement that white paper is. I say, do you remember that squiggly stuff with the face shapes on it, and how we filled them in with eyes and mouths all the way down the stairs? And wasn't Mother mad?"

Laughing and talking all at once, we arrived at the door of the lounge, which had been the chief living-room in the old days, and it suddenly seemed that the old oil lamp with the red-fringed shade should be standing in the middle of the white-clothed, heavily laden table. Father should be laying aside his book and his crooked glasses, and Mother folding away some piece of mending. Dahlia in her silvery frock, looking up with wide startled eyes, was, for a moment, a figure from a dream.

"These are my sisters. They've come after all," I said. "This is Penelope, and this is Megan." I turned to them. "This is Dahlia. I've told you all about her, haven't I? Now throw your things down anywhere and get near the fire. Are you hungry? What time did you start?"

I bustled round, turning on more lights and throwing logs on the fire, pouring drinks and fetching the chicken that wasn't yet quite cold. It wasn't until they had both eaten and I had taken away the trays that a kind of exhausted peace settled upon us and I could really look at them. We sat quietly for a little time; the air grew blue with smoke, and I looked at them.

Pen I had seen about two years before, but it was twice that time since I had seen Megan. Pen hadn't altered. Once only and that was after her accident when I first saw her scars, had I seen any difference in her appearance. The long pale plaits that had swung against her thin, childish back and whipped as she turned, were still there, a pale brown, almost unfadeable, colour. They were still neat, but bundled up rather ungracefully at the back of her head, exactly as they had been when she first put her hair "up." She herself had always been pale and thin, and there had always been frown lines between her eyes and beneath them where she screwed them when she read or looked at anything attentively. They had deepened a little, that was all. Her face couldn't sag or fall into folds because there was only the bony structure of it covered with skin that looked dry and rather hard. There was something slightly mummified about it, except when she was speaking or smiling. She had one supremely good feature, blue eyes, set deeply and fringed with up-curled lashes many shades darker than her hair. They might have been envied by many a woman more beautiful, and her brows had been nice, too; thin and mobile and dark; but one of the scars began just in the middle of her left eyebrow, dividing it in halves with a little bare patch and drawing it up. That gave her face a slightly supercilious expression which made people shy with her and even fear her a little. The other scar ran from just above her lip, through the hollow of her cheek to her ear. Both scars were on the same side, so that there was one profile untouched; and for several times after the accident when I saw her I used to take pains to sit or walk on her unblemished side. But after a time I got used to them; and they

weren't in the least horrible, just dry-looking white seams, like
pieces of cord.

Looking from Pen with satisfaction, I gazed at Megan with
surprise. Remembering, as I did, her letter, I was prepared for
change, a fading, a coarsening, a threat, if no more, of what havoc
the years could work. But any change there was seemed for the
better. Her hair might be hennaed, but it was bright and "live"-
looking, and more attractively arranged than I had ever seen it—
but then I thought that almost every time I saw her. It was cut
short and curled over the middle of her forehead in a style
reminiscent of the old pompadour, and after that it went back
sleekly over her crown until it broke into another cluster of curls
at the nape of her neck. Under the reddish gold of it her thin
pencilled eyebrows showed the darker and her eyes, paler than
Pen's, in fact, appeared to have the same deep glow. A vivid lipstick emphasised the curves of her mouth that hadn't sagged or
pursed or dropped into that vague expression of discontent that is
seen on so many faces in the middle years. Megan was still "our
pretty sister."

Why had she written me that eagerly miserable letter about
the lost joys of being thirty? I threw out a feeler.

"And how is Henry?" Her eyes softened.

"He's very well. Busy, you know, but blooming."

Curiosity nibbled at me. Why had she come home alone, a
thing she had never done before? On one of their holidays I had
heard her say, laughingly to some one, "Outposts of Empire
aren't safe for grass widowers." And once she had insisted upon
going back with him just after a sharp attack of 'flu when she really shouldn't have travelled.

Dahlia sat brooding over the fire while we three indulged in re-
constructive and reminiscent chatter, until Pen said, "I'd like to
hear some of these wonderful songs"; then she got up like an obedient child and sat down at the piano again. I took advantage of
the move to slip away and go upstairs to get out sheets and blankets. The dogs, glad to be liberated from disgraced exile in the
kitchen, pattered after me. I went out to the dark garden and
gathered blindly a handful of dew-wetted Michaelmas daisies.
And that reminded me of Pen's Austin. I got into it to drive it

under the cover of the cart-shed. It seemed very small and the miniature wheel and the frail willingness of the little engine were rather pathetic. Pen, I thought had been doing important work of the kind people call "good," for many years; Dahlia and I had merely enlivened a few of folks' leisure moments; but the barn held Dahlia's glittering toy-bright affair and my heavy roadster, while this little drudge chuffed itself into the cart-shed. There seemed a slight discrepancy in the awards, I felt.

Back in the house I took a childish pleasure in arranging the flowers and in slipping hot-water bottles between the new sheets, warm from the airing cupboard. And I thought about the next day, what we would do, how I would feed them, how Pen should rest and Megan sort out her troubles, whatever they were, in the peace and quiet of Pedlar's Green. As I passed Dahlia's door I thought about her and Roger Hayward. Perhaps I might even help her, too. I could at least point out to her the ruthless, hard, but effective path of reasoning that had led me out of the slough of infatuation to the upland of acceptance where I now, emotionally, dwelt.

Oh, I was full of plans and hope and confidence, bred, no doubt, of the fact that it was my house, that I had gathered the three of them into the shelter of my roof. Their physical well-being depended, for the moment, upon me. And that led me to think, with an arrogance like the arrogance of parenthood, that I could deal with their spiritual states as well.

I went down to offer night-caps, anything from whisky and soda to Ovaltine. It had been the most satisfactory evening of my life.

Remembering Agnes's departure, and the fact that Mrs. Pawsey never arrived until after nine, I had set my alarm-clock for six. It was still darkish when its twanging woke me. Block and Velvet who slept in my room, stirred and stretched, looking at me inquiringly through half-closed eyes. I put on my dressing-gown and slippers, ran a comb through my hair, and went down into the silent, sleeping house. The puppies got up from their mat in the hall and I opened the door so that the four dogs could go into the garden and not impede me. Stoves first. The boiler fire was still faintly aglow, so I fed it with sticks and laid on a few handfuls of coke, and breathed sighs of relief when it seemed not to resent the lack of thorough cleaning. The dining-room fire I lit as soon as I had cleaned the grate, and it went out twice. That soured my temper and made me think gloomily of the washing up that I must do before breakfast, for though I had plenty of crockery my supply of plates and knives was limited.

However, when at last the sticks were crackling, and I went into the kitchen, which faced east, the sun was rising, throwing a pinkish light on the whitewashed walls, and I felt better. I let the tap over the sink run until the water steamed, and then I plunged into the washing up with a will. I congratulated myself upon installing the hot-water system and thought with a kind of horror of the methods that had been in force in this very kitchen during my youth. I had a vision of the numerous chilled, chapped chilblained hands that had set great black kettles on the smoky fire of that Moloch of a range, which I could now ignore. Yet not one of the chilblained ones had ever, I was sure, walked out on Mother, or her predecessors, as Agnes had walked out on me.

Time before eight o'clock partakes, I discovered, of the slippery quality of the night hours. By the time that I had swept the most obvious dust off the flat surfaces in the dining-room and set the table and cut the rind off the bacon, it was full morning, the sun was shining brilliantly, and it was time for morning tea. I switched on the kettle and ran upstairs to make myself tidy.

I took Dahlia's tea first. She was awake, sitting up in the bed with a book in one hand and a cigarette in the other. She eyed me with startled guilt. "I forgot about your woman. I could have helped you; I've been awake ages," she said.

"Haven't you slept well?" I asked, with proper hostess concern, and something more. Dahlia detected the something.

"I always wake early in a strange bed," she said. "I'll just drink this, then I'll come and help you."

"At your peril," I said. "I've done all the work and I want all the credit."

I went on to the big room that I had once shared with Pen and Megan. I put the tray on the chest between the two beds and poured out three cups of tea. Pen sprang up, awake at once, and took hers, but Megan turned over and mumbled and moaned a bit. I sat on the foot of Pen's bed to drink my tea and gloat anew over the knowledge that here we were together again. I had not realised that the clan feeling could be so strong in me.

Suddenly, and for the first time, I missed the noise of hens cackling and cows lowing as they moved to pasture after the milking, and of jingling harness from the outgoing teams that had been the aural background of our childhood.

"Do you remember," I began on impulse with the almost threadbare phrase, "that red-headed boy called Alf Wicker who used to do the sticks and things?"

Megan hitched herself up in the bed and reaching for her tea said, "I should think I do. He was the first boy I ever kissed."

"You didn't," I said, recalling the red-scrubbed face and the gappy teeth and the manury smell that were indistinguishable from the memory that "Alf" called up.

"I did too. It was behind a haystack. I had the most awful yen for him. I must have been a most disgustingly amorous child."

There was a kind of caressing regret in her voice.

"I'm glad Mother didn't catch you," said Pen.

"So'm I," said Megan over the edge of her cup.

This morning, I noticed, she looked much older than Pen. Sleep had blurred the features of her face, whose chief charm lay in its delicacy; her skin looked sallow too and her hair was all flat and eclipsed under a net. Pen's pale plaits, slightly ruffled and falling over her shoulders, gave her an oddly childish look.

Standing about the room and casting prismatic colours on the white walls and ceiling were the cut-glass bottles and jars that made up the greater part of Megan's luggage. Skin foods and cleansing creams and astringent lotions and eyewashes. I had inspected them all in other bedrooms where I had visited her; and I had often wondered when, if ever, I should have time and money to invest in a similar display, and what, exactly, the result would be if I did.

I looked now from the bottles to Megan's face and was reminded of a soldier who, laying aside uniform and weapons, reveals himself defenceless. They rise and arm themselves again, the soldier and the beauty, but he may rise to possible victory; she faces certain defeat. For a moment I was sad and the stray sad sentences that wander homeless through time, sensing a harbour in my mind, crowded around. "A lady whom Time hath surprised." "Dust hath filled Helen's eye." "Beauty vanishes, however rare, rare it be." "Dear dead women, with such hair too." Trite, I thought, and hackneyed, and I shook them away.

"I must explain about Agnes," I said swiftly, and plunged into the story, ending with, "so I can't offer you breakfast in bed. You'd better get up, and you'd better do it now." They flung back the clothes, obedient as children. I carried the tea-tray away.

I kept a sharp look-out for Mrs. Pawsey, and when at last she arrived I shut myself in the kitchen with her and warned her to let fall no incautious word that would betray the true cause of Agnes's going. I asked her to carry on as best she could, promised that she shouldn't be single-handed for long, and said that we'd be out for lunch.

We all went in Dahlia's car into the town because mine would only seat two inside with any comfort. I was rather glad because with Dahlia driving I had more time to stare at the familiar landmarks which Megan insisted upon hailing with cries of recognition.

"That's where you used to meet us in the summer, Polly," she said as we flashed past the Green. "Do you remember the time when we tried to bring you home some ice-cream in a basin? By the time you got it it was like warm custard."

"And now the ice-cream boy is a familiar figure in every lane, and I'm sure there's not a child in England who thinks that ice-cream is tepid custard. I did for quite a long time. Things change, don't they?"

"Progress," said Megan. "Oh, look, Galley Wood, where the oxlips grew. And the gipsy boy's grave. I'd forgotten the gipsy boy's grave. Were there any flowers on it? Did any of you see? We went past so quickly."

"Some asters," said Pen in a tight voice.

"Fancy you noticing," Megan said. And I remembered that Pen had always passed the little mound with averted head. What a number of things I had forgotten until now. Megan's memory was far better than mine; but of course she had lived longer here.

"What is the gipsy boy's grave?" That velvety voice was Dahlia's, of course; and of course Dahlia didn't share our memories; she was in danger of feeling left out.

"It's a story—almost a legend," I said, "but you can't just dismiss it, because the flowers always *are* there in due season."

Pen interrupted me. "It's a horrible story. But go on, you might as well tell her. We've stirred up all the feeling of it now."

There was a little pause, and then, thinking that a great deal was being made out of a small matter—and after all it was the kind of thing to interest a visitor to the neighbourhood—I launched out into the story of how, more than a hundred years ago, a gipsy boy had been hired by a farmer to keep some sheep; and how some of the sheep were missing, and the boy, terrified of being accused of sheep-stealing, a hanging offence in those days, had hanged himself rather than report the loss; and how the sheep were found later, wandering in Galley Wood; and how from that day to this somebody, nobody knows who, but it is said to be other gipsies, puts flowers on the suicide's cross-road grave in season, even holly at Christmas-time. "We lived here for years," I finished, "and we, that is, Meg and I, were frightfully interested in it and used to watch. But we never saw anybody putting flowers on it, and nor did any one that I've ever heard of, but they're always there."

"Yes," said Dahlia, "that is an interesting story—and it is horrible too."

"Lots of horrible things happened in those old days," said Megan easily. "Did you ever read that story of the valiant little tailor?"

"Almighty God," said Pen, addressing the air, "what have I done?"

"Somebody has taken the Hall for a boarding school, I hear," I said swiftly as the grey stone gateway fled behind us.

"The Harrisons have gone?"

"Years ago."

"Do you remember that boy with the black hair who used to stay there? You know, the one who rode so well. We used to go to the Point-to-Point and yearn over him."

"I didn't," said Pen.

"Oh, you did. You were worse than I was."

"Well, anyway, not after you ruined the glamour by calling him Pete, out of some awful book you were gorging at the time."

"But he was," said Megan; "he was just like Pete. And it wasn't an awful book. It thrilled me to the marrow."

"Then it was a bad book."

"I don't see why."

"Well, I wouldn't lay down a hard and fast rule, but I should say that a book ought only to thrill you to the marrow if it reports or describes something that you know, either from the light of personal experience or from the light of knowledge, to be true, so that you can say, 'That is just how it happens, or that is just how it did happen.' That a book, purporting to be a love-story should thrill the marrow of a girl as ignorant as you were then, as inexperienced, proves, at least to my way of thinking, that it wasn't a good book. It wouldn't thrill you now, would it?"

"No—I suppose not."

"And why not, do you suppose?"

"Well," Megan blundered for a bit and then said, "I suppose you're right. I do know more about men, and women, and so on, now."

"But that," I said, irresistibly drawn into their arguments as I had always been, "isn't the fault of the book, surely. How ought a really good book, say about love, to affect an ignorant young girl, Pen?"

"With a sort of horror, I should say. You see, the girl is all full of dreams and illusions—and people shouldn't write books if they haven't got past the dream and illusionary stage themselves. Therefore what was written out of experience should disgust the inexperienced—as it does. Look at Hemingway and Aldington; people with permanently adolescent minds are disgusted with them still."

"Your argument would severely restrict the reading that a young girl could do, wouldn't it?"

It was Megan who answered the question, and surprisingly too.

"And rightly," she said. "It is that mock stuff that sends you out with all the wrong ideas. You kind of expect a man to be a cross between a cave man and one of Arthur's knights."

"Pete, in fact?" asked Pen. Meg nodded.

"I wonder where he is now."

"Who, Pete?"

"No, stupid, the boy with the black hair."

"Stiffening in the knees and heavy in the saddle wherever he is," I said brutally, and then I let my gaze follow Meg's out of the window.

It was a glorious morning, full of mellow sunshine and clear. On many old walls the creepers were blazing, scarlet, amber, and apricot. Here and there a solitary chestnut-tree that had changed colour before the rest—and chestnuts are most individual in their times of budding and changing shade—struck upon the almost incredulous sight in a miracle of yellow that set one thinking of Moses and the burning bush. If one could only arrest the process and preserve it so, with a few leaves scattered on the green grass like trapped sunshine!

The stubble was almost all cleared now, and the ploughs were out, moving slowly with the brown shining furrows turning and lengthening behind them. Even when we reached the outskirts of the town where the raw new houses clustered, the mountain ash-trees drooped their coral berries in redeeming beauty over gates labelled "Dunromin" and "Kosy Kot."

"Twenty minutes," said Megan, looking at her watch. "And old Gooch's cart used to take over two hours. We used to get so cold. Do you remember, Pen, when that brat was sick all over your lap and your brand-new handbag and you threw the bag away, contents and all, into a field? I *was* so shocked."

"Ugh! I remember. There was a half-crown in it too. I wonder if any one found it. I say, Polly, is Cope's bun-shop still in existence?"

"It's still called Cope's, and it looks much the same."

"We must take home some of those Chelsea buns for tea, mustn't we? I wonder if they're still as sticky."

"Oh, dear," Meg sighed. "I used to eat four straight off. How lovely not to have to consider one's figure. I can hardly imagine what that would feel like."

"Four would certainly make a bulge on you now," I said with a glance at the long slim lines of her black coat.

"Still, we'll buy four and eat them solemnly for auld lang syne."

"We'll buy three for that and one to introduce Dahlia to the joys of gluttony," I said.

"Where do I park?" asked Dahlia, half turning. I leaned forward to direct her and in a few moments we were tripping over the cobblestones of the ancient Market Place.

"I've got to go to the registry office, and I may be some time," I said. "You'd better meet me at the 'Castle' at about quarter to one. We'll have our lunch there."

"Oh, we can occupy ourselves," said Megan, thrusting one hand into the crook of Pen's arm and drawing Dahlia along with the other. "I want to walk past the school, and pull a long nose at old Mother Craske's and I'll buy those buns, oh, and heaps of things."

Her gaiety affected them as it always did people; she'd always been able to make a picnic out of a biscuit and a bottle of ginger-beer, and now, with gloomy Dahlia on one side and sober Pen on the other, she went lightly off down the street and before they turned the corner a shred of laughter blew back at me. For quite the millionth time I caught myself wondering why, in my secret heart, I liked Pen better. And I remembered one of Mother's sayings, one she said at least once a week to Meg, when she was in this kind of mood, "You'll cry before night." And often enough it had been true.

At the registry office I had a long session with an optimistic lady who had obviously believed all that the Reckitt's Blue advertisements promise about its white-preserving qualities, and applied what she had read to hair as well as clothes. The only trouble was that she had forgotten, or neglected, to rinse her hair afterwards, and the unreality of her colouring prevented me somehow from taking her very seriously. In that, as it turned out, I was wrong, for she "fitted me up"—her expression—with a middle-aged woman who filled Agnes's place to a nicety.

On my way to the "Castle" I left an order with the grocer, and one with the butcher, and bought a supply of dog food. I then called at the post office to complain mildly that nothing had yet been done about my request for a telephone. By that time it was ten minutes to one and I abandoned the idea I had had of buying stockings, and hurried in an undignified manner to meet my guests. Even then I arrived first, for Meg, who simply could not resist any kind of shop, had been indulging in an orgy, and as the three of them came strolling towards me I could see that they were loaded with small and rather insecurely fastened little packages. Just as they joined me, and Meg was launching out into a description of all they had seen and done, we had to stand aside from the doorway to let out two women, farmers' wives by the look of them, who were coming from the "Castle" yard. In the old days that had been *the* place to leave your horse and trap, and although the yard and the stables offered awkward and inadequate parking for cars, many people continued to use it from habit in preference to the new car park. These women met Dahlia and the rest of us, and there was that usual over-polite side-stepping and backing that occurs when people meet so. When that was over and our way was clear, one of the women, now behind us, said in a loud country voice to her companion, "Did you see that, Floss, a Negro!" I had just a hope that Dahlia, almost through the doorway, might not have heard, but her hearing was unusually sharp and a glance at her told me that she had heard all right. Bottomless hell! I thought. I swung on my heel; for a moment a passion of rage almost drove me after the fat red woman in the mangy fur. I could have smashed in her face and torn out her hair with all the pleasure in the world. But what was the use? There was the fact of Dahlia's colour, sticking out, as she herself had said, a mile. Why resent the observation of a fact? But why, oh, why, must it happen today? Just when she was feeling edgy, just when she was in my care.

I stuck my arm through hers, a foolish thing to do, since it betrayed the fact that I, too, had heard and considered it a matter of sympathy, and said as lightly as I could, "Well, what do you think of our genuine Tudor inn? Mr. Pickwick is supposed to have stayed here."

Pen lounged over to the framed sketches of Pickwick and Sam Weller, and the rest of them that hung on the wall and said, "That's an achievement, isn't it? To draw forth that remark from everyone who enters here, and to have them believe it."

"But it's a fact," put in Meg. "He did stay here. They'll show you a bed upstairs that he slept in, and there's a pump in the yard that Sam Weller washed at."

"Not really?" asked Pen, raising her other eyebrow level with the scarred one.

"Yes, really. You know it's true, Pen. He went to the 'Angel' at Bury too, and to the 'White Horse' at Ipswich."

"Who did?"

"Mr. Pickwick."

"There you are, you see. An achievement, as I said."

Meg stood puzzled for an instant, then she burst out laughing. "Of course, I see. An achievement indeed."

We wandered about the room with glasses of rather warm and sticky gin and vermouth in our hands.

"Drinking is frequently sordid now and must have been more so in the past, yet old pubs are romantic, aren't they? I wonder why they should be, more so than houses, I mean?" Pen asked.

"I should think because life passed through them. Houses only shut in the little stories of their occupants. An inn was like the highway," I proffered.

"Take that, for example." She pointed to some weapons, rapiers, swords; I didn't know which or whether they actually differed, that hung over the open fireplace. "They may have killed somebody, ended a life that was full of interest. And curiously enough the very breath I draw to remark upon it may be the one that came out in a gasp as the point went in . . . blown round the world for hundreds of years."

"Oh, grim," said Dahlia. "It might be a very nice breath, if you're going to think that way. The breath that Helen said 'Hullo!' with to Leander when he came up all dripping out of Hellespont."

"Oh, not 'Hullo,' surely," said Megan smiling. "Too dull, she'd have said '*Darling*,' like that."

"She more likely said, 'Come in and get those wet things off,'" said Pen.

Chatting in this fashion, we went across to the dining-room and dealt, each after her fashion, with the solid good fare provided. I made by far the best meal. Pen never ate much or cared what she ate. Dahlia was still off her food and Megan careful of her figure.

When the coffee came Dahlia looked at her watch, hesitated for a second, and said, "I think I'll use the telephone. Pour mine, please, white. I shan't be very long."

She went out with her peculiar lithe walk, and I noticed that the eyes of all the people at the other tables followed her with interest. I realised suddenly that this wasn't the best place in all the world for Dahlia. In a neighbourhood like this, where every one knew every one else even a casual stranger was likely to excite inquisitive interest. Dahlia's difference was bound to be noticed. However, when she returned after an interval of fifteen minutes, during which I had been glad that I hadn't taken her at her word and poured her coffee, she was looking better, relieved almost, as though she had at last made some decision and was glad of it. She drank her almost tepid coffee at a gulp, and then we went to the cinema, there being a matinée as it was market day.

Mrs. Pawsey was ready to leave when we arrived. I thanked her for staying and told her that help had been promised for tomorrow. Everything was spick and span; she had even, I saw at a glance, repolished the stove that had suffered at my hands in the morning. The boiler fire was roaring away and I was glad to think that there would be enough hot water for four baths. The meal was ready too; so I took my bath quickly, in order to get out of the way of the others, dressed, put on a thick coat, and set off with the dogs for their evening run in the fields. The peculiarly wide, red, autumn moon, either the Fishers' or the Hunters', I never knew which, was rising over the farthermost hedgerow. The dogs ran scuffling and snorting to and fro, three miles to my one. I walked for quite a long time, thinking about Dahlia and what I was intending to say to her about Roger Hayward. At least I thought about that to begin with. I was calm, resigned, immune, and I was framing sentences that would convince Dahlia that she was fretting over the passing of a shadow . . . and I ended in a state of mind where I wanted to fling myself on the bare damp soil and tear up handfuls of it in a rage of frustration and desire and self-hatred. I suppose it was like a fever that comes suddenly to a crisis after the blood has tried in vain to neutralise or annihilate a chance germ. Roger Hayward. R. F. M. Hayward, Esq. I'd written that on about half a dozen envelopes and watched it transform the lifeless paper into something significant and precious. Roger Hayward, whose interests covered a dozen different worlds, and who had invaded mine because he was a friend of old Worboise, who was making *Island Magic* that we were doing the songs for. Roger had once, years before, lived for about five years in the South Seas and old Worboise, with his incomparable skill in getting something for nothing, was busily picking his brains for information. I will say for old Worboise that he is a devil for information, his is all accurate and firsthand and almost all unpaid for. I paid, I suppose, for the bits he was scavenging that day.

Blast Roger Hayward! I know he's good to look at; but one day, quite soon, he'll be fat, and then his likeness to one of the more decadent Roman Emperors won't be attractive any more. I know he moves with a kind of restrained energy, especially on stairs, that I found wellnigh irresistible; but age and increasing weight will deal with that. I know that he's so utterly natural and frank, so openly selfish, so unashamedly self-centred, that even the people whom he hurts most can never complain that they have been deceived by him. I know that he has a gaiety and a confidence, a breezy lack of conscience that are like a warm fire on a cold night, but what is all that to me?

Those old fellows who wrote the Bible were wise in their generation when they talked about the lust of the eye and the lust of the ear. Dahlia and I were both prey to those lusts, and to a third, the lust of the flesh. For neither of us—and surely not one of Roger's many women—can possibly have been in love with him. No one could love so fundamentally unlovable a person. "Oh, son of man, according as thou art lovable those thou livest with will love thee." Who wrote that? With the exception perhaps of his honesty and his gaiety, which both arise, I suspect, from his lack of consideration for other people, he hasn't a single lovable quality. Lust of the eye. And yet he is the last person on earth to be called handsome. His nose is like Punch's, and his mouth is a firm, hard slit. There's too much muscle on his jaw, too; and when he looks at you and desire takes him, you can see

the movement of it, as though he were biting on something. God,
I didn't know I was so observant!

"There's something about that look," said Dahlia.

Yes, and it had knocked me endways when I met it first across
the table in old Worboise's overheated office. Calculating, flattering, critical, ready to be amused. "Play with me?" Bluish-grey eyes
under thick brows a good deal lighter than his hair. If I could
only see them looking at me like that again; if I could only be at
the beginning, the delirious, heady beginning once more, I'd see
if I couldn't handle it better. No, I wouldn't. I'd flee from that
look as I would from an infection. "If thine eye offend thee,
pluck it out." I wouldn't listen to a word of that talk about palms
and moonlight, about lagoons and beachcombers and the music
of guitars, with those eyes watching me and weighing me up all
the time. I'd go straight out of that office, and I wouldn't wait to
be caught up and swept off to lunch with some one I'd never seen
till that morning. And I wouldn't listen to a word of that talk
that was his special line.

". . . the most impossibly flattering things—things you might
read or imagine, but never expect to hear spoken," said Dahlia.
Things so blatant that you'd never think any one *would* say them,
my mind cried fiercely, but that was only to drown, or try to
drown the memory of the things that lazy voice had said.

"Will you take your hat off?"

"Why?"

"Never mind. Take it off. Ah, that's better: exactly like the
photograph."

"What photograph?"

"I don't know. I saw one in a paper. It had under it, 'Miss
Phyllis Field, Polly to her friends, who is half the Phyllida com-
bine whose songs in *Up and Doing* are taking London by storm.'
Will you be Polly to me?"

Oh, it oughtn't to have worked! I wasn't virgin. I wasn't even
young; and I'm not a romantic or susceptible person. I'd have
called myself hard-boiled. And perhaps that held the secret. He
was too. There was a directness, a clarity, a ruthlessness about
him that appealed to what there was of those qualities in me.

And the same things made us laugh. Dozens of times since I saw him last I've been in situations where I could just imagine our eyes meeting for a second before we collapsed into helpless laughter. At those times my nostalgia for him reached its heights.

I stumbled along on the narrow paths between the plough-land and the ditches, raking over the ashes of that affair; my mind occupied all the time by the slightly caricatured figures that memory throws up, caricatured because they are remembered by one or two individual and overemphasised features: Dahlia, Roger, and a blurry figure, Phyllis Field, myself. Myself, a scrap of life housed for a little time in a structure of blood and bones, flesh and glands that appeared to be identity's servant, and was in reality its relentless master. For, just because some of my bones and organs were arranged in a pattern called female, I, the indweller, had developed a passion akin to the hunger for food, for another structure and *its* indweller. Here, personality, is your Waterloo, and here, freewill, your Actium. For clear-sighted and unbeguiled, without tenderness and without a thought beyond the plane of the physical, I yet fell victim to the fevers, the disruptions, the desires that people lump together under the misleading name of love. I never called it so. There may be people who love unselfishly, who do not seek in that name either the flattering of vanity or the assuagement of lust, and only they should use the word. I eschew it. As we did. I don't believe the word was ever mentioned between us. Interest was there, and a certain similarity of mind, the same things amused or disgusted us. But actually the only bond between us was the desire of the flesh. I realised that with a complete insight that startled even me on the very first time I stayed with him—and that was the second time we met. He was still asleep in the morning when I came back from my bath and began quietly to put on the clothes that I had thrown off in a frenzy of impatience a few hours before. I found myself looking at him as at a stranger, impersonally, undesirous. I decided that it must have been curiosity that had brought me there. That was satisfied now, and the spell, I told myself, was broken.

He woke up just as I put on my coat, raised himself on his elbow, and shook back his hair. "What on earth are you doing?" he asked me.

"I'm going out," I said foolishly.

"But you must have some breakfast. Why this hurry?"

"I just want to go, that's all."

"Is anything the matter? You haven't got a conscience?"

That made me laugh. He reached out a hand and said, "Come here." I went over and put a hand on his. Now, I thought, angrily, I shall begin to answer again. Bottomless hell, why didn't I go through the door? But I might have been touching wood.

"When'll I see you again?"

"I don't know. I'll ring you," I said. Then Roger laughed, throwing himself back on the pillow.

"You are the *most* peculiar person. All right, but make it soon."

I walked along to the garage where I had left my car, and while they were filling her up I went into a place to drink some coffee. And there, quite suddenly, it burst upon me that the measure of this satiety was the measure of my satisfaction. I remembered, most unwillingly, two earlier affairs. For Clifford I had had an enormous deep feeling—or so I thought at the time, and Alec I had admired so much that with him I was always uncertain and diffident. But association with them had never been so complete, there had been gaps that we had tried to fill with talk, with the making of promises and the giving of presents. I realised the utter, rather cynical truth of old Raleigh's words, "The shallow murmur, but the deep are dumb." Something, either our maturity, or the affinity of our blood, something purely chemical, no doubt, had driven Roger and me into a unity that needed no words, no promises, no tendernesses, nothing but its own consummation. And from that moment I desired him again.

I knew all the time that from the romantic, the sentimental, the idealistic point of view it was a sorry affair enough. But I didn't mind. I saw it—until I went mad—clearly. I knew that I would never have laid down my life, my identity, or even my comfort on Roger Hayward's behalf; and, without wronging him at all I could make the same denial in his name. Heaps of people, I know, feeling not much differently would apply the word love to their emotions, blaspheming thereby a word that has led others to the stake, the gallows, and the Cross. But we weren't like that.

Our bodies found one another pleasant to look at and listen to and touch; they enjoyed the frenzy of feeling that they were capable of arousing in one another. We knew what we wanted, were able to take it, and lucky enough to enjoy it. And that was all.

Why, then, was I walking now in these dim fields, raging and impotent, prey to a gnawing hunger that I had no means of appeasing? And the answer to that was prompt and simple. Because I was a fool, a natural, congenital, dyed-in-the-wool fool. As long as I knew desire for a beast that must be mastered as well as fed, all was well. And then—ancient damnation—it was as if a lion-tamer had begun treating his charges like domestic pussy cats.

The season was against me too.

That year I was living in a funny poky little cottage that belonged to Maisie. She lent it to people when she didn't want it, and she'd lent it to me for the summer. I hadn't lived in the country since I had left Pedlar's Green, and the magic of it stole away my reason and laid my defences flat as the earth from which the bluebells and the cowslips sprang. It was that perilous season when the beech-trees followed the hawthorn's green and the blossom-time came hard after. I made my brief and only excursion into the cloud-cuckoo-land of the imagination, and I found Roger's name on all the banners that the spring had hung about it.

I fought. I reminded myself that this was the mating season, that something deeper than one's intelligence, and older than the human race was at work within fur and feather and petal in order that next year's sun might shine upon the new life that this season's disturbance would germinate and launch. I knew all that. And I might just as well have read a book of poetry, "hunting the amorous line, skimming the rest." Just as well.

On two lilac-tipsy evenings a part of me that was a stranger composed and wrote and posted indiscreet, traitorous screeds. Oh, Cranmer, that right hand of yours, paying in flame for its penmanship, how symbolic it was!

Once, waking in a dawn clamorous with birdsong and full of rosy cloud, I found myself rebelling against the material aspect of our association—the very thing that had made it rare and tolerable. My imagination, raw and untrained, set to work upon Roger's image, and when it had finished he was no more the philanderer with whom I had chosen lightly to philander for a little while—he was a lonely soul, seeking in many women, and never finding, the satisfaction of his discontent.

God, I can hardly believe it even now. I got to a state where I felt that he had come to me seeking bread and I had given him a stone. And then, instead of letting the dangerous moment pass, I, being a fool, telephoned to the Roger of my imagining, instead of the Roger of actuality who wouldn't have known the bread of the spirit had it been thrust beneath his arrogant nose.

An ill-timed request for a meeting; two letters that should have been destroyed immediately they were written; a stupid telephone conversation—more than enough to evoke that inevitable male reaction. "Here is another clinging woman who will be a nuisance." The frail, brittle bark of our mutual self-interest could not cope with the weight of the crumb of sentiment that I brought aboard it, in the time of the cuckoo calling, in the time of the hawthorn blooming, in the time of my folly.

One broken appointment—profusely apologised for—was sufficient to open my eyes.

All hell, I thought. Trying to make a questing soul, a searching pilgrim, out of Roger Hayward. You deserve to be pilloried where every woman you've ever laughed at or pitied could spit at you. I imagined him with one of his other women, immune from me, lapped away in a trance of new desire. Imagine, I said to myself, trying to run a hard head and a soft heart side by side. Poor bloody fool! Ophelia with your head full of lilac and birdsong and night running gently in over the fields of evening all on his account. How could you be so crass, so hackneyed, so jejune?

In a way mine was the victory too. For the perversity, that, incidentally must be hell for people like Roger, who shrink from what is offered and run hot-foot after what is withheld, this perversity swung him me-ward again as soon as I regained my sanity.

There were days of silence between us and then his voice came, in the evening, drawling and caressing over my telephone.

"Darling, I couldn't think what had happened. Why this silence?"

"I've been very busy."

"Busy as all that? Not a word or a line for days."

"I haven't noticed a lot from you either." Foolish, traitorous remark that would yet be spoken.

"You sound rather cross, darling. Are you cross with me?"

"Of course not. Why should I be? I'm just most awfully busy."

Something I didn't quite catch, it wasn't a very good connection.

". . . come up on Thursday, can you?"

"Sorry, but I shan't have a moment this week. I'm going to America on Monday."

"Where?" And the voice had changed too.

"America, Hollywood."

"What on earth for?"

"Fun. As a matter of fact, I've got a job there."

"Isn't this all very sudden?" Neglected maiden seeking anodyne to sorrow?

"Not very. I've been angling for it for ages."

"But why?"

"Wanderlust. Fresh worlds to conquer me and so on."

"But Polly, I simply must see you before you go. If you are going. I think I could dissuade you."

"I'd hate to see you try. And I honestly haven't a minute."

"I'll run down." Gosh! How he'd grumbled on the two occasions when he had made that journey.

"But I'm leaving here tonight."

"Then you're coming to London?"

"No. I'm going to my sister." A lie, but why despise so useful an ally?

"You are the cussedest person! How long shall you be there?"

"God knows. I say, I can hear my kettle boiling over on to the floor. Good-bye, Roger."

"Damn the kettle, I say, Polly, what about . . ."

I replaced the receiver. The kettle was not boiling. I had not got a job in America . . . but I had proved that I wasn't going to be a bore to Mr. Hayward. And later on I did get a job. I turned at the end of the next field and shouted to the dogs who came up breathless out of the darkness and were now content to follow me back to the house.

All that was more than two years ago, and except for one letter, forwarded to me, a few casual references from various people who knew us both, and, last night, Dahlia's admissions, I had heard nothing of Roger Hayward since. I'd been busy, and lucky, I'd met a lot of people and made some money. I hadn't missed a meal or a night's sleep to my knowledge because of him. And here I was smitten again with the fever I imagined cured. I gripped my hands and gritted my teeth. I've got rid of this obsession once and I will again. Before I go back into the house, my peaceful, happy house, I will be calm and whole again. Roger Hayward liked me to laugh with and to sleep with occasionally. I liked him for the same reasons. I became "intense," he was bored, I saw my error and we parted. Has he ever moped about in a moonlight field feeling as though vultures were tearing at his vitals? No. Then why should I? Suppose I'd never met him, should I have been conscious of something lacking in my life? Of course not. Why don't I now remember Clifford who had so much more of my life and was so much better a person? Or Alec? Or . . . or . . . any of them? Why can I remember the very way he walks, with a kind of chained vigour, especially when he goes up and down stairs? Simply because he happens to be the most vigorous and perhaps the most physically healthy person that I have known . . . and for that reason my body, blindly, biologically wise, craves for his. I'm like a cow. And Dahlia is like a cow. We're all cows. So here I am, with a whole, sound, independent body and an unsentimental mind. I should like to go to bed again with Roger. I should like a million dollars. Why should the failure to get one thing send me ripstitching about the countryside and the other not cost me a sigh? Why? Because failure in the emotional field is a thing that people sentimentalise over from habit; half our songs and books prove that. I will not be a partner to it. I will not be a cow.

V

We struck the lane again about a couple of hundred yards above the gate: and immediately I was thrown into something like panic by the sight of a car's lights approaching. None of the dogs was on a lead and the puppies were not yet completely obedient. There was no house but my own in the lane, and we had never met traffic there before. I called the dogs, and slipped my hand through two or three collars, and stood back on the rough grass by the side of the lane, waiting for the thing, whatever it was, to pass. It came very slowly, and then stopped. It occurred to me that it was some one who had missed the way, and as I walked forward, rounding the vehicle, and stooped over the dogs, I saw by the light of the taillamp a London taxi identification plate, which confirmed my belief. I reached the entrance to my drive just as a tall, massive figure in a pale overcoat turned, with a hand on the gate, and said, in a deep, musical voice, "Wait here. I'll see if this is the place."

Block began to bark and in a moment everything was pandemonium, through which I bellowed, "It's all right, they won't hurt you. What place are you looking for?"

"Pedlar's Green," said the musical voice.

"Oh," I said, "whom do you want?"

"Miss Dahlia Whitman." There was something vaguely famil-

iar to me in that velvety, trombone-like voice, but for the life of
me I couldn't place it. "She is staying with Miss Field."

"Yes," I said. "Well, this is Pedlar's Green, and I'm Miss Field.
Dahlia is here. Come in."

We had reached the door and I threw it open quickly. The
man passed me, I pushed back the dogs, shut the door and
straightening myself, looked into the face, the broad, black face
of Chester Reed, the Negro pianist.

For a moment I was staggered. I must still have been dazed by
my thoughts or I should have recognised that voice, noticed, even
under the shadow of the trees the lack of light about the face.
Then I could have pretended that I was the maid so that I could
have spoken to Dahlia before I admitted that she was here. Fool
that I was.

I suspected that Dahlia would be furious. Chester Reed had
been rather a bother to her in the past, hanging around, asking
her out, sending her flowers. She always protested that she
couldn't bear the sight of him, and I could understand that. "The
rock whence ye are hewn," I used to think. I looked at him rather
curiously as he stood in my hall. His close-cropped kinky hair
shone under the gentle light of the shaded bulb. There was dignity in his face, and kindliness, and he looked superbly happy. He
was a fine man, too, as big as Roger, that was my involuntary
thought. One part of my mind thought all these things while the
rest registered surprise. I must behave as though he were just one
of the people we knew, come to see Dahlia. I held out my hand.
"I'm so sorry I didn't recognise you before," I said, with truth. "If
you'll wait in here for a moment I'll fetch Dahlia. Have you come
from London? What a journey. Will you have a drink?" He
shook his head and smiled. Happy, easy, a superbly healthy animal I thought, nothing the firmness of his flesh, the brightness of
eye, the magnificent teeth. I closed the door and went across to
the lounge where only Penelope was reading by the fire. "I suppose Dahlia is upstairs," I said.

"Changing her frock, I think," said Pen. "She's beautiful, isn't
she?"

"I think so," I said rather absently. "Some one's come to see
her, and I don't think she'll be very pleased."

But Dahlia, when I told her, seemed neither displeased nor very surprised.

"He's a quick worker," she said, twiddling the little C-shaped curls into place over her brow.

"I can't think how he found out where you were. But you needn't see him if you don't want to. I can get rid of him for you." I was quite ready to remedy my mistake in letting him in.

"I'll see him," said Dahlia. "What frock shall I wear?"

"Depends what impression you want to make."

"Oh, a good one." I opened the wardrobe and ran my hand over the dresses, multicoloured, that hung there. I had my hand on a cyclamen-coloured affair with long filmy sleeves when Dahlia reached over my shoulder and snatched the dress that she had worn the evening before. Pulling it over her head and patting its folds she said, "This makes me look as black as your boot. Don't stare. I knew it. There! Now where have you put him?"

"Dining-room."

"How'd he get here? He had his licence suspended last week, and trains make him sick."

"There's a taxi outside, ticking up a nice little bill."

"Then it'll be a short session," said Dahlia, and glided away downstairs.

But it wasn't. I hung about the kitchen for a long time, playing put-and-take with the items of the meal, trying to keep everything hot without spoiling any of it. The soup thickened, and I thinned it down with milk as long as it lasted, then I used water, finally I considered that it would be uneatable anyway and pulled it off the stove. But it still smelt like tomato soup I noticed, and my mind drew, without arresting my whole attention, a likeness between my watered soup and Dahlia's Negro blood. I sauntered into the lounge where Megan and Penelope were talking with grave faces about some matter that they dropped as soon as I entered. We drank sherry, and I explained all about Dahlia and Chester Reed, as far as I knew. Pen said, "I should think she phoned him this morning. She came back looking like somebody who had taken a fence and was glad about it."

"Of course," I said, "I hadn't thought of that."

Presently a thought struck me. Ought I to offer him some

food? I looked at Megan. She'd lived in Africa and people like
that often had awfully strong feelings about colour. I remembered
a scene at a tennis club to which my aunt had belonged. A visiting team of eight had two Indians in it. The ladies of the club
had prepared tea and were about to serve it. One of them, the
wife of a retired Indian civil servant, picked up a plate of sandwiches and was approaching the guests when her husband struck
it out of her hand, and said, "You shall not wait on them!" I was
only a child at the time but the scene, and the general pretence
that the plate had fallen by accident, and that the words had not
been spoken, had stuck in my mind. I had been so surprised too,
for the man was usually so meek and inoffensive and subservient
to his wife. He must, I now reflected, have felt very strongly upon
the matter. Could I ask Megan to sit down to dinner with
Chester Reed? Yet there was Paul Robeson to consider, and the
Aga Khan . . . surely no one would ban them from their table.
Oh, dear. I said in a voice made small by my ignorance and embarrassment, "Do you think I ought to offer him some
grub . . . I mean, would you mind?"

Megan came back from some far-off place to which she had
gone when the conversation with Pen was broken, and said
vaguely, "Oh, I don't mind a bit. I'm not like that." It was Pen
who said, "Oh, must you? I hate Negroes, not for themselves, but
they give me such awful thoughts, all about slaves, and *Uncle
Tom's Cabin*, and lynchings in the Southern States. Their very
faces have the melancholy of the wronged."

"Why wrong this one still further?" Meg asked.

Pen laughed. "I know," she said, "it's nonsense. Part of my
mania, like the gipsy's grave. Ask him by all means."

As she spoke the door opened and Dahlia came in.

"I'm awfully sorry, Polly, to have been so long."

"That's all right. Where's Mr. Reed?" I said.

"He's gone."

"Oh. I was just going to ask him to stay for dinner."

"Were you really? How nice of you. Anyway, he has to play
somewhere at half-past ten. He'll have a rush as it is. We've just
got engaged." She tacked on the last sentence hurriedly, and
thrust her left hand towards me, exposing the ring with a dia-

mond about the size of a threepenny bit that blazed there. "I didn't really want this," she gabbled on. "We're going to be married as soon as possible; but he'd bought it this afternoon. I couldn't not have it, could I?"

"It's beautiful," said Megan. "Why didn't you want it?"

Dahlia raised one shoulder. "Oh, I dunno. It seems such an English thing to do somehow." And for the first time she looked me full in the face. Something—was it Dahlia's self, or the three-quarters white in her, or merely something I imagined?—looked out at me and cried "Betrayed."

I thought, she rang him up this morning, just after that woman had dropped the careless "Negro" in her hearing. It was the merest impulse; but Chester Reed went out at once and bought this "English" symbol which translated the impulse into accomplished fact. And that is the end of Dahlia.

"Congratulations," I said in a voice that I vainly tried to infuse with warmth. "Come on, we'll drink to you quickly and then we'll have this belated grub."

VI

I closed my bedroom door, settled Block and Velvet with a final pat, and dropped down on my bed. It had been, I thought, the longest day I remembered. Just to think back to the time when the sun broke into the kitchen was like remembering something ten years ago. I felt tired and hollow and troubled. And I had too, a most unreasonable feeling that I mustn't be tired, or hollow or troubled. I felt like some one who has been left in charge of three invalids. Only, there are things to do for invalids, useful, helpful things.

I undressed slowly, washed myself, gave my hair its regulation twenty strokes with a stiff brush, put on my pyjamas. And all the time I kept thinking about Dahlia. It seemed that every time I thought of her I could see a shadow behind her, soft and insinuating, waiting, ready to engulf her, the huge black shadow of Chester Reed.

It's nothing to make a tragedy of, I told myself firmly. Possibly he appeals to some atavistic streak in her. Anyway, plenty of perfectly white women marry Negroes. I must not think about this in the traditional, prejudiced manner. But I'm not. Whoever she had got engaged to today I should want to register some protest, because I should know that she wasn't in love with him. People shouldn't make loveless marriages . . . at least a few hard-bitten mercenary people can, and make success of it, but not people like Dahlia.

I looked at my bed, thought backwards to six o'clock that morning, and forward to six o'clock the next. . . . But I resisted the bed's invitation. I gave myself a shake, pulled on my dressing-gown, and went along to Dahlia's room. She hadn't started to undress. The curtains were pulled back from the window and shuddered in the strong current of cool air that came through the open casement. Between them Dahlia was kneeling on the window seat, staring out of the window. She turned her head as I entered and the whole of beauty was held for a moment in that slight movement, the lift and turn of the head, the flexing of the muscles in the slender back. She turned back to the window as she said, "Hullo, I was expecting you."

"Oh? Well, I damn nearly didn't come."

"Oh, Polly," her voice was teasing, "you couldn't resist an opportunity of wrestling with me for my own good. Could you?"

"I both could and can," I said rather sharply. "I don't want to wrestle with you, and I do want to go to sleep. So good night."

"Oh, Polly, please. I didn't mean it. Come here and look at the moon for a minute."

"Looking at the moon makes people mad," I said, but I went and knelt beside her on the window seat. The moon that had risen so wide and red—how long ago?—was small now and high, a silver shield held aloft over the dark fields of cloud.

"Do you believe it, that it's just a dead world, reflecting the light of the sun?"

"I've no reason to think otherwise."

"Then it's the female isn't it? I never realised before how right it is to call the moon 'she' and the sun 'he.' Awfully right."

That called for no answer and I made none.

"You're right about the madness, Polly. You can stare and stare until what you are and what you do, what you think and feel are of no importance at all. Can't you?"

"No," I said truthfully; "it's only the moon, after all. What is important to me is important to me, and would be if there were suddenly six moons in the sky."

Twisting her head slightly, she looked at me thoughtfully.

"You're a lucky devil, Polly, you know. You've got a lot of sense, just sound sense. Have you ever fallen badly for anybody?"

"Dozens of times."

"Incredible. Has it ever made you do anything utterly foolish?"

"Amongst other things it sent me to America."

"Father in Heaven! I never guessed that that was why. Still, that was a good move, really, wasn't it? Not to be compared with what I've done today."

"That's what I came here to talk about, fool," I said. "But I can't talk with this wind blowing or with you staring out of the window." I swung the open casement to with a crash and tugged the curtains across. Then I said bluntly, "Look here, Dahlia, if you saw a hat you wanted and couldn't have it for some reason, that wouldn't embitter the rest of your life."

"I'm no good at parables," Dahlia said stiffly.

"Well, that's what you're doing. Just because you can't have Roger Hayward you've picked on the most unsuitable person in the world for you."

"You can't compare picking a husband with choosing a hat."

"Why the hell not? It's exactly the same. You pick something that takes your eye, suits you, and looks as if it'll please you. And being disappointed over a man is no more than being disappointed over a hat."

"What rubbish!" said Dahlia. "There's your heart to consider —and your soul."

"Oh, spare me," I said. "And, anyway, if your heart and soul drive you to marry a man you do not love you'd do better not to consider them."

"But that isn't the only why."

"What do you mean?"

"I mean that isn't the only reason—Roger isn't—or even the chief one. You heard this morning, didn't you?"

"Heard what?"

"What that woman said."

"Oh, what of that? They're all ignorant clods round here."

"Maybe. But an ignorant clod often says what other people only think. You needn't pity me, Polly. There's quite a lot of vanity in it. I thought, 'Well, there's one person on this earth to whom I'm white.' So I went and rang him and asked if his offer was still open and it was. So there you are. He makes lots of money, and he's generous, good-natured, and crazy about me."

"Poor deluded devil!"

"Why?"

"So nice for him, isn't it, to be married like that, by a person who, a fortnight ago, found him about as useful as a sick headache. You aren't in love with him, that's why, noodle."

"That's not his fault, is it? It's my fault. If Chester were white would you be so concerned?"

"Oh," I said wearily, "we're not getting anywhere. Dahlia, I don't want you to marry Chester Reed. I'm specially concerned now because you took that silly ignorant word to heart. Don't you see that if you do this you'll have given that woman power over you, let her influence your life? Whereas if you ignore it, it might never have been spoken. After all, it can't be the first time, things being as they are, that you've had to face something of the kind. Why mind this time?"

"Oh, because of Roger, I suppose. I'm really all on edge. I just want to tear my hair and scream."

"Well do. Nobody'd mind. You might feel a lot better."

For some reason that I could not myself exactly understand, I had spoken all this time harshly, with a minimum of sympathy. But now, looking at her suddenly and seeing the strain and misery on her face and the littleness of her, I was smitten to the heart. I took both her cold little hands in mine. "Listen to me," I said. "You think I'm hard, I know. I've been trying to *sting* you out of this thing. Now I ask you, Dahlia, at least not to do anything in a hurry. Stay here with me for a bit. Then, when the weather gets really bad, we'll go somewhere where there's some sun. And you'll get over Roger Hayward. Believe, I *know*, he's only a passing infection of the blood."

"Oh," said Dahlia, as one upon whom a great light breaks, "so that is how you know. Oh, my God, how richly funny! Oh, yes, do by all means let's stay here together and form a new order, an enclosed order, Little Sisters of Frustration. We could get a copy of that bronze Sheldrake did of him, and set it up on high and cry, 'Holy, holy, holy,' in the night watches." She laughed suddenly, a high, staccato peal that caught my breath.

"Hush," I said. And when she went on laughing I raised my voice and shouted, picking on the one shred of sense in the whole hysterical outburst, "Then you will stay? I'll get rid of Chester for you."

She was calm just as suddenly.

"It isn't any use, Polly. I am going to marry Chester. I want to. Despite all you may think and say it's the most sensible thing, really. He wants me, and I don't see why somebody shouldn't get something out of this. And I do like him. We can understand one another. And he's a man. After Roger I want a man, at least, and how many are there? Frankly, I'm as lecherous as a tomcat, you know, and I've got to cater for that somehow. Don't you give it another thought, Polly. I'm not worth it, truly. There's only one thing I want to do now, and that is . . ." She got up suddenly and went with her strange panther tread to the dressing-chest that stood on the far side of the bed. I watched her. She opened a drawer and took out a photograph, unframed, still in its folder of stiff paper. She dropped the folder on the floor at her feet and fumbled in her manicure case for a pair of pointed scissors.

She was going to cut it to pieces. Without seeing it I knew that it was a photograph of Roger. Where had she got it? I'd never had one. Something in me wanted to cry out, "Let me look at it for a second." With a feeling akin to food hunger I longed for one sight of that hard, unkind face. Had they caught that alert eye, that thin-lipped mouth, ready with sneer or smile, that arrogant nose? I crushed down the request. I would not be like a child, pressing its nose against a pastrycook's window. Dahlia said, in a still, quiet voice, the lowest note on a mellow fiddle, "How much civilisation has helped barbarians. Once on a time this would have taken ages of work in clay or tallow and hair. And now . . ."

Was it pure fancy, or did the room darken and draw itself together in sudden premonition of evil? Was it pure fancy or had Dahlia darkened, too? And why did I think of forests and vile things crawling? I said, "Dahlia, stop it," but my voice did not reach her. Holding the photograph in one hand and the bright scissors poised in the other, she said clearly:

"Roger Hayward, may you fall into the pit that your own lust has dug. May all that any woman has suffered through you come back a hundredfold." And she drove the scissors clean through the cardboard.

I said foolishly, "That's silly. He can't help himself. He only obeys his nature."

"As I do," said Dahlia. She twirled the scissors so that the photograph whirled like a paper windmill and then fell to the floor.

"That'll fix him," she said with horrid certainty.

"You don't seriously believe that that mumbo-jumbo has any power," I protested.

"Wait and see," said Dahlia. She came round the foot of the bed. "I must go tomorrow and see about things and get rid of my flat. It's been lovely of you to have me, Polly, and I'm sorry to be such a bore. Good night."

She held up her face. But I had seen, as the scissors went home, the gleam of her eyes and the flash of her teeth. Fiendish. I couldn't kiss her. I ducked my cheek so that it touched the peak of her hair.

I thought of why I had come there; and I shrugged the thought away. After all, Dahlia wasn't the first woman to marry a man she did not love. Sometimes it worked.

"Good night," I said flatly. And as I looked at her before leaving, something—was it Dahlia's self, or the three-quarters white in her, or something I merely imagined?—looked out at me and cried "Betrayed."

Part II

GOING

I

Waking next morning with the sunlight lying across the foot of my bed and spilling pools of light on the floor, I lay for a little while smoothing out my mind, pressing out, as it were, the impression that Dahlia's affairs had made on me. After all, I could do nothing about them now, and to be saddened by them was foolish and futile. She would go to London and she would marry Chester Reed and that was that. What I had to think about was whether she would still work with me. That, I thought, as I kicked back the covers and made a hasty toilet before tackling the early morning tasks, was the real thing, the only thing that really mattered between Dahlia and me. What did fondness matter? Why the very word, in its true sense, meant foolish. And I was too old, too battered by many contacts, to let fondness for a person whom I could not control cast even a momentary shadow over a day when I might live and be happy. It was in that mood that I started the day.

Just before Dahlia left a tall thin woman, dressed in black and carrying a large cardboard suit-case, arrived and announced that she was Miss Finch, and had been sent from the registry office. I took her into the kitchen, introduced her to Mrs. Pawsey, and then showed her Agnes's old room. I wondered, as I looked at her gaunt, ramrod-straight body and long flat feet whether Kipling, who so clearly defined the born cook type, would have allowed her to make him a piece of toast, but she settled down to the discussion of the day's food in a capable and fairly amiable manner, and I hoped for the best.

I went round to the barn with Dahlia to get out her car. She had run it in very awkwardly on the previous evening and muddled the exit so badly that I said, "Here, let me do it. If you're going to bungle like this all the way your licence will be suspended too."

"There are days when I can't drive, or do anything at all. This is one of them, but a special Providence watches me on those occasions."

"You'd better not go," I said doubtfully. "Stay just another day. I seem hardly to have seen you, what with the chores and people coming and going. Do stay."

"I can't, darling. I promised I'd be back today. But I'll see you soon, won't I? There're the rest of *Slave's Saga* and all those songs for *Patchwork Paradise*, you know. All this," she dismissed the situation with a wave of her hand, "won't make any difference to our working together, will it?"

"Well, thank God for that. I was wondering."

"Oh, but you needn't, Polly. You know—don't you—that nothing, nothing would ever make any difference to that. I'm yours. In fact, apart from gratitude, I think you're the only person that I've any real affection for. If I weren't such a worthless character I'd be willing to spend the rest of my life with you."

She looked at me with such sincerity in her eyes that I was uncomfortable, thinking as I did of my own thoughts about her that morning.

"Here, drive your own car," I said.

She shuffled along into the driver's seat and settled the skirt of her coat over her knees.

"I've left something on your bed," she said with a peculiar little smile.

"Thank you," I said.

"Wait till you've seen it."

The girls had come down to the front gate to see her off. I joined them and we stood there waving and calling out farewells, to which I added, "Be careful."

"I will. Good-bye. I have enjoyed myself. I'll write. . . ." She put in her gear with a noise like tearing calico and shot off down the lane.

"Well," I said, "I hope her Providence is on the job today, she'll need it."

Megan closed the gate.

"Remember how Mother used to hate us to swing on this gate?"

"And now it's Polly's and you could swing on it as much as you like, you don't want to. Life is like that," said Pen.

"Just for that I'm going to have one," said Megan. She opened it wide, perched on the lowest bar, and with a loud cry thrust off. The gate crashed to and she jumped down, brushing her hands.

"Well, I wonder what possible pleasure we got out of that. I suppose all kids are crazy."

We dawdled back to the house. I had a feeling that with Dahlia's going something had closed in on the three of us. What it was I had no idea, and as I hate feelings that I can't explain I thrust it away.

About ten minutes later I went upstairs to lay out sheets for Miss Finch's bed, and going past my own door remembered Dahlia's words. In the middle of my eiderdown lay the photograph of Roger with the gaping hole in the jacket about where the heart would be. There was a piece of the cover with it, and scrawled on it in thick pencil were the words, "May you be the woman."

"Damn and blast!" I said aloud, and turning the thing plain side uppermost, I tore it into shreds. I went down the back stairs and dropped the pieces into the kitchen stove. I should have slapped Dahlia hard if she'd been anywhere near. Then I thought that I was taking the whole thing far too seriously. It was funny, really, all this cursing and wishing and not daring to look at a pictured face. I shuffled that off too, and smiled as I went through and asked Pen and Meg, "Now, is there anything you'd like to do?"

Megan, with her unfailing flair for doing the "right" thing, answered my question with another asked in a quiet voice. "Have you put any flowers on the grave?"

Slightly startled, I said, "No, of course not. Ought I to have done?"

"Oh, I do think so. Of course I know it's kept trimmed and so on, but now that you're living here there ought to be flowers on it. Whatever will people think?"

"I'm afraid that pretty little problem never even occurred to me. After all, there haven't been any flowers there for eighteen years."

"I don't believe you've even been near the churchyard at all."

"Perfectly right. I haven't."

"You really are the most amazing creature."

"But why? Simply because I don't do something that would be certain to either bore me or depress me, although actually I never even thought about it. We'll go now if you like."

"I think we'd better. Can we take some flowers from the garden? And we shall need a bowl of some sort; something heavy enough to withstand the wind and deep enough to hold a good lot of water."

"I think you are the amazing creature," I said, preparing to go in search of the well-defined receptacle. "What do you say, Pen?"

"I'll come with you," said Penelope, evading the question.

By the time we had reached the churchyard my old dissatisfaction with myself had convinced me that it was indeed most unnatural of me not to have come here before. I filled the bowl I had chosen at the pump in the wall and then stood back, while Megan, on her knees, most correct in demeanour, arranged the sprays of Michaelmas daisies and the rather scraggy chrysanthemums and asters, which were all that the garden afforded. I looked at the names on the headstone: Arthur William Field, who had been dead for eighteen years and had been sixty when he died; Catherine Mary Field, who had predeceased her husband by two years and had been fifty years of age. Father, whom we had liked very well and laughed at for his unpunctuality and absent-mindedness; Mother, whom we had respected and feared a little because of her sharp tongue. A man and a woman, who, out of their loving, one supposed, though the thought was strange, had created the three people who stood here now in the sun of an October morning. Bones now, and names on a headstone and the faintest of memories in the three minds of their children. I at any rate had never understood either of them.

I knew that Father had once been well-to-do, and had idled away his days reading and collecting books, visiting strange places, and writing verses more remarkable for scholarship than beauty. Faced with penury through some mismanagement of money that even he never thoroughly understood, he had taken to farming in the middle years of his life, not because he knew anything about it, but because he liked living in the country and could not bear organisation of any kind. That was how it was that we had come to live at Pedlar's Green when I was a child of about two. Mother had far more iron in her. Bred in idleness and comfort, she had never flinched in the face of changed circumstances, and my only memory of her is that of a busy bustling woman who knew the prices of eggs and chickens, the value of the calves, and exactly what Father ought to get for the pigs. Had she despised him? Did his inefficiency, his unpunctuality, his serene imperturbability exasperate? There was never a sign of it in her behaviour. Perhaps his academic mind exacted from her practical one the tribute of respect and admiration that practical people pay, all the world over, to something that is just beyond their strong but limited grasp. Or it may have been the other way round. Perhaps they were a perfect pair. Perhaps they were very happy. And their happiness, or their differences, their secret hopes and fears, their egoism, their very identities had ended here, under this curtain of smooth turf and that was all.

I shuffled uncomfortably as Megan, still on her knees, pulled a spray, settled a flower, snipped off a leaf. It was to avoid thoughts like this that I had ignored the churchyard; the ignoring had been unconscious, certainly, but it had been wise. What was the use of hanging above a tomb? Whom did we serve by remembering? Forget them, forget all the dead who trod the ground and used the moment that we have now inherited. There is food to be bought, and drink to be enjoyed; over in Stoney there are shops where we can buy things. I want to feel the rush of air and the thrill of speed when the needle touches fifty.

I said to Megan, "Come on. You won't improve on that."

"Don't grudge a moment," said Penelope, answering my mood

rather than my words; "they used to sit up o' nights when we were young."

I set off down the path. The thought wouldn't be borne. And the comparison was faulty. It was not to the living but to the dead that I was grudging. But I didn't trouble to explain.

We dawdled back to the house in silence. I couldn't think of anything to say, Penelope was as quiet as usual, and Megan was muted. There is no other word for it. Her face had a strange, withdrawn look, and I had an uncomfortable feeling that it hadn't been an attitude, after all, that had taken her to the churchyard. Perhaps she did have deep, warm feelings under all her gaiety and poses. And I'd been unsympathetic! I sighed to myself. I'd offered both Dahlia and Megan all that I had yet they seemed all the time to be making dumb demands for something I hadn't got. Yet I knew that if Pen and I had, for some reason, broken down the eighteen-year-old defences and stood there shedding tears over that grave, Megan, after joining us in our weeping, would have been the first to recover, would have offered us words of comfort, her arm, her handkerchief. Then the full circle would have been described, the tribute would have been paid, and Megan would have had a sense of fulfilment. It was all too silly. I broke silence with, "Shall we go to Stoney now?"

And then Megan put the last elegant touch upon her picture of visiting the past in the correct manner, and said, "Not this morning. It's so nice. I want to go blackberrying."

"It's too late in the year," I said promptly.

"Much too late," Pen seconded. "It's after the Equinox when the devil looks over the bushes and blights them all."

"Never mind. Let's go out on the brakes like we used to. I've thought about doing it every autumn since I did it last."

"All right," I said, "if that's your fancy. Must you have a basket and a crook stick, or will a paper bag do?"

The place that we called "the brakes" was a piece of waste land, very little good even for grazing. The soil was sandy and there were clumps of wild thyme and outcrops of bracken amongst the grass. It was scattered with blackberry bushes and low scrubby hawthorn-trees, so that it was like a series of grassy passages and little rooms with living walls.

Once upon a time it had been a favourite place for playing in. Penelope and Megan used to take up their abode in two adjoining nooks and pretend that they were neighbours. They had washing days and cooking days and neighbourly quarrels and reunions. There was, however, only one of those domestic completions—children, and that was myself. So one time I was Penelope's child and the next Megan's. A large doll played, so to speak, opposite me. They quarrelled very often about whose turn it was to have me. I always sided with Pen in these arguments. I liked her better, even then. Sometimes our combined evidence resulted in her having me as many as three times running.

Once in the brakes we were sheltered from the wind and conscious of the gentle warmth that was left in the sunshine. It *was* late in the year for blackberrying, the berries fell at a touch, and those we salvaged collapsed into purple mush that stained our fingers and the paper bags. I was rather sorry that in the early days of my living there I had never once thought of this once-so-looked-forward-to pastime. I'd always loved blackberrying-time. There had always been a strange charm about the season, the imminence of change. There was, too, a sense of luckiness about finding a thickly fruited clump, a special warm *black* taste about the berries themselves. It's difficult to explain exactly. Either you enjoy grubbing about for blackberries and nuts and primroses or you don't. But I have heard most surprising people admit a weakness for that kind of thing—women with sophisticated-looking, white hands who can't resist digging up celandines with a nail-file.

I could have blackberried in the brakes by myself quite happily, I'm sure of that. And I could have taken my spoil home and been gluttonous over the pie, the jelly, or the jam, and never given a sorry thought to the fact that we three had had such merry, appetite-raising times there, three lanky children with scratched hands, stained mouths, and plucked holland frocks. But today it seemed for a moment, as I stretched out my hand to the plucking, that they couldn't be gone, those children. They must still be there, gloating over good finds, calling to one another through the gaps in the bushes, yelping to invite sympathy over scratches.

We were lucky, I thought, to have been country bred; to have known the joys of nutting and primrosing in the woods, to have been allowed to try our hands on softened teats at the end of the milking, and to have ridden the cart-horses that had such surprisingly sharp ridgy spines, despite the breadth of their backs. We'd been lucky too, to start off with bodies fortified by fresh air and plenty of milk and eggs and butter. God, I thought, I have a mercenary mind! And just then Megan came round a bush with a most peculiar expression on her face, and said to me, in a voice between tears and laughter, "Do you remember the wash days? And the day when I took off your liberty bodice to wash with the doll's things, and you got a cold and Mother was so cross . . ." Her face worked for a moment, and then she dropped the bag she was holding and bowed her face in her hands. Some tears splashed down between her fingers. Bloody hell, I said to myself, that's torn it! But even then I didn't think. . . .

"You were a fool ever to come here," Pen said harshly.

"It's nothing to cry about, Meg," I added, calling up my difficult kindness again.

She stood there, bowed over her hands, with the tears running down and her slim shoulders shaking with racking sobs while Pen and I stared at one another in helpless consternation.

At last I went to her and put my arm round her shoulders, bracing her against the impact of her sorrow. She was small, I realised, smaller than Dahlia, to whom I was always so kind. To Megan I was seldom kind; she had evoked admiration, not pity, from me—until now.

"Don't," I said awkwardly. "What is it, Meg? Is anything wrong? Tell me, tell us. We'll put it right for you. Darling, don't cry like that, it's so bad for you."

She drew a deep quivering breath and I felt her body stiffen. Now it was coming. What was it? And would it be anything that we could cope with? Was it a love-affair? Was she in some trouble about Henry?

The breath she had drawn came out in a long miserable sigh, and then she said in a surprisingly calm voice, "Oh God, I was mad to come here. Mad."

"But why?" I asked in genuine bewilderment. "I thought you'd like it. You can go away again, darling, if you don't like it here." I was remembering how boredom could always drive her butterfly soul to desperation, how sometimes in the middle of something that she had seemed to be liking she would spring up and say, "Oh, I'm so bored I could die." I thought, perhaps, the quietude of Pedlar's Green had worked like that already on her. I was not prepared for her to turn and say, "It isn't that I don't like it. I wanted to come. And really, it doesn't . . . Oh, it's the years, the time, the knowing that life is over . . ."

"But Megan—" A dreadful thought struck me. I remembered that haggard look she had before her face was done up. Perhaps she was ill. Maybe that was why she was so thin. Perhaps she had come over alone and gone to London to consult a doctor, perhaps he had told her something dreadful.

I tightened my arm around her, but she shook herself free and said in that same calm, dead voice, "Don't mind me. I'm mad. I can't explain it. It just comes over me at times and I just can't bear it. I wish I could die now and not have to face it any more."

"Face what, Megan? Are you ill?"

"In my mind I am." She looked at me, haggard and appealing, her eyes smudged with tears and her powder streaky. A silly quotation slipped through my mind, "Canst thou administer to a mind diseased?" I glanced at Pen, passing on to her the appeal that Meg had made to me. Pen responded.

"Come on," she said in her dry voice. "This is a damn silly thing to be doing, haunts of childhood, and all that. Let's get down to the house and Polly will fix you a drink and you can make up your face and you'll feel better."

"I'll never feel better. I've been making up my face and having drinks for years in order to forget it. It won't be forgotten. Every day is a day lost, and age sets in and the grave is waiting."

I had never heard anything approaching this from Megan before. I was dumb.

"Well," said Pen. "What of it? We all know that, and it's the same for everybody."

"I know that. What I don't know is how people bear the thought. Think of us. Just yesterday it seems we were running about here with all the future before us, and now here we are, not Polly, perhaps, so much, but you and I, Pen, spent, with no future left. We've used all the life that we're going to have. What we were born and reared for, over, done, finished."

"You just have to accept that, and not dwell on it. Other people don't."

"I've never even thought about it," I put in, foolishly.

Megan turned to me.

"I usen't to. God knows, there never was a less thoughtful or introspective person than I was. And then one day it just happened. At least it was in the night. I woke up and I could hear Henry breathing in the other bed, the way people do when they're asleep. And I realised suddenly that every breath he drew meant one less to draw. I was frightfully keen on Henry then, that was why it hit me so. And then I thought it was the same for me, for everybody. We were all dying slowly. Nothing could stop it, not love, not anything. And the day would come quite soon when love even would be unthinkable between the old bodies we'd have then. And everything I've thought or done since has been coloured by that thought. I tell you I'm mad."

"Oh, no," I said. "I should think it's simply that your nerves are out of order. You ought to see somebody about it."

"What could anybody do? I'd just look at him and think, 'You are going to die too.' I think that about everybody. Just now I remembered us in our holland frocks with scratches on our hands —and then I saw us dying."

I remembered my own thoughts about those same children, about how lucky they were to have their bellies full of food and I was most curiously ashamed.

"I think," said Pen, speaking slowly as though deliberating her words, "that you happen to be one of those people for whom religion, some belief in a future life, is a necessity. What you can't stand, really, is the thought of annihilation. If you could once get a good hold on a belief in the immortality of the soul you wouldn't mind the decay of the body any more."

Megan turned towards Pen this time.

"I know. I want to be a Catholic."

"Well, go on, then. Be one. Why not?"

"I don't think I have enough faith."

Pen hitched one of her pointed shoulders in a fidgety way she had.

"Be something else then. A Baptist, or a Transmigrationist, or a Buchmanite. It's all the same ultimately."

"But I don't think I have enough even for that."

"Well, I can't give it to you. You must cultivate it. That is the whole point. Faith, like all other habits of mind, grows with its own practice."

"I know," Meg said dolefully. "That's the trouble. I know you think I'm pretty futile. That's why you say, 'Have faith,' just like you'd say, 'Have an aspirin.' You don't sound as though you'd got any yourself."

"I haven't. But, then, I don't have to. The idea of Penelope Field, who was a child and then a young woman, becoming an old hag and eventually a corpse doesn't raise a qualm in me."

"You aren't very fond of yourself, are you, Pen?" I asked in a sudden flash of curiosity.

"I haven't much cause to be."

"Then you think it's self-love?" Megan asked, unoffended.

"Unconsciously, yes. I quite see that it's more difficult for you than for me. You've always been pretty; naturally and rightly you're fond of your body. Watching it fade and become less attractive must be hell for you. That's why I recommend religion."

"But it isn't only the body, Pen. The mind is blotted out too. All your memories, the good times and the grand people you've known. It makes everything seem so futile. Oh, I know I'm no good at this kind of talk, but to think that even all the love you've known, everything you've felt, everything that makes you *you* is bound for oblivion, that is what is so appalling."

"What's wrong with it? You've enjoyed the good times and the grand people. You can't ask more than that."

"Oh, Pen, I can't talk to you. You don't sound human. You understand, don't you, Polly?"

"I begin to," I said. And my own words frightened me. I pushed away the thought. This was just one of Meg's moods, like the tantrums that she had as a child, which had upset every one

in the household so that our nerves were still quivering long after
she had recovered.

She had turned and begun to walk away. Pen tossed her bag of
blackberries over a bush, and I dropped mine into a clump of net-
tles. Then we followed her.

"You've forgotten," Pen began again, patiently, "that I'm a bit
older than you and have had, if I may say so, a rather different
kind of life. I'm resigned. You've been a bit late arriving at this
stage, I think. Most people get it settled earlier, and either go gay
and forget it, or evolve some theory, most suitable to themselves,
regarding immortality."

"No other alternatives?" I said.

"They're the only ones I ever heard of. The only ones that 'the
Good Book' as Grandmother used to call it, has to offer. Either
'Prepare to meet thy God' or 'Eat, drink, and be merry.'"

"And which," I asked, "have you chosen, Pen?"

Pen laughed.

"Once I actually prepared to meet my God, but He didn't like
the look of me. Polly, don't you think a drink would be an idea?
Come on, then." She took hold of Megan by the elbow and we
began to hurry away into the house as though the brakes had suddenly become haunted.

Going out by the back way to take the dogs into the fields that
evening, I noticed that the dustbin lid was tilted. I went to put it
straight. But the dustbin was full beyond the brim with bottles
and jars. Mary Castle's Eye Lotion, Powder Base, Night and Day
and Pore Cream, Petal Powder, Bloom Rouge, Eye Shadow, and
a flask three-quarters full of Lotus Blossom perfume.

I fished them out and brushed off the tea-leaves and ashes that
clung to them. When I had set them on the shelf in the wood-
shed the last rays of light wakened the prisms in the glass again.
Too nice, I thought, to throw away so. After all, it was not they
who had let Megan down.

Dinner was a ghastly meal, despite Miss Finch's excellent cooking. I had to make a determined effort not to look at Megan's un-
decorated face. With that cluster of curls on the brow, with its

suggestion of youthfulness, it looked like the face of a child that is frightened of the dark. I wished that I could think of something that would console her. But there just wasn't anything. Mortality is the burden of us all, and if she couldn't bear it unconsciously—as I had done, or carelessly—as Pen did, well, that was just her damned luck! All I could do was to try to provide diversion and keep up a flow of chatter.

Afterwards Pen started the gramophone, and Megan went up to her room to write a letter.

"I do hope," I said idly to Pen when we were alone, "that she isn't in the habit of writing that graveyard stuff in letters. She got me properly jacked up with it all this morning. It's the last thing I should expect from her."

"Is it? Actually, it's so normal as to be pathological. Pretty, romantic-minded women often go gaga that way when their sexual impulses begin to weaken. Either religion or nymphomania gets nine out of ten in the end."

"Well, nymphomania may be uglier, but it's easier to cope with, I think," I said. "Let's hope she chooses that, if choice is inevitable."

"It doesn't matter much, either way," said Pen, and it seemed to me that there was just a suggestion of a sigh in her voice. For the first time—perhaps because the events of the last day or two were beginning to have effect upon me—I caught myself wondering what lay behind the cool, hard, impassive front that Pen turned to the world. Her detached attitude towards Megan's state of mind, the way she discussed women's reactions, struck me, for the first time, as being queer. After all, she was a woman herself, not far separated from Megan in age, widely as their lives and experiences had differed. Had she, I caught myself wondering, cultivated her intellectual side until the emotional had withered? Or had she met with some unfortunate experience that had hardened and chilled her? She'd never been pretty, never had vivacity enough to hide the stark fact; and as I looked at her I had a kind of vision of the pale, leggy, clever little girl going determinedly down the years, choosing her work, choosing her attitude, perfecting it, and all the time being conscious of something missing. Perhaps when she said, "pretty romantic-minded women" in that impersonal analytical way, she was envying them all the time.

But I put that thought away as soon as it was formed. There was no envy in Pen, and, almost I dared have sworn it, no frustration either. Because there was a power in her. What she wanted she would have taken. No doubt of that. Not for the first time I was conscious of shame in comparing my life, my character with hers. My drifting years, my shoddy affairs, my present forlorn hankering after Roger, my love of cash and the things that its possession brought me . . . cheap and unworthy all of them. Ugh! I thought with a mental shrug, Pen always did fire my inferiority complex, being older and so much cleverer. Perhaps I'm still seeing her with the eyes of a schoolgirl. Perhaps she's quite ordinary, really, just a virtuous old maid. Then I was ashamed again. You couldn't class Pen like that.

Megan came down with a coat slung over her shoulders and a couple of letters in her hand.

"Going to walk to the post?" she asked us, and we tore ourselves out of our comfortable chairs to go with her.

"How I used to dread coming up this drive alone," I said, as we went through the shadow of the laurels.

"So you did," said Megan. "And now you don't mind living there all alone. Or do you? Don't you get jittery when the wind howls?"

"Not a bit. Fears are funny things. I can trace mine exactly. It was wolves first, in the shrubbery, and there was a black bear, too, in that corner of the passage by the back stairs. Then they went and I was terribly afraid of burglars, and after that of ghosts. Then, I suppose, I grew up and found real things to fear, and I wasn't afraid of being by myself any more."

"Real things? What are you afraid of now, Polly?"

"Having teeth out, and being poor," I said, with prompt truth.

"Fancy," said Megan. "Now I go to the dentist's like a lion. And dread my looking-glass. Are you afraid of anything, Pen?"

"Well, yes," said Pen. "I am. I'm terrified to death of being afraid, and I bet it gets me into more bother than either of your phobias. If I ever catch myself wondering what will happen if I do this, or say that, or question the wisdom of any of my plans, I just say, 'Ah, you're scared.' And then I simply have to say it, or do it, whatever it is. And God, what it lands me into sometimes. Simply because I'm scared."

"How absurd," said Megan. "If you really did that you'd be behaving like a lunatic all the time. For instance," she looked up at the top of the telegraph post to which the letter-box was fixed. "Would you be afraid to jump from the top of that pole?"

"Yes, naturally."

"Well, then . . . according to what you said just now, you ought to climb it straight away and throw yourself off it."

"That isn't so at all," said Pen, in a reasoning voice. "It would never occur to me that any useful purpose could be served by doing that, therefore it would never occur to me to do it. But if any purpose could be served, and it did occur to me to do it, and then I felt scared, well, then it would work. Half of me would cry out, 'Aha, you're scared,' and I should be so terrified that I should do it right away."

"You wouldn't."

"I've done worse things than that," said Pen in a dead way.

"Aren't you going to post those letters?"

Megan separated them and studied the top one in the faint light of the moon.

"Letter for Henry," she said, and slipped it in. The other she held a moment more, raised it half-way, and then lowered her hand sharply.

"Christ," she said violently, and the sudden word sounded more like a prayer than an oath, "I've got the mind of a jellyfish!" She tore the letter across several times, using all her force on the good tough paper, and flung the pieces over the hedge. "Come on, talk, say something, say anything! You, Polly, why are you afraid of having teeth out?"

Almost hysterical for the first time in my life, I gasped, "B-b-b-because I've got t-t-twisted roots," and began to roll about the road, helpless with laughter.

II

First down in the morning, it was I who picked up the letters from the mat and took up, on Megan's tray, the missive that changed, it seemed, her mind from jelly to granite. It had been forwarded twice, that letter, once from a London hotel to Pen's place, and from there to Pedlar's Green.

Pen met me on the stairs; she preferred, she had told me, to breakfast at a table. She said, with a kind of bleak humour, jerking her shoulder towards their room, "We've had a hell of a night. Turning and tossing and yappering about how one joins the Roman Catholic Church. Would I know? God, it'd be funny if it weren't so beastly pathetic."

"I know," I said. "I'll be down in a minute. Ring for the breakfast, will you?"

In the room that seemed curiously bare without the jars and bottles, Meg scrambled up in the bed when she saw me. She looked grim: hollow-cheeked, hollow-eyed, and frail to a degree. Her eyes fell immediately on the letter, and at once the hollowness and pallor of her face was washed over and drowned by a flood of colour that began at the chiffon frill of her nightgown and rushed up to lose itself in the tangle of her unnetted hair. Her lips parted and her eyes darted over the single page. I watched her. When I withdrew my eyes it was a second too late. She looked up and saw me staring. "It's from someone I met on the boat," she said, smiling; but the smile and the words denied our sisterhood. I was a stranger caught staring and the explanation sounded as though I had asked for it. I almost blurted out, "I wasn't curious. I just wondered if this would cheer you at all." But, instead, I said, "Have you got all you want?"

"Yes, thank you," she said, and the words didn't really apply to the loaded tray.

Megan's post had often been a matter of family interest in those distant years. There would be a letter from some boy who had got her address, and Mother would ask, in a voice that demanded an answer, "Who is that letter from, Megan?" Once Megan had said, "From Evie," with a look that convicted her of lying, and Mother had said, "I don't believe you. Give it to me." Megan had looked helplessly at Father, who said, reasonably enough, "If there's anything in it that your Mother can't read, Meg, Evie is an unsuitable friend for you." We all waited, tensely. Tears gathered in Meg's eyes and hung on her lashes in a very disarming fashion.

"I am waiting," said Mother.

Meg bowed before the inevitable.

"That was a lie," she said. "It's from a boy."

"What boy?"

"A boy who sometimes walks to school with me. He's a nice boy, Mother, really. And there's nothing in the letter, but it would . . . it would seem silly if you read it."

Mother read it. Worse, she read it aloud, in a peculiarly mocking voice. It did sound silly. She intended it to. Megan began to cry in earnest. "I didn't want him to write to me," she blubbered. "I told him not to."

"And for this," said Mother, tapping the offending sheet, scrawled all over with boyish writing, "for *this* you lie to your parents. For this you waste your time at school for which we have to scrape and save the fees. I am pained, surprised, and disgusted at you."

I regret to say that the rhythm of "pained, surprised, and disgusted" impressed us more than the import, and we used to express disapproval amongst ourselves in those terms for a long time.

But Megan had other letters. Almost every holiday the scene would be repeated. And Mother always read the letters, and Megan always cried. Then Mother died and the first time that Megan had a letter after that—though of course her letters had been uninspected for some time by then—she looked across to Mother's place at the table and burst into tears. Pen, who happened to be home at the time said, very puzzled, "But you never *liked* showing them to her, did you?"

And here, after all those years, in the very same house, Megan was holding a letter in her hand, tugging on a dressing-gown and following me down the stairs to the telephone. I heard her asking for a London number as I closed the dining-room door.

I told Pen. "There's a letter from someone she met on the boat, and she's telephoning now."

"Aha," said Pen, crumbling a piece of toast, "I'm afraid God will have to wait a while longer."

Megan was down and dressed by the time that I had drained my last cup of coffee. Pen had gone out into the garden.

"Hullo," I said, "you have been quick."

She put on the expression that had gained her Heaven knows how many favours.

"Polly, darling, will you do something for me? Take me into Stoney now, at once, will you?"

"Of course," I said. "Are you leaving today?"

She nodded. "If you don't mind. You said you wouldn't. Only you see—I can't go straight to the station. I did such a fool thing yesterday. You see . . ." she hesitated and traced a pattern on the carpet with the toe of her shoe. "I got all worked up, and I thought I wouldn't ever bother about anything so trivial as my face again. I put all my stuff in the dustbin. And I wrote that letter, calling off all this other affair. And then I couldn't post it. I'm so *glad* I didn't. Now I must go and arm myself again. Would you think there's a shop in Stoney that has heard of Mary Castle?"

"I doubt it very much. But come with me."

I led her to the wood-shed and pointed to the shelf.

"Oliver Cromwell was a very sensible bloke," I said. "He gave vent to this remarkable statement, 'Trust in God and keep your powder dry.' You should remember that."

Megan threw her arms round me and squeezed out all my breath.

"You dear, you darling, you sweet Polly! You've saved my face, as the Chinese say." She lifted the hem of her skirt and began gathering the bottles into the lap of it. In less than half an hour she came out to me in the garden. The delicate vivid mask of her make-up was on her face again, and the mask of gaiety was on her soul. She twined an arm round my waist and turned me away from the house and fell into step beside me.

"You don't mind, darling, do you, my going, I mean?"

"I shall mind, but I want you to do what you want, of course."

The mental mask slipped a trifle.

"I don't know what I want, and that's the truth. But I can't stay here, Polly. You see what it does to me, don't you? All that atmosphere of the past and the years . . . and the . . . the innocence of it all. I've tried to get back, to wash it all out. It's no good, Polly. I think about the years till I feel like an ant, and about the space beyond the stars till I'm mad. And the only thing that can save me is a shattering affair, a feeling, a traffic in the flesh. While you're feeling anything you're not finished; and while you can have fun you're not old."

"And are you going to have fun?"

"Yes," she said, "I'm going to have fun."

"And Henry?" I asked foolishly. I didn't like Henry, but he had a certain soundness and was terribly attached to Megan.

"Oh, Henry," she said, and her voice was a shrug. "Henry's all right. But he can't save me any more. All that is like an old coat —nice enough, but no good to keep out the wind. But a fine new coat, a fine new coat, that will keep out the wind."

"What wind? You're full of parables this morning. What wind?"

And then Megan said a strange thing. "The wind of the spirit that bloweth where it listeth. And the queer thing is that it blew on *me*. I wonder why. But it was no good. I'm one of the carnally minded—you know about them?"

"No," I said harshly. "I didn't have so long a course of Grand-mother's Bible reading as you did."

She ignored the gibe.

"Then you won't remember the scarlet woman of Babylon, whose cup was full of fornication and other abominations. I am she. But oh"—she let go my waist and stretched her arms out from the shoulder, bracing her slim body against the wind—"it's heavenly to feel something again, to want something. I've been numb for so long. And to think that I've been playing with the idea of being a nun!" She dropped her arms and laughed. "Come and help me pack, darling. I'd like to catch the two-ten."

III

"I guess I'd better go tomorrow. Work's piling up all this time," said Pen, as we stood on the platform waiting for Megan's train to pull out.

I said, "Oh, no, you must stay," rather absently, for I was looking at Megan. The prospect of pleasure, which simply meant another conquest for her, had made her radiant. The smart little hat with the eye veil that just brushed her nose, the trim town suit and the silver fox fur slung carelessly over one shoulder, the perfume, the good, much-travelled-looking luggage, built up the impression of a woman, well cared for, beautiful, assured, elegant and well-to-do. I thought, I haven't seen you for a long time, and it may be years before I see you again. I may never see you again. And how on earth shall I think of you? Smiling from the first-class carriage? Blubbering amongst the blackberries? Brooding over Time by the fire? Which are you? Which is Megan? Which is my sister?

The guard raised his green flag. We exchanged the last hasty kisses, the last insincere promises about writing regularly. A white-gloved hand waved a handkerchief as the train rounded the bend and Megan had gone.

"I'm afraid she's a trifle cross with me," said Pen as we reached my car. "I begged her to wait for a little."

"Oh, did you? Perhaps I ought to have done, too. I just accepted it when she said she was going. She seemed so much braced—and—and I'm afraid I'm not very moral, Pen."

"Well, don't sound so apologetic! Neither am I. I'm simply pessimistic, and I think she's just in the state to make a pretty fool of herself."

"Oh, dear," I said, "what a problem it all seems."

"Simply because she's discovered that she won't live for ever. That's what it amounts to. But, of course, she always was like that, suddenly seeing that two and two were four and never realising that everybody else had known it for ages."

I looked ahead along the road where the russet and yellow leaves were dancing in the sunshine. And I thought, it's a golden autumn afternoon, and I'm seeing it. There have been hundreds like it, and the people who saw them are dead. There'll be hundreds more and we shan't be here to see them. Hell! I've caught Megan's bug.

"I see what she's driving at in all that talk," I said.

"So do I," said Pen, turning her uplifted brow on me. "But it seems a poor reason for adultery."

"You don't need a reason for that," I said, and my words were lighter than my mood.

"I suppose not," said Pen, and began to talk about something else.

I had been on the verge of asking her then, "Pen, have you ever been in love?" I felt that if I knew the answer to that I should know something more about her. There might be a story that would explain things. Besides, I really wanted something that would take my mind off Megan. But the moment slipped and I didn't get a chance to ask that impertinent question until after dinner when Miss French had slipped away like an attendant shadow with the coffee tray.

"Pen," I said, "have you ever been in love?"

The sound eyebrow went up to match the other, and she gave me that old quizzical look.

"Whatever makes you ask that?"

"I've often wondered," I said, a little uncomfortably. "Just as I've often wondered about your face—that accident. Oh, don't tell me if you'd rather not. I suppose you think that curiosity is vulgar. You're never curious, are you? Only . . . it's struck me in these last few days that really . . . we don't know much about one another, do we?" And an undertone in my own mind added: "Of course *you* don't know much about me, and there's a lot, about me and Roger for example, that I'd hate you to know."

All the same, I did wonder about the "little accident" to which Pen had attributed the bandaged head and palsy-shaken limbs with which she had faced the assembly at father's funeral. She said now, with a most odd detachment, "Oh, those scars on my face!" as though they were something quite apart from herself. She slumped lower in the chair and tucked her hands under her folded arms.

"Preparing to tell the story of my life," she said, jibingly. "I've never done that before." But there was a brooding, a remembering look in her eyes that told me that it was coming.

"You wouldn't remember the Andrews, would you? They were kind of relatives of Mother's."

I shook my head. I had perhaps heard the name before, but it conveyed nothing to me.

"They lived just outside Oxford," Pen went on, "and when I went there Mother said I was to go and see them. I did go. I went quite a lot. They were always asking me, and though it wasn't the kind of house that gave you any pleasure to visit I seemed to have to go all the more for that. They were poor, they'd only his pension, he was a retired colonel, and the house was far too big. The fires were always tiny, only just alight, in fact, and in winter it was agony to stay there because the blankets were so thin and scanty. I felt these things more then than I should now. Also the house was full of the most horrible souvenirs, old, odd weapons, beastly brass ware, animals' heads and photographs of people in pith helmets. They'd spent a long time in India—you knew that as soon as you opened the door. It was quite nice in summer, there was a big wild garden with a lot of trees, and the roses all going back to the cabbagy sort. Well, there's the background, as you might say." Pen paused and twitched her shoulders.

"It was in the war, as you know, and Colonel Andrews' main occupation was putting little flags and tape lines on an enormous

map of Europe that hung in a cellar of a room that was called his
study. I always had to go and see that the first thing when I went
there. I used to have the most awful struggle remembering what
it had looked like last time so that I could make some intelligent
comparison. Mrs. Andrews spent her time trying to save enough
sugar from their rations to preserve the currants and things from
the garden. One of the girls who used to come out there sometimes with me was diabetic and didn't use sugar, and I'd given it
up, so sometimes we used to take some in a bag when we went.
That used to please her no end."

Pen paused and twitched again. I realised that all this had been
hedging. I said, "Hell, Pen, I'm sorry I asked you that silly question. I've stirred up something you'd sooner forget."

She said, "It isn't the sort of thing one can forget, my dear,"
and went on in a kind of rush.

"One day when I was there they were in the middle of a savage
discussion about asking Charlie to stay. Charlie, I gathered, was
the son of one of Colonel Andrews' erstwhile fellow officers, he
was an orphan and had no people. He'd been wounded, and the
old man wanted to ask him there while he recuperated. Mrs.
Andrews, thinking of food and the servant problem, was equally
anxious not to have him. The old man was obstinate, however. I
remember he said that day, 'There's nothing I wouldn't do for
Jim Lawrence's boy. He can come here and run around for a bit
with Penelope. They'll be company for one another. Do them
both good.' He had a kind of simplicity of outlook that you often
find in his type. It was very disarming. It made it impossible, for
instance, for me to give any hint of what I was thinking, which
was that a young officer's idea of doing himself good would not
be to run around with a plain earnest student. I knew the kind of
girls young officers liked, and the thought of them made me feel
leggy and gauche. I'd seen Megan at work!

"However, there I was, roped in as part of the entertainment,
and after I'd seen the lad once or twice my shyness wore off, for
he was shy too, quiet and young and thin and sunk, utterly sunk
in some mood of abstraction to which we had no clue. Throw me
a cigarette." She lifted herself in the chair to reach for the box I
held towards her, and cupped her hand round the match,

thoughtfully. Once more I had the feeling that the story would end now. It was rather like those old, old films where you were suddenly faced with the words, "End of Reel 1."

"At first the old man made a frightful fuss of him, opening his precious port and urging him to drink burgundy because it was 'good for the blood.' But he cooled off, because, as I discovered, Charlie not only took very little interest in the marvellous map, but showed a marked reluctance to discuss the war in any way. In his more flowery moments Colonel Andrews had been known to refer to it as 'this twentieth-century crusade,' and that, Charlie told me afterwards, nearly made him sick at the table.

"We, that is Charlie and I, got to know one another very well. It began over a dance that a club I belonged to got up in aid of the hospital funds. He'd taken tickets on condition that I went with him; and though the thing wasn't much in my line I was kind of bound to go in any case. We enjoyed it—about the only thing we ever did, incidentally. He got hold of some whisky and cheered up quite a lot. Oh, dear, the further I go the more explanatory I'm bound to be. There was a doctor at the hospital that I knew through doing a bit of work there, he'd been wounded very early, and had a stiff leg, so he ran a funny little old car, and he'd taught me to drive it. That was a help to him in a way. And on this night, when he knew that I'd come in from the Andrews' house and was going back, he said I might take the thing and drive us home if I could get it back by nine in the morning. He meant well, but it started the whole thing.

"On the way out I went over a rabbit. It squealed, and I got out and went back to see if it was truly dead. Charlie came too. The thing was all squashed, and its insides and blood were all spread out on the road. I was sorry, of course, but not upset. I'd been in the hospital quite a bit, and blood wasn't exactly new to me. Nor to him, I should have thought. So when he went to the side of the road and was violently sick I just thought it was the whisky he'd drunk, or the bump, or something.

"He came back after a moment or so, looking rather sullen, and I felt a bit awkward—being there, you know—so I began to start the car again, very attentive. Then he said, 'I suppose you think I'm drunk. Well, that's where you're wrong. That's the

way nasty sights take me, so you can imagine how I enjoy this
twentieth-century crusade, can't you?' He spoke very truculently,
but underneath there was an appeal—bitter, definite, unmistakable. I had a kind of flash of understanding and saw all that
that sulky sentence implied. I was probably a bit out of myself too,
for somehow I didn't feel shy or constrained any more. I made
some sort of sympathetic noise, and then I got the whole flood of it.

"I'd read things, of course, and I'd seen wounded men, but I
hadn't begun, until then, to realise what it meant to people who
were in it, and who were cursed, through no fault of their own,
with queasy stomachs and badly balanced nervous systems. My
own were both excellent. Actual physical things had never
affected me. But Charlie's talk went straight to a sensitive spot
that exists, I suppose, in my imagination only, the spot that used
to make me dread that gipsy boy's grave because it could con-
struct out of that mound over a heap of dry bones the terror and
the despair that had overtaken him in that last hour of his poor
little life. Yes, it was like that. Out of the mound and the bones
of the thing that we had got used to, the thing we glibly spoke of
as 'the war,' Charlie evoked for me the living horror of the thing
seen from the inside. Can you understand that, Polly?"

"I understand," I said. "Go on, what did you do?"

"Very little. What could one do? I know I finished up with my
arm round his shoulder and his face pressed into my shoulder—
the traditional attitude of defence that comes naturally to
women. But the arm couldn't shield him and the shoulder
couldn't blind. After a bit I had to start the car again and drive
home, and the only thing of comfort I could think of to say was,
'You've had a shattering time. You're unstrung. Perhaps you'll
feel differently when you're better.' Then he laughed, and said,
'Not I. I felt this way before ever I saw anything.'

"I had an idea that in the morning he would hate himself for
having talked as he had done, and me for having listened to him.
But no. From that night on he followed me about like a dog. He
raked up a rusty old bicycle from somewhere and rode into the
town with me, hung about while I was in lectures or at the hospital, and accompanied me home. The Andrews were mildly

amused by it all, and teased us rather. Our talk wasn't by any means all raw bones and bloody heads. He was awfully intelligent and had thought and read a lot. I *am* making a long story out of this, am I not? Anyway, I fell for him.

"I suppose that was the only way I could be in love with anybody; I'm not the kind of person who could engage in a jolly flirtation, or who could bear being swept off her feet, as the phrase goes. I want to cherish and comfort and support, odd as that may sound coming from the dried-up old hulk I am now. And all my nice motherly instincts had full play through that long spring and the early summer. And the better I knew him the worse I felt about him. He was so gentle and sensitive. I suppose that sentence is capable of misconstruction, especially nowadays when every one is on the lookout for that kind of thing, and men have to almost parade the hair on their chests to prove that they *are* male. But it wasn't like that at all, though I'm sure he wasn't normal. He was just shattered and utterly incapable of recuperation. And the days fled past until the day came for his examination by the medical board.

"Now I was certain they wouldn't pass him. His whole make-up seemed to me to be so obviously out of gear that I didn't think he'd ever be passed for active service again, although the wound that had sent him home was perfectly healed. The board wasn't in our town, so we rode to the station together in the morning and I propped my bicycle over his by the railings and went on to the platform. He got into the carriage and stood by the door talking to me, and then, just as the train was leaving and I stepped back, he went an awful colour and looked at me, and said, 'Penelope, come with me.' I tore open the door and scrambled in, just as I was, in an old skirt and jumper, with no hat and no gloves. That doesn't sound strange nowadays, but it looked funny then. They passed him, of course. I realised later that they were turning blind eyes to obvious physical disabilities in that dark hour, so they couldn't be expected to consider nerves.

"And that began the last lap.

"I can't tell you it all. It was like a nightmare. He'd talk about it, his dread of going back, and his worse dread of doing some-

thing that would disgrace him for ever, and then he'd break off
and talk about something else, striving after the normal, the ordinary, the sane.

"I went at last to the colonel. I hoped I'd make him understand. 'You know people,' I said, 'you can do something, pull
wires, use influence . . .' It was awful. He called me a hysterical
female, and Charlie a coward. He spoke of Charlie's father who
had died the death of a hero. He spoke of England with her back
to the wall. He said that if only they'd abolish the age limit . . .

"I fired at the 'coward' and said that for Charlie to face one
day of modern warfare without cracking was a braver thing than
for an insensitive block of a diehard to go through a whole
death-or-glory campaign. And then the old man surprised me.

" 'Young woman,' he said, 'you talk like a fool. Do you think
we weren't frightened? The Afghans torture the wounded, you
know, and I've ridden into many an action knowing that if I were
wounded and hadn't strength or means to finish off myself I'd die
slowly under the knives of the women. I've ridden with a palsy of
fear in my knees so that it was hard to hold the horse between
them, but I've ridden . . . and forward.'

"I was a little ashamed of the things I had said and thought,
then. And I could see that there was no help to be hoped for
from that quarter.

" 'He isn't frightened, he's sick,' I said, and came away. After
that the colonel hardly spoke to Charlie, and there was no more
port or burgundy.

"He—that is, Charlie—didn't sleep much, any more, and we
got into the habit of sitting up together, or going for long walks
in the night. I think perhaps we were both a little crazy. I know I
seduced him—just that. I thought it might take his mind off, but
it didn't.

"So the day came nearer, and at last he said there was only one
thing to do, stand up again to be shot through the head and pray
that the fellow had better aim than the last.

"I said, '*Did* you do that?' He said, 'Yes, and I will again.' And
I thought, what good are you?—even to England with her back
against the wall.

" 'Do you want to die?' I asked him.

" 'It's the only thing that can save me, now,' he said.

"And I knew it was true.

"So, to cut short this frightfully long-winded tale, I borrowed the poor little Rover one evening and drove up to the Beacon, which was a highish hill, an escarpment rather, and the road was railed in in places where the drop over the side was sharp and dangerous. We sat at the top and watched the sunset, and we talked a bit. Most of my talk was aimed at delving out new justification for what I was going to do. And I delved out plenty. I thought about watching the sunset for the last time, and that I wouldn't be there tomorrow. I realised that every day is some-body's last one. It's quite an easy thing to accept really. And then I drove down and straight over the edge at a bend. He didn't know anything about it. I had just one wild fear for a moment that the railings were stronger than I thought and weren't going to give way, but they did, and we dropped.

"I didn't wake up for four days, but when I did I was quite clear instantly. There was a nurse in the room and I said to her, 'What about the boy who was with me?' She fenced for a bit and frightened me like hell in case it should all have been wasted, but at last she told me that he was dead when we were found. I went straight to sleep again and slept for the greater part of a week, which shows you what the strain must have been, though I hadn't been conscious of it. And then almost immediately Father died, and I really had to stir myself to get to the funeral. I was all right after that. At least, I hated myself. I can't think why. I'd do it again. And I am not *sorry*. I just hated myself. I wanted to do a kind of penance. Of course I was young.

"The first thing I tried to do, as a kind of atonement, was to leave Oxford and get a job and look after you. But Father had ar-ranged for your future—about as badly as he did everything. And then I heard of the Mary Montague—just starting, short of helpers—made for me. It's good work, and I hate it. The squalor, the regulations, the horrible things you have to see and do. I'm not fitted for it really. I like colour and life and violence and lux-ury. I like lovely, intelligent people. But I've been there eighteen years, and I shall be there till I die. My God, what an egotistical outburst!"

She broke off abruptly on that note of scorn, reached for a cigarette and lighted it. The flare of the match showed up the scars
on the hard thin face, the satirically lifted eyebrow, the deep
steady eyes, the beautiful blue eyes of a woman who loved life
and violence and colour, and had renounced them all. I thought,
so this is what happened to the little girl who used to take prizes
at school: this is the thing that Pen has carried about with her all
these years. Dear God!

I couldn't say anything at all. If respect and homage and appreciation of a person's sheer character were tangible things that
could be made up into a parcel and held out like a present I
could have offered Pen a surprising amount. But these things
have to be spoken, and I could find no words at all.

Presently she said, flicking away ash, "I bet Megan's having a
fine time now."

"Yes," I said, "she's hugging the chains of her mortality tonight."

"Well, that's the only thing to do with chains, you know,
Polly."

I thought suddenly, with a sickening vividness of my chains,
desire and lust and hunger for Roger.

"You're right," I said. "Have a drink?"

IV

Pen left next morning. I tried to dissuade her, knowing the uselessness of my arguments, even as I uttered them.

"You'll come again, anyway, won't you?" I urged her. "Come for Christmas."

Pen smiled. "Do you think you'll be here at Christmas?" she asked.

"Of course. I'm here for good," I said.

The little car, the patient donkey of the automobile world, pegged away down the lane, and as I turned from watching it and closed the white gate behind me, a sense of dire enchantment, such as my prosaic mind had never known before, fell upon me. The circle had narrowed ripple by ripple after each departure, and now I was alone. I was alone before that last interview with Miss Finch who, lingering after clearing away my luncheon things, told me that she must leave, the country was getting on her nerves.

"You can go now, at this moment, if you like," I said with spurious kindness. I gave her a week's wages and hardly noticed her going.

The evening, falling appreciably earlier today than yesterday, came on dull and cold. I built up a huge fire and let in the dogs to sit by it with me. I heard the footsteps of the stockman from the Hall Farm go down the lane. He would be the last person to travel that way tonight. Mrs Pawsey had gone, long ago after laying the table in the dining-room for my meal. I didn't go near it. I sat by the fire and gave myself up to the enchantment that had befallen my peaceful home, my happy life.

Of what was it made? And how had it fallen?

Three days ago I had welcomed them in, those guests who had taken away something that they had not brought, and left at the same time so much behind. I thought about each in turn. And I thought about them not as solid people but as little marionettes, hurrying down their appointed paths under the leaden eyes of the unseeing sky.

Dahlia, my first guest, my foundling, my mascot who had let one part of her, like a black procuress, offer the white Dahlia to Chester Reed for his pleasure. I saw her going down the years, hiding God knew what regrets, losing her looks, going heavily, going gravewards.

I mourned over Dahlia, as she was, and as she would be. And Megan, my pretty sister. Lovely Megan, with her laughter and her bluff; happy Megan with her clothes and her bottles and her men. Megan had come back stricken with a strange disease, and Pedlar's Green had made it worse. "Saul, Saul, much thinking hath made thee mad." Who had said that, and why? Just a little thinking had made Megan mad, and like a victim of hydrophobia she had bitten me in passing and now the same madness moved in me. For I could see her, too, moving under the leaden sky, from one diversion to another, from this lover to that, until at last the time for diversion and the time for lovers alike would be gone and Megan must turn towards the grave that she dreaded. Laughing Megan, who had kissed Alf Wicker behind a haystack, was it for this you were made?

And Pen? Ah, surely I could think of Pen with comfort, for Pen feared nothing. As she enjoyed nothing. And I knew then that the measure of our fear is the measure of our enjoyment. We fear to lose what we enjoy. And Pen would not fear death, having been dead these many years. Her very strength had been her undoing. Where weaker people had wept and wrung their hands in the face of what was too strong for them, Pen had acted as though she had been God, or, at least, His deputy. And this strong sad woman had been a little girl who had played at keeping house, and had enjoyed blackberrying, and had sat here by this very fire, munching apples and walnuts on just such a night as this.

What does life give in exchange for what it takes away? I asked. And there was no voice, nor any that answered. Only the wind howled round the house in the way that I remembered; and Block got up and went to the door so purposefully that I had to rise to let him out.

"Make one errand of it," I said, and drove them all out into the garden.

I did not go back to the fire. I made the round of the house, pressing on lights before me and darkening them behind. I'd loved it so. All my white paper, all my corners and shining spaces. I'd offered it freely to those three women who had passed through it quietly on one certain spot of their different paths and who had left me with this weight of melancholy to grapple with as I could. I hated the house now. I could only think of those children who had banged its doors, played in its corners, laughed, growing every day towards their destiny, beginning even then, and all unconscious of it, to serve their death sentence. I went back to let in the dogs, and we all sat down again by the fire.

"I think I'm going crazy," I said to the bright eyes in those hairy faces. And the ears pricked at my voice, and the tails stirred lazily. Dear adorable faithful creatures, but there is no comfort in you. Between me and you there is a gulf wider than that which separated Dives from Lazarus. They were both men. Lay your unthinking heads upon your earth-dampened paws and sleep, my friends, you cannot help me now. For I, Polly, Phyllis Field, am the third child. I have known hardship, and a scrap of success; I have had an affair or two and have been a little in love. Not much, like Megan, not greatly, like Pen, but a little. And I, too, travel down the years under the sky towards certain oblivion. And there I stopped.

Almighty hell, I said to myself, are you going to spoil what days you have because the day comes when you won't know it? You must escape, break this chain, forged of quietude and loneliness and three guests who were unfortunately chosen. Take a drink and get hold of yourself.

So I poured a stiff one and drank it quickly, and another to keep it company. And I said to myself, "Polly, you need a treat. Your entertainment has been a failure and you're alone in the house. Autumn is here and the wind would drive any one nutty. What is the most self-indulgent thing you can do yourself?" The answer came with stunning promptitude: "Ring up Roger Hayward. Remember that letter."

I remembered it. It had been one of the major surprises of my life. It had been written some time after our break and had done quite a bit of travelling to reach me. It was so essentially Roger's letter that I was forced to admit its sincerity, and for that reason I had preserved it in the inmost flap of my notecase. I took it out now and read it, though I could have repeated it word for word.

Polly, my dear [it ran], it is some time since you went off huffed or satiated, whichever it was, and I dare say think it odd of me to write to you now. As it happens I've been thinking about you. You know how I loathe introspection, and I know how you loathe sentiment, but something impels me to write this. Perhaps age with its vagaries is overtaking me! Generally, I am relieved at the end of my affairs, but about ours I am sorry. There was just something, I can't say what, in it, and in you, that I haven't found elsewhere. I wish I'd seen that sooner. You've finished with me; but if ever I can do anything for you in any way, if only to while away a dull half-hour, I wish you'd let me know. I'd go a long way and I'd wait a long time to prove that I remember you with much kindliness and some regret.

Now that was something to have received from Roger Hayward —who should know better than I? And, sitting there with my crazy miserable thoughts for company and the wind howling like a fiend out of hell round the house, the thought of Roger and the sight of his writing was as stimulating to me as—as—well, there just is no comparison.

Roger hates introspection. Roger does things all the time—

makes love, eats, drinks, plays games, talks, travels, makes love again. The fact that his legs and his eyesight will one day fail him has never occurred to him. He'll begin to worry about that on the day that they do so. Roger is like I was before this set in. And if I could be with him . . . and never mention these three days—that is important—he could save me.

Never mention these three days. Is that important? Or would he just laugh and say in that lazy voice, "Well, what can you expect? Shutting yourself away with a lot of introspective women. Come on, Polly, snap out of it."

But you couldn't dismiss this all as the vapouring of a lot of introspective women. It had been a very real experience. It was concerned with essentials. I knew that. But mine was not a nature to cope with essentials in any other than a practical sense. I couldn't escape either by Megan's road or Pen's.

I must be saved.

I went into the hall and gave Roger's number, and in the interval I thought over what I should say. Oh Roger, my house has been spoiled for me, and my peace shattered. I've had three people I loved here and now I can't think about any of them with any comfort. I've looked out through the safe curtain of this physical being and I've seen us all spinning down the slopes of time like willow leaves on a swift stream. I know it doesn't matter a damn whether I get this call through or not, whether you answer or not, whether I ever see you again or not. There's space beyond the stars that makes you sick with a sense of futility every time you think of it; and every time your heart beats you're a beat nearer the inevitable end. I know that you can be like Pen and accept all these things and still be counted amongst the quick when really you're dead. But, Roger, please, out of your sanity, save mine. Save me from thinking about the menace of the years . . . save me from the horror of impersonal space, save me from seeing people as only God could see them and stay sane. Restore to me the pleasures of the flesh that were given us as a means of blinding the soul. Give me back the kisses, the wine, and the roses that can make all summer in a day that I wouldn't change for the certainty of heaven.

"You're through," said the voice at the exchange.

"Hullo," said Roger.

"Hullo," I said. "This is Polly, Polly Field. I say, Roger, are you doing anything very much tomorrow?"

YOU'RE BEST ALONE

CONTENTS

PART ONE

KIT BY HIMSELF

The late October wind, tearing its uninterrupted way across the plains of Europe, the wastes of the North sea and the flat spaces of East Anglia, flung itself, baulked at last, against the stone walls of Kit Shelfanger's little farmhouse. Outside it could set the loose straw whirling in the stackyard and rip myriads of yellow heart-shaped poplar leaves from the trees by the little pond; it could wail in the chimney and draw great spires of flame up the wide brick opening; it could batter, furious and impotent, at door and window. But the kitchen was snug and secure, a little cave of fire and lamp-light, and Kit, listening to the wind, decided, not for the first time, that it was the time of year he liked best.

Something, perhaps the contrast between the weather without and the cosiness within, or the fact that he had just realised that this week celebrated his tenth anniversary at Heath End, made him unwontedly conscious of his surroundings and he looked round the kitchen with approval. One wall was completely occupied by the fireplace and the latched door which led to the stairs. To the right stood a heavy oak dresser, devoted as its maker had intended, to use, not to ornament, the china upon it unmatching and unsymmetrically arranged. Opposite the fireplace the wall was broken again by a door that gave upon scullery and dairy, the rest of the space occupied by an old-fashioned bread bin beneath which in an orderly row stood Kit's array of footwear. The fourth wall held the yard door and the window, the former covered by a heavy red rep-curtain for the better exclusion of draught, the latter shrouded by short full curtains of red-and-black check which hid for the moment the row of potted geraniums that during the day struck a slightly incongruous note in the utilitarian apartment.

Beneath the window stood a red rep-covered armchair, twin to the one in which Kit sat by the fire. Close behind him, with two legs on the bright hearth-rug and two on the clean primrose-coloured bricks of the floor was a big wooden table. The end nearest the door was bare, scrubbed clean and white; the fireside half bore a cloth of the same red-and-black check as the curtains, and the arrangement of crockery upon it gave some clue to the orderly, perhaps slightly old-maidish character of the man who intended in a few minutes' time to eat his supper there.

The implication of the neatly set table was borne out by the man's appearance. It seemed to hint at an affectionate, neat-handed woman in the background. The heavy boots and leggings thrust out towards the fire were splashed now by the day's mud, but they had been blacked recently; his grey breeches were clean and whole, carefully patched at one knee; under his tweed coat with its reinforcements of leather he wore a coarse blue shirt, collarless, but clean.

Without rising from the chair where he sat, he leaned forward and opened the door of the oven which flanked the stove on one side. Using a piece of clean dry sacking for an oven cloth he drew out and inspected a brown dish wherein a jointed rabbit, under a shroud of shredded onion and pink and white salt pork, spluttered with an appetising sound. On the lower shelf two big potatoes were browning in their jackets.

The small Welsh collie which had been lying on the rug rose a trifle stiffly and nudged her greying muzzle against her master's knee. "Ready for supper?" he asked her. Her luminous eyes were raised towards his face and her plumy tail waved gently. "It's just ready," he said, and setting the dish back on the oven shelf closed the door again and rose to his feet.

Standing he was revealed as a tall man with the stoop which tall men acquire in a world where everything is just a little low for them. His shoulders were wide and thin, his waist, girt with a heavy leather belt, narrow, and before the stoop had come upon him he should have been an imposing figure. Now however the bowed shoulders and a certain curious tilt of the head gave him an air of humility, almost of uncertainty, a look emphasised by the extreme mildness of his blue eyes below their straight brown brows.

He moved deliberately, without grace but with a singular deftness, setting a plate to warm on the fender and bringing a golden-crusted loaf from the bin. Then, after a glance at the white-faced clock which ticked loudly from the high mantelshelf he sank into his chair again and took up his pipe. Just time to light up and finish the pipeful before the meal was done to a turn, said the action. He tore a narrow strip from the edge of *Farmer and Stockbreeder* which he had been reading, made it into a spill and leaning forward thrust it between the bars of the stove.

At that moment Guess, the collie, scrambled, stiffly but swiftly, to her feet, stood for a second with ears pricked and then launched herself towards the outer door in a mad tumult of barking. Withdrawing the unlighted spill Kit said, "Quiet, Guess!" and the dog was silent, though she kept her ears up and her eyes on the door. Now that queer tilt of the head was explained; it was the listening attitude of a slightly deaf man, the best-ear-forward gesture of a man who has been deaf for a long time. He could hear the howling of the wind as it rushed thwarted about the house and the crisp rustle of the leaves it bore with it and for a moment or so those were the only sounds he could hear; and then, sudden and unmistakable, came the slither of the unaccustomed foot upon the cobbles that lay between the house door and the yard. Guess yelped again, sharp and denunciatory. With an exclamation of surprise Kit put spill and pipe on the edge of the table and went to the door.

Even in daytime visitors at Heath End were rare enough, not averaging one a month; for the place was extremely remote and Kit Shelfanger exceptionally unsociable. In the early days after his arrival curiosity had brought a caller or two on some flimsy excuse, curious to see what kind of fellow this was who had bought derelict Heath End and was reported to live there completely alone. In this corner of England where little that was dramatic ever occurred, his arrival had given rise to all kinds of rumours. They flourished especially after it was known that Kit had been a sailor. Some romantic soul suggested that he had married a black woman and was keeping her hidden at Heath End. The rumours had died as quickly as they had arisen—and all interest with them—as soon as it became known that the new owner of Heath End was a very ordinary man, a bit deaf, quiet-spoken, fortyish, quite unremarkable and completely unromantic.

Nowadays not even the most enterprising salesman of cattle food, fertiliser or farm machinery would risk his springs on the track that led from the road to the farm, for everyone in the neighbourhood knew that Kit Shelfanger could be found at Welford market on alternate Thursdays, regular as the calendar.

Yet now, on this wild October evening, at hard on eight o'clock there was that indisputable strange step on the cobbles.

Kit said, "Back, Guess," and edged himself between the eager dog and the door. As he opened it the heavy red curtains billowed inwards, almost horizontal on the current of air, the little checked ones fluttered madly, the flame of the lamp leaped and the fire sent out a gust of smoke. Holding the door steady with one hand Kit leaned into the night, keeping his good ear forward, and called into the darkness, "Hullo. Who's there?"

Whoever it was had missed the door in the darkness and had gone stumbling on as far as the corner of the house. Kit called again, and heard, before he could see anything, that stumbling, dragging step coming back again. Then a voice, cultured, hoarse, exhausted, asked, "Is this Mr. Shelfanger's place?"

"I'm Shelfanger," said Kit simply. His eyes, growing used to the darkness, could now discern a man's figure, holding to the wall, making its way back to the door.

"Thank God," said the voice, heartily. "I'm Jamie. Can I come in?"

Always distrustful of his hearing, Kit stood wondering if he had heard aright, and if so what "Jamie" might mean. It was clear that the name had been proffered in the certainty of recognition. To Kit it meant nothing, and as he hesitated for a second the stranger reached the door, crossed the threshold as though blown on a gust of wind and stood in the kitchen. The same gust, receding, tore the door from Kit's clasp and banged it heavily. The curtain swung into place, the lamp flame leaped and Guess advanced a pace or two, growling, her grizzled face a mask of bare-fanged hatred.

"God, what a night!" and "Is that dog savage?" said the newcomer in the same breath.

"It's all right, Guess, all right. Lie down," said Kit in answer. He raised his own eyes from the dog to the face of the intruder, now well within the circle of lamp-light, drawn by the fire, and it was his turn to take a step backwards and give a gasp of astonishment.

"Jamie! Eva's boy! Good heavens!"

He looked at the young man with eyes that were at once avid and reluctant. This pitiable scarecrow in the dirty, frayed, cottony grey sweater with a greasy polo collar, in the filthy torn flannel trousers and broken shoes—Eva's boy. It seemed incredible. And yet, in the haggard pale face with its hint of vanished beauty, above all in the overgrown tangled mop of chestnut coloured hair there was incontrovertible resemblance to the one person of whom Kit Shelfanger still thought sentimentally, his eldest sister, Eva. Yes, that was right, the boy had been named Edward Jamison. "I'm Jamie." This was Eva's son, blown in on the breath of the autumn wind, tearing aside the merciful scars that twenty-five years had grown, baring the old wounds. Ghosts. Memories. No time now to dwell upon the past.

Jamie half turned from the fire.

"That's better," he said, and the deep musical voice, less hoarse, reviving already, set the chords of memory twanging. "God, I thought I'd never find you. Everybody in that one-eyed town could tell me how to get here, but once I'd turned off the road I couldn't believe . . . I kept on . . . it was like the end of the world . . . incredible, and that wind . . ." He shuddered.

"It's five miles from the main road," said Kit. And then, "How did you come to look for me? Did Eva . . . did she send you?"

A curious expression crossed Jamie's face, like a shutter falling. "Didn't you know?" he asked. "She's been dead six—no seven years. I found this among the things she had treasured. Poor dear, they weren't many towards the end." He dragged out of his ragged pocket a folded sheet of paper, fraying and dirty about the edges and two pennies.

"My sole assets," he said with a curious smile, tendering the paper.

Kit shook his head at it. He had no wish to touch it. It was the letter which he had written to Eva just on ten years before, as soon as he had settled in at Heath End.

"She never answered it," he said.

"She was proud," said Jamie detachedly, neither praising nor decrying a quality to which he himself made no claim.

He turned back to the fire, leaving Kit with all his questions unasked. To what end had Eva's brightness been brought? What of her husband? Through what straits had Jamie made his way here to Heath End? Ah well, there was time for all those questions.

His instinct of hospitality, almost atrophied from disuse, stirred and asserted itself.

"I was just about to have supper," he said almost shyly.

"Very tunable words," said Jamie. "That is, if I am invited."

"Oh, but of course," Kit said, awkwardly. And then, edging past to the oven, he thought he detected a suspicion of malice in his nephew's brown eyes. Another memory stirred uneasily. That was the Liddell look. Eva's husband had always delighted in any sign of discomfiture among the Shelfangers, and had often gone out of his way to embarrass them. Of course, he had despised them all. And even now, a quarter of a century since he had last seen it, Kit recognised the Liddell look and hated himself because it could still administer a pin-prick. After all, he thought, drawing the hot dish from the oven and scooping up the two potatoes, why should he make me feel awkward? He's the beggar. I've had to take him in and share my supper. But when he had set the food on the table and reached fresh plates and cutlery from the dresser, he turned and surprised such a look of avid hunger upon the sunken young face that, all unbidden, pity stirred in him. Eva's boy, he thought again. And in a warmer voice than any he had yet used he said, "There, draw up, boy," and plunged in the spoon, seeking the choicer portions, piling Jamie's plate high.

It was later than usual when Kit retired. He had not been able to bring himself to share his own big double bed with Jamie, and no other mattress or bedclothes were aired and fit for use. The pair had spent the latter part of the evening with a barrier of bedding between them and the stove. The food and the beer and the warmth of the kitchen had made Jamie drowsy and he had dozed for an hour before the bed was ready. As soon as it was made up he had gone to it, pausing at the door of his room to say, with Eva's sweet smile, "You've been marvellous, Uncle Kit. Thanks awfully."

But now, sitting over a last meditative pipe before the dying fire, Kit was conscious of dissatisfaction, both with his own behaviour and that of his nephew. He could dimly remember an uncle of his own, and he imagined what the old man would have said if he, Kit, had turned up at his house, ragged and dirty and obviously destitute. "Well now, young man, what have you to say for yourself? Here's a pretty pass. What's your explanation?" Some such speech had been forming in his own mind, all through supper, all through the long session by the airing bedclothes. But somehow the words had remained unspoken. Why? And why had the boy himself proffered no explanation? Walking in from the night like that and settling down, almost as though he had been invited—it was a queer way to behave. Kit wondered whether any other young man were capable of behaving so—and whether any other uncle would have been content to accept such behaviour without question or comment.

But deeper, and in fact more urgent than his dissatisfaction with the evening's happenings, was his concern for the future. Would the boy take himself away? Would he have to be assisted financially? Had he any plans? Kit had no means of knowing; but one thing he did know with a certainty that permitted no evasion, and that was that Jamie's arrival had threatened something that he held very dear indeed. He sighed as he considered it.

Kit Shelfanger had been born a misfit. He had a naturally solitary soul. And he had been the sixth child in a family of twelve.

The old farmhouse on the Cumberland fells, where his father conducted a tolerably successful business as a sheep breeder, had been solid and spacious, but in that family, all lively, quarrelsome, active, privacy had been an unattainable luxury. When Kit was eight years old he had fallen from a tree and injured the side of his head. For the concussion that followed the doctor had ordered absolute quiet, and for many years to come the boy had looked back at the period of his illness as the happiest time of his life. For the first time he had a room to himself, he became involved in no disputes; as he recovered he was able to read a book without someone saying "Oh, put that old book down and come and do this and that." It was the acme of happiness, sharply emphasised by the misery of his return to family life. For the fall had injured his ear and the deafness proved burdensome. To children there is something perennially comic in deafness and every misunderstanding, every failure to hear upon Kit's part was joyously seized upon as cause for mirth. At school the well-meaning master insisted that the deaf child should sit near the front, which meant that Kit, at eight, at nine, at twelve, even at fourteen, sat among the "young 'uns," his long legs cramped in a small desk. His robust, thoughtless father seemed never to distinguish a defect in hearing from mental stupidity and would roar at him impatiently. Nobody was guilty of deliberate unkindness to him; and nobody understood that his naturally solitary nature was being driven into misanthropy.

Like all other creatures who find themselves at odds with their surroundings, Kit Shelfanger developed an escape mechanism. It was the result of the books which, despite the teasing and cajoleries of his family, he persisted in reading. One day, he told himself, he would escape from all the things that irked him; one day he would go to sea. The thought of wide stretches of lonely shining water, dotted with islands of surpassing loneliness and loveliness, supported him like a religion, a religion with *Robinson Crusoe* for its Gospel, *Coral Island* for its Psalter. Only one worldly tie held him back from going in search of the promised land; and that was his love for his sister Eva. Eva was five years older than he, the second of the family and its beauty. When the whole brood was assembled about the table her blazing head among the brown ones arrested the attention, her pale oval face looked alien amidst that crowd of square tanned ones. She was physically a misfit just as Kit was mentally apart. But Eva was a Shelfanger in everything except her looks, she was nosy and high-spirited, tough enough despite her frail appearance, perfectly at home in her world. Everything was well with Eva until she met Edward Liddell.

Even now, looking back over a period of twenty-five years, Kit could wince at the memory of Eva's stormy courtship, the social and psychological disturbance which entered the old farmhouse with the slender, dark-haired, superior young man who wanted Eva and yet hated the homely family from which she had sprung. Oh those miserable months, with Eva's bright spirit clouded, her self-confidence shaken; the resentful family; those dreadful parlour meals with everyone unnaturally tidy; the inevitable rebellion and disgrace upon somebody's part. And no one in the family was so tortured by the affair, no not Eva herself, as the glowering deaf young brother, doubly concerned because of his love for his sister and because he was naturally a bystander, an onlooker.

On one occasion (and the middle-aged man's ears burned at the recollection) his misery and concern had found vent in speech. Edward had missed two appointments, had been formally invited to Sunday supper, had neither appeared nor sent an excuse; then he had written asking Eva to meet him for tea in Listhamouth. Eva, miraculously restored, had asked one brother after another to drive her there and by some trick of fortune Kit was the only one who was free. Half-way there he had halted the horse and said,

"Don't go, Eva. Don't encourage him any more. He isn't any good to you. He thinks he's too good for us all; and pretty soon he'll think he's too good for you. You'd do better with somebody that looked up to you, like a man should look up to the girl he wants to marry. He wouldn't come to supper, Sunday. Don't you go to tea today. Let's drive on to Picton Cross and have tea there. That'll show him."

She had looked at him with wide icy blue eyes, blank with astonishment.

"You must be mad," she said. "You're like all the rest of them.

158   *Requiem for Idols* and *You're Best Alone*

You just don't want me to better myself. You don't try to help me."

"Better yourself," said Kit bitterly. "With a little stuck-up nincompoop like Ed Liddell."

"Don't you call him names. And drive on, Kit Shelfanger, I'll be late."

"Listen Eva . . ." In his agitation he reached out and held one of her white-gloved hands; and then, suddenly and dangerously articulate, he told her everything that he had noticed and concluded about the man she had chosen. His reading, limited and specialised as it was, had given him a mastery of words which was unlike anything that Eva had ever heard; and his love for her, his habit of observation had brought him insight into both her character and that of Edward. The very truth of his statements made them offensive because they chimed with Eva's own hidden fear. Sitting there, perched in the stationary trap on the wide fell, with the harebell blue sky above them, the scent of thyme in their nostrils and the bleating of many sheep in their ears, this brother, who adored his pretty sister, and the sister who was noticing her silent queer brother for the first time, worked their way through a quarrel which was the more violent because its true cause and ultimate issue was not understood by either of them. Eva attributed to family prejudice, stupidity and stubbornness what was really the fruit of burning thwarted affection; and Kit thought that he spoke from an altruistic desire for Eva's well-being, when all the time he was activated by sexual jealousy. The bitterness which resulted was out of all proportion. Eva could never forgive Kit for his exposure of Edward; Kit could never forgive her for her blind allegiance. He ended:

". . . and he probably won't marry you after all."

"He will so," said Eva, hardening her jaw. "He'll marry me before harvest."

And a month before harvest Eva was married. Kit stayed on the farm until the busy season was ended and then announced his intention of going to sea. His father, with six other sons to work in the present and be settled in the future, made no hardship of the defection of the one he had always thought stupid. And so Kit went out in search of lonely islands.

"There are no islands any more." And few places are so crowded, both physically and psychologically, as a ship which is a compact, self-contained world afloat in space. Kit had made a bad exchange; for at home there were at least empty open spaces at the door, he could walk alone. Here he seemed always to be surrounded by men who, whatever their natures, were bound to make some impact, conscious or unconscious, upon him. They sought his friendship, or his support in some scheme; or they found him amusing with his silence and his deafness; or they disliked him; or they confided in him. There was contact upon every side. And with the pressure of the contact his mania for solitude grew. He automatically sought a new avenue of escape. And this time it was a more possible one, one capable of translation into reality. He would work and screw and save and one day he would have a little bit of land, a small house. He would work on the land and live in the house, and he would have a dog, his pipe, his glass when he felt like it. And he would be alone. Absolutely alone. There should be no claims on his pity or his time; no longer should he bother to turn his better side to any man.

This dream took him more than twenty years to realise, because men are cheap, land comparatively dear. But the day came when Heath End was his own and he could move into it and be alone at last.

And now, for the first time in ten years, he was not alone under his own roof. He stirred uneasily, and looked up at the ceiling, above which Edward Jamison Liddell was sleeping the sleep of exhaustion. Already, thought Kit, sourly, his coming has disturbed me, reviving the past, stirring up things I had forgotten and wish to forget. Already he has made me conscious of my deafness, of my lack of social graces, of my weakness of character which dare not ask even a simple question, "What are you doing here?" What more will he do? What of tomorrow? And suddenly, with a gesture of determination, he knocked out his pipe and put it in his pocket. So far as Jamie Liddell was concerned there would be no tomorrow. He would offer him money to tide him over and he would tell him that he must go. Upon that decision Kit went upstairs, careful to tread lightly, not to wake his unwelcome guest.

PART TWO

KIT AND JAMIE

The wind wore itself out during the night and morning broke still and clear, the stripped tops of the poplars sketched thinly upon a sky of palest turquoise. Kit, who had not slept well, went about his early morning tasks with the feeling that something unpleasant lay ahead of him.

He loved his animals, lavishing upon them the depth of feeling that most people reserve for their own kind; but this morning the pushing greediness of his pigs, the gentle nudging noses of his work horses as he filled their manger, the calm friendly eyes of his cow, as he entered her stall with his pail—all these dear and familiar things failed to distract his mind from his problem.

He kept forming certain leading questions in his mind. "Now Jamie, exactly what do you want of me?" "What are your plans, my boy?" Most of the questions were shrouded, like that, by a spurious kindness: but a few were stark and frank. "Where will you make for now? I'm afraid I can't ask you to stay." "Have you got into some trouble?" Once even he mentally voiced a fleeting suspicion. "Are the police after you?"

But when he had finished his before-breakfast tasks and reentered the house, set the table for two, cooked the meal and called Jamie twice and was at last seated opposite him, none of the sentences he had rehearsed would come to his lips. Even in retrospect they sounded crude, churlish, impossible. Instead he asked whether Jamie had slept well, whether he ate porridge, preferred thick or thin rashers, hard eggs or soft. These questions settled, he made a remark about the pleasant morning after the rough night and then fell silent. Jamie was not, evidently, a breakfast-table conversationalist. He answered questions briefly and did not volunteer any remarks at all.

Across the table Kit regarded him. The boy looked ill. The morning light showed a yellowish tinge in his face and eyeballs which had escaped notice in the lamp-light. His lids were puffy, his hands none too steady. But his appetite was hearty and once again Kit knew the kindly feeling that should accompany the gift of food. Moreover, Jamie had owned, or borrowed, a comb, and this morning the beautiful chestnut hair lay thick and close upon his skull—and it was very like Eva's hair. And Eva had kept that earnest, stumbling, apologetic letter among her few treasured things! It was utterly impossible to show Eva's son how unwelcome he was.

"And you live here entirely alone?" Jamie asked suddenly.

"Quite alone."

"Don't you find it depressing?"

"Not a bit. It's what I'd always wanted. I suppose I'm a solitary man by nature."

There, he had said it. With instant compunction he added, "Let's have your plate. There's some more bacon."

"Excellent bacon it is too. Your own? As a matter of fact I'm damned hungry. I've been ill. I've a lot to make up."

"What's been wrong with you?"

"Sort of malaria—very beastly."

"I didn't know you could get that in England."

"I didn't," said Jamie quickly. "I was nearly two years in Africa." Both voice and manner showed plainly enough that he did not intend to follow the statement with any further confidence.

But Kit asked: "When did you leave the Bank? It was the Bank, Eva put you to, wasn't it?"

Without lowering his eyes, or even his lids Jamie contrived in some curious fashion to veil his glance, so that once more Kit thought of a shutter falling between them. It was a thing to which he was to become accustomed. It could mean almost anything. At the moment it rebuked Kit for tactlessness. But he answered with apparent frankness:

"Let's see. I went in at seventeen. Oh, I was there for about two and a half years all told."

Jamie would be twenty-four now, Kit reckoned. Two and a half years at the Bank, nearly two in Africa, that left a considerable period unaccounted for. Oh well, that was none of his business. But the future was. Now was the moment to put his question, "Well, my boy, what are your plans?" "Now Jamie, exactly why did you come here?" It was no good. He couldn't say that kind of thing. And anyhow Jamie had by some means or other already made it plain that he was not to be questioned. What plans he had he would divulge—or act upon—in his own good time. He was, in some curious fashion, master of the situation, although every external thing was against him. Once again Kit thought of Eva. She had been like that too. He had read enough to know the modern word for it, "personality," that was it. Eva had had it, and Jamie had inherited it. It was the most desirable thing in the world, better than beauty or brains or virtue; without it you could do nothing, with it you could do anything you set your mind to. Mildly Kit reflected that it hadn't done much for Eva, and Jamie in twenty-four years hadn't got very far. But that was the point. Jamie, with twopence in his pocket, in rags, in need of charity, had it in him somehow to sit at his uncle's table and defy questions, baffle curiosity and make Kit feel uncomfortable.

Conscious that his own personality must be very weak and defective, Kit drained his cup and stood up—defeated.

"Well," he said, hitching his belt, "I must be off. I'm working the Top Field today and I shall take a bit of food in my pocket. I'll be back about five. You'll find something to eat in the pantry. Make yourself at home."

For the first time since his arrival Jamie showed a slight uneasiness. He dropped his glance and fidgeted with his cup.

"Is that all right? I mean, for me to stay a bit? Sure you don't mind?"

"I don't mind—for a bit," Kit said. He went out hating himself. His answer had failed both ways; it was neither true, nor was it really hospitable. And as he said it he felt a strong distaste for the prospect of finding Jamie there when he came in from the fields, of having Jamie's company at an indefinite number of meals, of spending his evening, doing his cooking and cleaning under Jamie's eye.

I was best alone, he said to himself as he led out his horses. And all day long, up and down the sunny spaces of the Top Field he carried his dissatisfaction with him. Jamie's coming, setting so many things in motion, self-consciousness, pity, memory, had ruined the peculiar happiness that had been his for ten years. It was like a draught cutting through the comfort of a warm bright room.

It wasn't much to ask, thought Kit, with a pang of unusual self-pity, just to be left by myself. Selfish perhaps, but it didn't hurt anybody. And after ten years it's going to be damned hard to get accustomed to having somebody about all the time. But then, he thought again, the boy may not stay. Heath End is hardly his cup of tea and he looks like a rolling stone. Kit took heart and strengthened his grip on the plough handles.

October passed and November, mild, damp-drenched, fog-clouded, came, and still Jamie lived at Heath End and still Kit alternated between pitying and hating him. Outwardly their lives assumed a steady pattern. Careful not to over-exert himself, Jamie nevertheless took on some of the minor tasks about the farm and the house. He had some knowledge—how and when acquired?—of machinery and would tinker for hours with the car or with some bit of farm gear, always, Kit admitted, leaving it better than he had found it; but also invariably scattering tools about and leaving them with a carelessness that irked the older man's thrifty nature. With animals he was useless, having neither patience nor kindliness—and for that Kit hated him, both because it was a trait that he hated for itself, and because it was a Liddell characteristic. On that long-ago day when he had spoken his mind to Eva one of Kit's arguments had been, "You've only to see how he treats his mare. A man like that'll never use his wife properly." Must he, Kit wondered angrily, on an evening when Jamie said roughly to Guess: "Get out of the way," be reminded again of that argument?

Withindoors Jamie was handy, though lazy and careless; and sometimes Kit found it pleasant to come in from the fields and find the kitchen tolerably tidy, the fire burning and the meal in preparation. He had never actually minded doing the work himself, but because this evening welcome was the most pleasant thing about Jamie's presence, Kit's simple mind seized upon the advantage and made the most of it, appreciating it out of all proportion to its value.

On the whole their relationship was friendly enough, though the friendliness was always in danger. It was rather like the bloom on a plum, the slightest lack of care in handling it might result in its disappearance; and Kit was subtly irked very often to realise that it was always from him that care was demanded. Sometimes in the evening they would talk, Jamie doing most of it, and then he would tell a story or refer to something in his past. Kit was always very interested, always half-expected to be told the whole history of Jamie's life; but the stories always stopped short of any really significant revelation, and then Kit was sometimes tempted to ask a question. Often it was a harmless question enough; but Jamie's resentment was instant and sure. He would look at his uncle with hatred and suspicion, brush the question aside and soon relapse into silence. And Kit, knowing that the question had been innocent—or, if deliberately curious, justified—would nevertheless feel snubbed and apologetic, as though he had been guilty of a lapse of taste. Then he would hate himself for feeling so.

But beside these psychological sparrings there were other things to mar the peace. One dull afternoon, shortly before darkness, Kit, from the stable, heard the car engine roaring in the barn which was used as a garage. He noted the sound and attributed it to Jamie's testing of some piece of tinkering. Later, going past the barn and seeing the door open he paused to close it, thinking: "Blast the boy, he never shuts a door or puts away a tool." Then he saw that the car had gone.

Indoors the remains of Jamie's midday meal still stood on the table, the fireplace had not been cleared, nor the lamp filled with oil. Slowly and methodically, as he did everything, Kit moved about, tidying, restoring, preparing to cook. He was half afraid to rejoice in having the house to himself, for the respite was bound

to be brief, and the more whole-heartedly that he enjoyed his solitude the less welcome would Jamie be when he returned. But as
the evening wore on he did permit himself to wonder. Was it just
possible that Jamie had taken the car and gone away for good?
Kit knew him well enough by this time to think him capable of
making just such an exit. He was rather appalled at the warmth
of his pleasure as he contemplated the possibility. The car, an
aged, if willing vehicle was worth thirty pounds at the outside.
Freedom would be cheap at the price.

At eight o'clock he ate his supper, cleared the table and settled
by the fire with his *Farmer and Stockbreeder*. Jamie's chair, the
less-worn twin of his own, remained by the wall, out of the range
of the fire's warmth; and Guess, instantly adaptable, lay in her
old place on the rag hearth-rug, the place where Jamie's feet had
of late been planted.

"You're glad too, aren't you, old girl?" Kit asked her once when
his eye fell on her. She beat the floor with her tail. All the same,
Kit thought, when next he glanced at the clock and saw that it
was half-past nine, I don't like that way of parting. I meant to do
something for him. He *is* Eva's boy after all. And not even to say
good-bye.

He stayed by the fire, musing and dozing, until after his usual
hour. Once or twice the idea slid through his mind that Jamie's
absence might be involuntary; he might have had an accident, the
car might have broken down. But even so there was little Kit
could do. He had no other means of transport, no telephone.
Moreover, by that time he felt sure in his heart that Jamie had
slunk off. He had wanted money, been ashamed to ask for it, and
seized upon the car as a means of making a little. It was
significant that Kit saw such an action as a typical piece of
Jamie's behaviour; it marched alongside his secretiveness, his
slyness, the almost tangible atmosphere of shadiness that he
carried with him even when he was at his best.

But when, just on eleven o'clock, Kit, from his bedroom, heard
the car bump over the cobbles to the danger of its springs, and
stop by the barn door, he knew that the story he had told himself
about Jamie's running away had had its roots as much in his own
wishing as in his estimate of his nephew's character. And the old

compunction seized on him; hurriedly he tumbled down the steep stairs in order to unlock the kitchen door. Not for worlds would he have Jamie find it barred against him.

As he turned back from the door to draw the embers of the fire together under the kettle, he heard, though the sound was muted by his deafness, Jamie singing as he crossed the yard. The singing was loud and raucous, the words of the song blurred. Jamie had been drinking; and alongside that realisation a new suspicion shot through Kit's mind. There had been no evidence during these last weeks that Jamie had more than the twopence which he had showed with that pitiable defiance on the night of his arrival. How then could he go out drinking?

Jamie pushed open the door and stumbled over the threshold. His eyes for once were wide open and brilliant, his cheeks brushed by a reddish glaze. A thick loose wave of hair, almost a curl, drooped sideways across his forehead. His likeness to his mother was very obvious in that moment.

"Hullo, Uncle Kit, still up? Thought you'd be abed before this." His manner was boisterous. "I found my way into Welford. You've got a nice little pub there, the Magpie. Know it? Full of stout fellows."

"I use it, when I go to market."

"Ever meet a chap named Tillingham? Keeps a garage."

"I've heard of him."

"Very stout fellow indeed."

("You shouldn't have taken my car like that. Or gone off without a word. I might have wanted it myself for all you knew. I might at least have wanted an errand done in Welford. And what did you use for money?")

Aloud he said: "The kettle's hot. Would you care for a drink? Tea, or coffee?"

"I've got a better idea than that. How about a hot toddy?" With an almost comic look of craft and cleverness he pulled from his ragged trouser pocket a little flat quarter-bottle of whisky and set it, with a ridiculous flourish, on the table.

"Come on, Uncle Kit, let's have a drink together, on *me*. I've had your beer every night. So let's have a drink now to Kit Shelfanger, Uncle Kit, one of the best as I told the fellows tonight. One of the very best, I said, and I meant it."

Kit felt hot. Although he gladly dispensed with the company of his fellows he was not quite indifferent to their opinion of him. It irked him to think that Jamie, in his dirty unmended old pullover and horrid trousers should have gone into the Magpie and announced, drunkenly, to all and sundry that he was related to Kit Shelfanger of Heath End. Far as he had removed himself from the company and traditions of his own family he knew suddenly that the old yeoman blood moved in him; every male Shelfanger had a "market suit" and would not dream of appearing publicly in his working clothes. And Jamie's weren't even that. He looked like a tramp—though of course he sounded like a gentleman; probably people thought he was just eccentric. It was strange, thought Kit, that he should derive comfort from that thought. It just showed how small-minded he really was. He was a little ashamed. And the shame weakened the resistance that he had intended to put against Jamie's suggestion that they should drink together. Without protest he watched him divide the whisky between two glasses.

"There now, isn't this cosy?" Jamie demanded, sinking into Kit's chair, leaving him to take the one at a distance from the fire. "You and I must go on a binge together pretty soon. Get to know one another better. That's what we want, isn't it? Break down the barriers. Did I ever tell you about the fellow in the pub at Freetown . . ."

He embarked, with thickening enunciation, upon one of his mysterious, unconnected, unrevealing stories. And Kit was free to try to remember exactly how much loose cash he had had in the old Player tin in his left-hand top drawer. Not very much, for since the only time he needed money was when he was in Welford where the Bank was, he was not in the habit of keeping much ready cash. And he never counted it. There might have been three pounds, or four, in the tin, in assorted coins. Hopeless to try to check up on it. Yet he was almost as sure as though he had seen him do it, that Jamie had been at that drawer. He registered a resolve to move the tin to a drawer which had a lock.

So far from breaking down any barrier; that evening erected a
new one.

Next day Jamie was yellow, sour, withdrawn into himself while
Kit, a victim of nagging doubt about the money and the conviction that he had handled the whole situation very badly, was
more than usually morose.

Jamie recovered his spirits first; made one or two tentative ad-
vances; and then with a disarming frankness, asked:

"Are you mad with me for taking the car without asking? I
would have, you know, but I wasn't sure where you were."

(Indeed! And what else did you take? That's what I should like
to know.)

Kit said, with a grudgingness of which he was ashamed:

"Oh, that's all right. Forget it."

Out of Welford, along the Pickthall road, cultivation ceases. On
either side for as far as eye can see the scanty grass barely covers
the hummocky sandy soil. Wind-warped thorn trees, like twisted
gnomes, Scots firs and pine trees, break the surface here and
there, and in summer wide belts of bracken froth greenly. The
whole area is honeycombed by the warrens of multitudinous rab-
bits. Infrequently a narrow bumpty track leads away towards
some lonely dwelling. Ten miles from Welford, and almost as far
from Pickthall, which is smaller and less important, one such
track leads up to Heath End, which is itself a result of a
geological freak which has thrown up, in the middle of the infer-
tile hearthland, a few acres of cultivable soil. At the mouth of the
track stands a post, to the side of which is nailed a locked letter
box, marked "K. Shelfanger. Heath End." It is the only sign of
human presence in that inhospitable region.

Very, very occasionally, the postman would ride his red bicycle
more slowly as he approached the box, draw in to the side of the
road, prop himself against the post without dismounting, and slip
into the slit in the side the dull, impersonal missives that were
addressed to the owner of Heath End. Kit never made a special
journey to collect his post, but when some other errand brought
him near the box he would open it with a key on his watchchain
and claim the belated, and often rather dampish, letters that lay

within. There was never anything addressed to him as a person. An Income Tax Form; an official communication telling of the latest decisions of the Milk or Potato or Pig Marketing Boards; a tradesman's circular; an appeal from the Farmers' Benevolent Fund: a specimen copy of some paper which hoped to supplant the *Farmer and Stockbreeder* in his affections. Nothing more. Once, for perhaps six months after he had dispatched his one letter to Eva he had opened the box more regularly, with some quickening interest, but nowadays his post meant as little to him as it did to the postman.

One day, a week or two after Jamie's visit to Welford, Kit returning from a visit to Pickthall paused at the box and opened it. As he walked back to the car he turned the letters face uppermost, recognised two receipts for bills he had paid, snorted to see that the Committee of the F.B.F. were giving a dance in the New Year and cordially requested his presence, and then stared with some surprise at two communications addressed to Jamie. One was a postcard, headed in thick black letters, "The Mitre Garage, Welford. Prop. G. Tillingham." Sprawled across the blank space below was a message which Kit read without hesitation or shame.

What about our bit of business? Write or call. Urgent.

G.T.

The other, a cheap bluish envelope, somewhat limp with damp, bore a London postmark and was addressed in an ill-educated, unformed hand to "E. J. Liddell, Esq." So someone besides Gordon Tillingham knew where Jamie was. Secretively, as he did everything, he must have written a letter.

When Kit handed over the post at supper-time Jamie glanced at the card, tore it in two and flung the halves at the fire. The letter he put unopened into his pocket. After the meal he lit his candle and went upstairs for some time. When he came down he asked, almost immediately: "Uncle Kit, you're going to Welford on Thursday, aren't you?"

"All being well. That's my day."

"Can I come with you?"

"Of course."

(But not in those clothes! Yet you can't wear mine, they're too big for you. And how can I mention the matter without offering you money to rectify matters? Oh, dear.)

Futilely, as was his almost predestined manner in anything connected with Jamie (he was beginning to realise that now), Kit toyed with suggestions for washing and mending the sweater, for scrubbing the soiled trousers, for offering a loan so that Jamie might rehabilitate himself. But Thursday dawned and nothing had been either said or done about the defective wardrobe, and when, at about half-past ten on the last murky Thursday of November they climbed into the car, Jamie was dressed as usual, though he was clean and his hair, now very long, was smooth and burnished. Kit wore his good dark "market suit," and a pair of boots slightly lighter than his working ones, well-blacked. His gold watch-chain brightened his dark waistcoat and his unobtrusive tie was neatly knotted. He looked exactly what he was, a farmer in modest but comfortable circumstances dressed for market day.

He was foolishly but inescapably self-conscious of driving with Jamie beside him. He suspected that Jamie was a far better, if less careful, driver and probably despised his conservative speed. He resisted a temptation to drive more quickly than usual. This feeling, combined with the fact that he was on the verge of offering his nephew money, preoccupied him and kept him silent during the drive. They were nearly into Welford before he spoke.

"You haven't any money, have you?" he blurted out at last, his voice brusque from embarrassment.

"Not a stiver," said Jamie cheerfully.

"Well, I think you should have something else to wear, something warmer." Without taking his eyes from the road ahead he dived into his own left-hand pocket where, all ready, separate from his own money and folded into a hard square parcel, he had laid three pound notes, one ten shilling one and three half-crowns.

"Get yourself a good warm jacket. Thompson's is the best place I think. That's all the spare cash I had, but if it isn't enough I'll have some more when I've been to the Bank."

Jamie's warm thin fingers came to meet his and closed on the money. "Thanks most awfully, Uncle Kit. It's only a loan, mind.

I'll make it right with you pretty soon." His voice was easy and quite without the embarrassment that had roughened Kit's. Gosh, thought the elder man as he negotiated the now thickening traffic, if he knows why there was only that much in my box he's a damned cool customer.

They had reached the centre of the little town and Kit halted the car.

"Thompson's is about ten yards along there," he said, pointing. "I must take the car round to a few places, I've got a lot to do. I shall have some food at the Magpie at about one."

"Well, don't wait for me," said Jamie. "I may be busy too. When do you start home? And where shall I meet you?"

Kit hesitated. For ten years his market day procedure had been invariable and he had always enjoyed his simple and solitary programme.

Immediately upon arrival he had made a round of the shops he patronised and bought his supplies. It meant concentrated activity, for besides the farm things, to which all the farmers must attend, he had to deal with matters which most men could leave to their wives. He had plumbed the mysterious, net-shrouded, carpet-hushed precincts of the draper's shop in search of butter muslin and mending wool; he had threaded a careful passage between the menacing stands of glass and porcelain in the china shop and earnestly matched a broken saucer; he had pushed through a crowd of perspiring country women in order to reach the household counter at Woolworth's where the best egg-timers were to be found. And he had enjoyed it all. After the domestic came the agricultural hour, an implement part to be mended or replaced, cattle food to be ordered, a visit to the veterinary counter of Boots'. And then a short walk to the cattle and corn market, where he made the only contact with his fellows that he could really be said to enjoy. Men would nod to him, greet him by name, stand for a moment and talk shop about crops, the weather, the market and then move on again, undemanding, uncritical, transient.

One o'clock found him at his table near the window in the Magpie dining-room, enjoying, for the first time in fourteen days, the taste of food cooked by other hands than his own. The meal hardly varied, roast beef, Yorkshire pudding, two vegetables in season, fruit tart and custard, cheese, the whole washed down by a pint of the local brewer's beer. After lunch he had his hair cut, collected things he had ordered in the morning, looked back at the market, had the car tank and the two spare cans filled with petrol. And at five o'clock, having decided which of the two cinemas was showing a picture more to his liking, he solemnly bought a one-and-sixpenny ticket and joined the throng of oblivion-seekers in the stuffy, plush-filled dark.

He particularly liked films that had foreign settings; he always chose one of those if possible, despite frequent disappointments. They were worth while for the few times when an actual photograph or a clever construction could evoke a memory of his wandering days. He knew now that this was how he had wanted to see Singapore, Madagascar, Zanzibar, San Francisco, not from a ship, in the company of other people, but alone, from some vaguely spiritual standpoint. In the cinema's darkness he could recapture the delight, the magic with which he had regarded the far places of the earth, long ago, on a Cumberland sheep farm. Apart from films which offered him this re-enchantment, he liked those that featured Gary Cooper, Katherine Hepburn or Margaret Sullivan. If he had analysed this preference he would have discovered that it existed because he sensed in these people that inner loneliness, that natural apartness of spirit which was at once his own strength and weakness.

He was usually out of the cinema by seven o'clock. He never waited for the secondary picture—usually a comedy—or for the news. Back in the Magpie bar he had a final drink, beer in summer, whisky in winter. He was always home by eight o'clock to do his belated milking and final chores.

Now, on this November Thursday morning when Jamie asked him to say when and where they should meet at the day's end, he felt that his pleasant programme was threatened. Jamie would tire of Welford and want to return early; or he would wish to remain later; or, worst of all, he would suggest visiting the cinema as well.

Curtly, because he was frightened, Kit said, "I never leave earlier than a quarter past seven, or later than half-past. I shall be in the Magpie somewhere between the two."

"Oh, all right," said Jamie, almost soothingly. "I'll be there." He had not missed his uncle's hesitation before replying, nor the tone of voice in which he answered, and as he turned towards Thompson's a knowing, faintly salacious smile curved his lips. Between the end of the marketing and seven o'clock the old buffer did something that he wanted to keep dark. He'd bet there was a woman in it somewhere. And not unnaturally. After all he wasn't old, in the early forties somewhere; and the Shelfangers as a family were far from continent. But it was amusing to think of old Kit, sober old thing, solemnly visiting, once a fortnight, some plumpish, prettyish, rather faded blonde (you could guess his type at once) and growing so hot and huffy at the very idea of anyone's guessing. Really!

At ten minutes past seven Kit walked happily into the smoke-blue bar of the Magpie. He had enjoyed his lonely day; the usual programme had gone like clockwork, and the picture, with its wildly fantastic story against a realistic background of the China Seas, had been completely satisfactory. He had almost forgotten Jamie. He edged his way to the end of the curving bar, ate two pleasantly salted potato crisps, ordered a double Haig and added some water from a jug that stood handy. As he raised his glass he saw Jamie at the other end of the bar; at least he saw somebody vaguely familiar but not instantly recognisable. With his brilliant hair closely cut and smoothly brushed so that only the faintest breaking of a wave behind his ears betrayed its curliness, with a jacket of sporting cut and warm chestnut colour, a new shirt and a dark green tie, Jamie looked very different from the shabby figure which had descended from the car in the morning. He was talking and gesticulating with indolent animation. As Kit watched he finished the sentence and the man on his far side gave a bellow of appreciative laughter. Jamie threw back his head to drink and Kit recognised his companion. Gordon Tillingham of the Mitre Garage. Their eyes met across the space and Kit saw Tillingham lay a hand on Jamie's arm and say something. Jamie turned quickly and smiled. In a second or two they had dodged their way round to Kit's end of the bar.

Tillingham said, "Good evening, Mr. Shelfanger. Haven't seen you for ages."

Jamie said, "Oh, you know one another? Good." Kit, battling with his dreadful shyness muttered, "Hullo Jamie, evening Tillingham," and picked up his glass. He did not intend to empty it at a draught, but when he set it down it was empty.

Tillingham seized it at once, "What are you drinking, sir?" The respectful address from Tillingham who respected no one, made Kit feel odd suddenly.

"Me? Oh, I've finished," he said.

"Finished? Nonsense," cried Tillingham boisterously. He sniffed the glass. "Ah, good old Haig. Here Elsie. Double Haig three times. Soda or water, sir? Right. Well, here's luck."

Kit looked at Gordon Tillingham and decided, not for the first time, that he did not like anything about him. The young man had taken over the Mitre Garage from a couple of slow, honest, old-fashioned brothers who had sold Kit his car and who always did any repairs that were necessary. For a time under the new régime Kit had continued to patronise the place, but several small incidents and one large one had convinced him that Tillingham was neither a good mechanic nor an honest business man. He had quietly taken his old car elsewhere next time it needed attention. Tillingham aped, desperately and with dubious success, the manner and accent known as "Public School." Something flamboyant and aggressive about him defied his efforts. He lacked something that Jamie had, even in his worst moments. Jamie with his no-good gentleman father and his respectable yeoman-bred mother might be dishonest, secretive, idle, vicious, anything you could name; but he would be all things as it were in his own right, he would not be sticking to some alien, superimposed code or creed. It was quite clear that Tillingham, probably unconsciously, knew that already. His manner to Jamie was familiar, but it was a deliberate familiarity which noticed and enjoyed itself. Dull, stolid Kit, with his plebeian watch-chain and blacked boots, could see clean through Gordon Tillingham, in a way that would have astonished that astute young man.

Both Gordon and Jamie seemed anxious to include Kit in their conversation. Gordon asked knowledgeable questions about farming; Jamie inquired, with rather a queer look, whether he had had a good day. The glasses were empty again. Kit had them recharged; he did not intend to be indebted to Tillingham for anything.

"Still driving your same bus?" Tillingham asked. Kit nodded.

"Ah. That was the best model they ever put out. It'll see two new ones off the road yet. Of course, from a business point of view it was *too* good. Didn't give the trade a chance. Between you and me that was why it was discontinued."

It was the first time anyone had ever praised Kit's ramshackle conveyance; and the fact that an expert was now praising it in somewhat extravagant terms merely made him wonder, a trifle ungraciously, what it could possibly be that Tillingham wanted from him. It was with a sense of escaping from something that he said, after a glance at the old-fashioned watch, "Well, Jamie, I'm afraid I'll have to be moving."

"One for the road," Jamie invited with hasty earnestness. But Kit, still suspecting something in the offing—though what it could be he had no idea—this time refused firmly and turned towards the door. Jamie hung back for a moment and engaged in a last, hurried speech with Gordon and then caught up with his uncle. The car, its rear seat and dickey piled high with goods, stood in the yard.

"I'll drive if you're tired," said Jamie obligingly.

"Bless you, why should I be tired? It's the easiest day I have." Kit seated himself heavily in the driving-seat and switched on the lights and the engine.

There was silence for a little while, and then Jamie said, "He's a good chap, G.T., don't you think?"

"He's all right," said Kit, rather grudgingly. "I used his place for a bit and he mucked up a job or two, so I left him."

"Oh." Jamie's tone was rather deflated. "As a matter of fact, from what I can gather, he has rather more business than he can properly handle. He's a good mechanic, but he can't give enough attention to that side of it. He's too busy with the new cars and the second-hand ones, especially the latter."

"Oh," said Kit in his turn.

"As a matter of fact he made me a pretty good offer—"

(Now it's coming, Kit thought. A partnership for three hundred pounds. Well my boy, apart from the fact that I can't spare it, I haven't sufficient faith in Mr. Tillingham to invest money with him.)

"You see, what he really needs is a partner. But as I explained I haven't a bean. So then he said if I cared to help him overlook the repairs and take on a second-hand end of the business, he'd take me in without cash. Only you see—I can't very well do it—without your co-operation, Uncle Kit."

"Oh, how's that?"

"Well, you see, he'd only be able to give me a very nominal sum, not more than a pound a week. The commission of course would be up to me. But until I began to collect on that I would have to live somewhere. I thought . . . for a bit . . . if I could live at Heath End and pay you the pound for bed and breakfast and supper . . . and use the car every day. Would you mind that?"

And he had been bracing himself to refuse to lend a matter of hundreds of pounds! Kit's relief was really boundless.

"But of course not," he said, with unaccustomed warmth in his voice. (But that of course was why Tillingham had praised the old car; had wanted to indicate that it could do thirty miles a day regularly, in order to bring him a cheap workman!) "And you needn't think of paying for a bit of food. Lots of what we eat at Heath End doesn't cost anything. And you'd find this old wagon would begin to cost money when it worked regularly. The tyres aren't too good. But Jamie . . . it seems to me that if you're going to make the effort to get into Welford every day, you might contemplate a better job than that."

"But I wouldn't get one that suited me better. You see, I'd have the air, and be my own master. I'm not everybody's man either. I have off days when this malaria lays hold of me, you know. That wouldn't matter so much in this job."

"No, I see that. Quite."

"So it's fixed, is it? Well, thanks a lot, Uncle Kit. You've been a friend to me, and no mistake."

It was the kind of speech that assailed Kit's shyness like a blow. He grunted and drove a little faster. Presently he said, "And when do you start?"

"Might as well look in tomorrow, I should think."

So tomorrow, between breakfast and supper, the place would
be his own again. A sweet sense of relief flooded his spirit. Tomorrow at midday he could go in and have his bite of food, and
move about doing his bits of cooking and tidying without the
sense of having another eye upon him all the time. Oh very good!
And no doubt as soon as Jamie was making any reasonable
amount of money he would go and live in Welford. And Kit,
without having it on his conscience that he had turned out Eva's
boy, would be left in the blessed solitude that he craved. Things
had worked out much better than he had sometimes feared.

He was blissfully unconscious of the lack of realism in his
reflections. Jamie could have told him that there was little chance
of his being left alone so long as he was willing to provide free
board and lodging and the use of his car. Jamie knew when he
was on a good thing, and for the last few weeks of the year he
was very well contented with his home, his job and his surroundings. Tillingham, regarded in the more conservative circles of
Welford trade as a tricky customer, could, nonetheless, be shown
a new trick or two by his new partner. If he ever suspected that
Jamie, so expert a cheat, would eventually cheat him as well, he
gave no sign of the suspicion. Jamie, confident, debonair, and,
when he chose to be, charming, was exactly the person for whom
Tillingham had been looking—the person in fact that he would
have liked to be, one with all the advantages of good looks, apparent breeding, social knowledgeableness, yet unhampered, as so
many gentlemanly persons were by inconvenient scruples when it
came to driving a bargain or taking advantage of a sucker.

At Heath End, too, the new arrangement worked very well.
After the first week or so Jamie often missed supper and came in
later and later. Kit grew accustomed to having his hearth to himself. Yet sometimes, when Jamie was present, the evenings were
pleasant. Jamie's facile tongue and ready, if sardonic, wit often
provided entertainment as he recounted stories about clients and
customers. It was as if, during his weeks of immolation at Heath
End his mind had lacked material and now seized eagerly upon
anything of interest. For a full three weeks he seemed contented
and happy and when he was in the house was a pleasant companion.

But one morning, shortly before Christmas, he appeared at the breakfast table with the old sour, yellow, withdrawn look on his face. He had been very late the night before and Kit, watching him, came to the conclusion that he had been drinking. It was a cold morning, the car was slow in starting and finally Jamie got out and swung it savagely. Kit was glad to think that Gordon Tillingham, or some other more sanguinely constituted person than himself, was to have the benefit of Jamie's company all day. But, leaving the car running, Jamie came back to the kitchen door and said, with an obvious effort at pleasantness, "I shall be back early today. Is there anything you want me to bring?"

"I don't think so. I'll probably be going in myself tomorrow."

"O.K., then. Good-bye."

The car drove into the yard just as Kit was entering the house at about six o'clock that evening. He paused on the step and looked up at the stars, piercingly bright. He called back to Jamie, "You'd better let the water out. It's going to freeze hard." But Jamie followed him into the kitchen and seized the bellows and began to blow up the fire. Kit leaned across and pulled out the damper and then, going to the larder, brought out and began to truss the chicken which he had killed and roughly dressed earlier in the day.

Jamie sat on the end of the fender, his hands held to the stove, but his face turned towards his uncle, watching, with a curious speculative gaze until Kit was nervous. He was relieved rather than surprised when the young man, after sighing impatiently, burst out, "There's something I've got to ask you, and I don't know how you'll take it."

Kit drove home the skewer and laid the trussed fowl in the baking tin and then said, "Well? What is it?"

"Would it put you out very much—I mean would you very much mind—if I asked somebody to stay over Christmas?"

Every nerve in Kit's body sprang to attention and prompted an uncompromising "Yes, it would." But he gave no sign of discomposure. He spread fat generously over the chicken's breast and asked, "Who did you want to ask?"

"Well," even Jamie's assurance was shaken this evening, "it's a bit awkward. It's a girl, a young woman."

Kit opened the oven door and pushed the tin inside. Then he closed the door carefully and straightened himself. There had been a strong tang of whisky as his head neared Jamie's and for a moment the wild hope went through him that the boy was drunk, joking. But one glance at his nephew's face killed that hope.

"Well, that is *very* awkward," he said unhappily. "We've only the two beds. Besides, we live very roughly, you know. I don't think a young woman would be very happy here. I'd think better of it if I were you."

Jamie sprang to his feet. His face had hardened and his manner had lost its faintly placating diffidence.

"Unfortunately I can't. I wish I could. I've no wish to inconvenience you, Uncle Kit. I wish to God I'd never let her know where I was. But I did, like a fool. And now she'll come, whether I let her or not."

"But," said Kit, speaking for once on impulse, "she can't. No woman has the right to invite herself like that. I'm . . ."

"This one has," said Jamie. "You see, I married her."

Why should that be somehow shocking as well as startling, Kit asked himself. There was nothing unusual in being married, surely. The oddity, if oddity there were, lay in Jamie's having kept quiet about it all these weeks. But he had kept quiet about so many things; his past was still quite obscure; it could probably offer many other surprises. Rather unhappily Kit evolved and rejected several replies. (Well, that's a surprise. But why? Why shouldn't Jamie be married? Why didn't you tell me? Again, why should he? Who was Kit to hold him to account?) He compromised with, "Well, of course that does make a difference. Naturally."

"I'm glad you see that," said Jamie, rather glumly. "So what's the verdict? Can she come?"

"Just for Christmas, you say?"

"I don't think she'll stay longer. It's only that she is curious to see where and with whom I am living. I shouldn't think she's ever spent longer than a day in the country in her life. She's a townee to the bone." He spoke with detachment, as though discussing the character of a complete stranger.

Kit felt himself chilled by the tone. He found it possible to ask, "How long have you been married?"—a question he might have shied from had Jamie's manner been less impersonal.

"Oh," said Jamie, with his usual vagueness over dates, "About two years."

(And where has she been all this time? Have you ever lived together? Have you helped to keep her? Who was she? Were you in love?)

"How long will supper be?"

"About an hour."

"Then I think I'll run into Pickthall and telephone. She's been writing me very impatient letters. I'd better let her know it's O.K. and that she can arrive and be met like a reasonable being." Jamie, since his going to Welford had had the key to the letter-box and emptied it night and morning.

He drove away, leaving Kit to his cooking and his thoughts. He found the idea of the new incursion very disturbing. It was impossible for him to visualise with carelessness or composure the presence of a young woman at Heath End; carrying her jug of hot water to the sink in the scullery, for instance and washing there, as he and Jamie did; spending the evening by the cooking-range fire; sharing their rather haphazard meals. Moreover Jamie's manner had given rise to a suspicion that relationships between husband and wife were not very happy; they might argue, and quarrel, and there would be the old business of taking sides. Again, Jamie had given no idea of the woman's character or type; she might be anything. Arrogant perhaps and scornful, despising Heath End; or common and grating. Searching for a clue Kit remembered the cheap blue envelope with the childish writing which he had found in the box. If that had been from Jamie's wife she was not a socially terrifying person, at least. But there was no proof that she had written that letter; the later correspondence he had not seen at all. And even if she were homely and decent her coming was going to lead to domestic and mental re-arrangements which Kit dreaded with all his heart. Why, oh why, hadn't he had the power and the spunk to say, "No, Jamie, if you want to entertain your wife you must do it elsewhere."

He hadn't said it. He had, as usual, mishandled the situation and must pay for a momentary weakness with indefinite discomfort. He almost groaned as he basted the browning fowl. Yet when, shortly before the hour, Jamie returned with the news that it was fixed and Rosetta would be coming by an afternoon train on the next day, Kit's response was practical and had a spuriously hospitable ring. "We'll have to get a proper wash-basin and things for upstairs. She can't wash in the sink."

"Oh, it wouldn't be the first time," said Jamie carelessly. "Still," he fished in his pocket and drew out some pound notes, "I drew some cash today. I'd like to pay for anything that's needed." He peeled off five notes, folded them and held them out.

Kit, with every justification in the world for taking them, was suddenly, and without reason affronted. He said stiffly, "I don't want your money. It's my house. I can buy what's needed for it."

Jamie, looking a little startled, said, "Oh, all right. I didn't mean anything. *I've* been perfectly comfortable here. It's a damned nice house—nicer than it will be with a fretting female in it. But I'll shove her off as soon as I can. And I would like to pay for things. It isn't fair that you should be put to a lot of expense."

"You know her," said Kit. "You could buy some fancy things that she'd like to eat. And—a Christmas present perhaps."

"Damn that," retorted Jamie hotly. "She shouldn't have married me if she wanted Christmas presents."

He lay awake in the night reviewing his furniture and planning what he must buy. When he had come to Heath End he had furnished, from a secondhand furniture store, the kitchen and two bedrooms. That is, he had bought two arm and two kitchen chairs, the big white-wood table, two beds, three large rugs, a chest of drawers and some crockery. Vaguely at the back of his mind there had been then the thought—or hope—that there would be an answer to his letter to Eva. If she should come to stay how gladly he would put the other necessary things and the little refinements into the spare bedroom. And now, after ten years, his letter had brought him, not Eva, but Jamie, and after Jamie some dreaded, unknown female named Rosetta. The irony of it! He groaned as he turned for the twentieth time upon his erstwhile comfortable bed.

PART THREE

KIT, JAMIE AND ROSETTA

The morning, with its winter-blue sky and crackling frost was cheerful and invigorating. And Welford, thronged with good-humoured Christmas shoppers, had an infectious gaiety. Not even the deliberate commercialisation of the festival that honoured the birth of the least mercenary of men, could quite obscure or spoil the quality of the season. Even Kit Shelfanger was touched by the contagion and looking back upon his many solitary Christmasses, recanted a little and wondered whether it was not, after all, more natural and more pleasant to be shopping for three than for one. Perhaps he *had* been a selfish old curmudgeon who needed to be jolted out of his rut. The surface of his mind made this response to the world about him, but deep down, the real Kit, that mixture of instinct, habit and experience, knew that he dreaded the hour when Jamie and his unknown wife would cross the threshold of Heath End, and the door would close, and all the currents and cross-currents of human intercourse would begin to make themselves felt.

The train was arriving at four-fifteen and since the station was on the way home it had been arranged that Jamie should meet Kit at the car and that they should go to the station together. Kit, with his last parcels in his arms, reached the car at five minutes past the hour and spent some minutes arranging his stores so that a passenger, with luggage, might be accommodated. Then he took the rug from the bonnet of the car, folded it, hung it across the back of the driving seat, got in and tried the engine. It had retained enough warmth under the rug to start without trouble; and through the noise of the responsive engine Kit heard the clock on St. Nicholas' tower chime the quarter. It had not occurred to him that Jamie might be late. He hesitated for a moment or two, then replaced the rug on the radiator, turned off the engine, got into the driver's seat and fished out his pipe. There was nothing he could do, for he did not know Rosetta by sight and at this time of the year the trains from London would be crowded with holiday-makers.

Just as the chime broke out again to mark the half-hour, Jamie, quite leisurely, entered the yard, swung open the car door and seated himself. He shuddered a little and said, "Beastly cold day it's been." He jerked impatiently at the loose mica in the screen that was supposed to protect the old car's passengers from side draughts.

"We're late," said Kit.

"Not to matter. Trains are always late at holiday times." He hitched a careless shoulder.

But at the station there was none of the thrice-daily bustle which at Welford preceded and followed the arrival of the down train. A few heavily-moving country people, weighed down by parcels, pushed through the barrier towards a local train. A man whom Kit had noticed earlier in the day in the market-place was seizing his last chance to sell off some mechanical toys; a boy offered the newly arrived evening paper. Between the two, in the middle of the entry, under the harsh glare of the unshaded light stood a solitary female figure, with a suitcase and a round hatbox at her feet.

Jamie said in a flat voice, "Well, she came," and got out of the car without alacrity. Kit, anxious to make the most of his one chance to study his visitor unobserved stared eagerly at the young woman. Of her face he could see nothing, for it was only a narrow smudge of pallor between the sharply down-sweeping brim of a fantastic little hat and the huddled-up collar of a short coat of some fluffy fur which gave to the upper half of her figure a look of solidity and luxury, a look not substantiated by the thin short skirt which clung about her knees, the too-spindly legs in pale stockings, the fragile high-heeled shoes.

Kit, who was tall himself, preferred small women and credited all tall men with a similar preference, was faintly surprised to see that she was almost of a height with Jamie. Without reaching up at all she put out her furry arms and clasped him about the neck. Jamie kissed her briefly, picked up the suitcase and led the way back to the car beside which Kit was by this time awkwardly standing.

"This is my Uncle Kit," said Jamie.

Kit, in a sudden agony of shyness said falsely, "I'm glad you could come," and held out his hand into which Rosetta put a small one which, even through the kid of her glove, struck icy cold.

"I'm afraid we've kept you standing about," he said apologetically.

"Oh Jamie's always late for everything, aren't you darling?" said Rosetta without resentment. Her voice was high, desperately refined and sent a shiver of dislike through Kit.

"Give me the bags. They can come in the back with me. You drive, Jamie."

The short journey through the streets with their patches of light and darkness and their crowding pedestrians was, for Kit, used to his own steady driving, a breathtaking business. But once out on the straight heath-bordered road he was able to relax. The vibration of the car—always helpful to his hearing—enabled him to listen to what conversation passed between Jamie and Rosetta, and he listened carefully, anxious to glean some clue, some guidance, some knowledge upon which to rely in what he felt were going to be difficult hours ahead.

He was disappointed. Rosetta would have been talkative; indeed, though he found her voice displeasing and faintly alarming, Kit pitied her as simple irrelevant statement followed simple irrelevant statement and elicited no more than a grunt, a negative or an affirmative from Jamie. Finally she said, "Mother asked to be remembered to you."

And to that Jamie said, "Oh, *very* kind of her, I'm sure," in a voice that revealed his feeling for his mother-in-law, his dislike for the conventional phrase and his complete boredom in about equal degree. Rosetta must have sensed the lack of response then, for she fell silent and no one spoke during the rest of the journey.

As soon as they arrived at the house Kit was seized by a heavy sense of responsibility and that old self-doubt which he dreaded and which was his normal reaction to company of any kind. It had been wrong, he decided, for him to go to Welford today. It meant that the house was cold and unwelcoming and would make an even worse impression than he had feared. He did not stop to ask himself why he should mind Rosetta's opinion of his home and the welcome extended to her. If she had gone straight back to London his own feeling would have been one of relief. Nevertheless he suffered acutely as he unlocked the door, fumbled for a match and revealed the cold dark recesses of the kitchen. True the lamp was lighted instantly and it was only a moment's space before the plentiful dry sticks were blazing and crackling in the stove—but it was long enough to make him turn to Rosetta with apologies.

She stood awkwardly, still holding the hatbox, on the far side of the table. Her face was whitened and puckered by the cold and upon its surface the rouge and the lipstick stood out with a startling vividness. She was certainly looking about the kitchen, but her gaze was not interested, not observant, and when, in answer to Kit's apology, she turned her eyes towards him and smiled and said, "Oh, it doesn't matter," her expression, despite the smile, remained blank and unresponsive. Kit found it oddly disconcerting.

"It'll be warm very soon. If you kept your coat on and sat here . . ." he suggested, pulling his own chair close to the stove. "I'll have the kettle boiled in a minute. Of course, we ought to have had tea in Welford, I'm afraid I didn't think."

She gave another meaningless smile and sat down in the chair. Presently she took off her thin poor gloves and held her hands to the strengthening flames. They were thin hands, Kit observed as he set the kettle in the midst of the fire, thin and square with blunt fingers. The nails, of uneven lengths and ugly spatulate shape, were painted a peculiarly lurid purple shade, as though

frostbite had seized on her fingertips. Like the high-pitched gen-
teel voice they repulsed Kit.

Jamie came in from putting the car away and crouched on the
fender end, stretching *his* hands towards the fire. With his coming something of animation returned to Rosetta's face and manner. She leaned back and loosened the collar of her coat. Next she
took off the crazy little hat. Her hair was very fine and silky like a
child's, and yellowish white in colour. It was curled up over her
brow and at the back fell into a smooth flowing line, like a silver
bell. Beautiful, thought Kit, setting it against the voice and the
purple nails. Into Jamie's face too, he noticed, came a look of
arrested attention as the lamp-light fell upon her uncovered head.
Soon the white look went from her face, pink cheeks and crimson
mouth retreated into the natural colouring of her skin and her
normal commonplace prettiness established itself again.

By the time the kettle boiled Kit had set the table with the
ham, the cold pigeon pie, the butter, honey and cheese which had
seemed to him suitable for a meal which must be quickly ready
and yet substantial enough to nourish a traveller. He was pleased
by Rosetta's appreciation of the food. Bits that he had read here
and there had led him to believe that no modern girl ever ate a
square meal for fear of spoiling her figure. Rosetta's obviously joy-
ful consumption of ham, pie and honey was a pleasant surprise.
Jamie's moodiness eased as the meal progressed. When Rosetta
began to chat again, mentioning people of whom, naturally, Kit
had never heard, he listened with more interest and even once or
twice prompted the flow of gossip by a question. The worst of
Kit's shyness passed. Rosetta's voice, though not pleasing, was at
least easy to hear and so his deafness caused him no embarrassment. A faint reflection of his morning mood came upon him.
It might be quite a happy Christmas after all.

Still feeling hospitable Kit rose from the table, leaving the pair
with their cigarettes, and stole away to fill an oilstove and set it in
their bedroom. He was out of the kitchen for a long time. He had
to empty his own things from his chest of drawers and drag it
into the other room; he had to set out upon it the toilet set
which he had bought in Welford, an elegant affair of pink roses
and bluebirds; he had to spread upon the austere bed the plump

new eiderdown covered with fluted silk of a pink that differed wildly from the roses on ewer and basin. It gave the bed an opulent air which pleased him. He looked about when he had finished, half satisfied, half dubious. There flashed into his mind a vision of Eva's room back at home. It had always seemed like a shrine to the loutish boy who dared hardly venture even to peep within it. Being the eldest daughter, Eva enjoyed the privilege— greatly envied by Kit—of a room to herself; being a young woman of character she had stamped it as her own. Across twenty-five years there came the memory of a dressing-table shrouded and skirted in spotted white muslin with blue bows looping it here and there, of a ruffled satin sachet that held Eva's lavender scented handkerchiefs, and the larger sachet which matched it and which, with Eva's nightdress secreted within it, lay just below the swell of the pillow on Eva's narrow, virginal bed. Poor Eva, she had so liked nice things. It was her taste as much as anything that had led her out of the safe normal path. Kit sighed as he closed the bedroom and went down to tell Rosetta that the room was ready and warm enough to unpack in.

Jamie carried up the suitcase and Rosetta followed upstairs. While they had gone Kit cleared the table and washed up. Then he arranged three chairs on the hearth, placing the two padded ones side by side and setting the ordinary hard kitchen chair for himself. On the table he laid out a dish of homegrown walnuts and one of apples and a packet of muscatel raisins. His hospitable instinct satisfied by this gesture he sat down on his hard chair, got his pipe lighted and picked up his book. It was called *Africa Is Not Dark* and blended travel, adventure, history and geography in just the mixture that he most enjoyed. At first he read with divided attention, a consciousness of Jamie and Rosetta coming between him and the full impact of the printed words; but gradually the old spell asserted itself and he was far away, meditating with the book's author upon the romantic implication of the chain-mail discovered upon the banks of Lake Chad, when the stairs door opened and Rosetta made a clumsy entrance into the kitchen. Jamie followed her. He looked a trifle sheepish, and this, combined with Rosetta's triumphant manner, informed the watcher that they had been to bed together and found, as such

ill-assorted couples often do, a brief but certain solvent for all
their differences.

Rosetta had taken off her coat. The thin dress had an even
thinner top of some transparent material. Its little sleeves ended
well above her elbows and on one arm she wore a collection, a
dozen or more, of bangles of assorted colours. They made a constant jangling noise.

Kit saw that Jamie noticed the apportioning of the comfortable
chairs. He hesitated before he sat down and glanced at each
chair in turn. Nevertheless he sat down without saying anything.

And now there came upon Kit one of those indecisive moments
that made company a misery to him. Should he continue to lose
himself in his book? Or should he give his guests his attention?
They were newly united, they should have plenty to say to one
another. Was his company an embarrassment to them? He decided that he would go to bed early. But meanwhile . . .

As usual he compromised. He continued to read, but not
wholeheartedly. He looked up now and then, cracked walnuts for
Rosetta when he found that she liked them, made it obvious that
he would respond instantly when addressed. This was perhaps a
mistake. Rosetta resumed, as though it had never been disturbed,
the stream of gossip with which she had tried to beguile the
homeward journey and enlivened supper. Jamie, after some rather
grudging responses, said sharply, "You might remember, Rosetta,
that all this is pretty boring for Uncle Kit. He doesn't know any
of these people. A matter for congratulation, by the way."

All Rosetta's gaiety and confidence vanished at the sound of his
voice; but she rallied and turned to Kit with her bright, mechanical smile.

"I'm so sorry, Mr. Shelfanger. I'm afraid I do run on, and it's
such a long time since I saw Jamie." The smile vanished suddenly. Kit, watching, saw her look towards Jamie with an expression wherein doubt, yearning affection and misery mingled and
for the first time he realised that there were depths in Jamie's
wife, depths at the moment in torment.

But there was resource too.

"Let's play cards, then. We can all do that."

"I'm afraid I haven't cards," Kit confessed.

"That sums up Uncle Kit's attitude to card games, my dear," said Jamie, cruelly.

"Not at all," Kit protested. "I've no one to play with, that's why I haven't any cards. I'd enjoy a game."

"I brought cards with me," said Rosetta with a touch of reproof in her voice, "otherwise I wouldn't have mentioned them."

She fetched them down and they provided the needed diversion. Very soon Kit and Rosetta and Jamie were just three people playing cards for small stakes at a clean scrubbed table, their attention focused upon the chances of the game, personalities in abeyance. Kit, rising at the end of a game to fetch beer from the pantry, was amazed to find that the evening had fled; it was eleven o'clock.

"Late for me," he explained with a smile for Rosetta, "but never mind. It's holiday time."

Upon that note he tried, poor earnest man, to maintain the atmosphere. A dozen times a day he would be aware of a psychological danger threatening, and a dozen times a day he would endeavour to forestall it. He worked hard to make his guests physically comfortable; he cooked prodigiously; he did chores unobtrusively; he fell in with any plan. But he was very miserable. The thing he most dreaded, becoming involved with other people's feelings and lives, being forced to take sides—even tacitly—in other people's quarrels, had come upon him in a place and at a time when no escape was possible.

He had never imagined, nor had his very eclectic kind of literature prepared him to imagine or understand, a relationship like that which existed between his nephew and his nephew's wife. It was obvious that any affection which Jamie might ever have had for the girl had vanished long ago. In its place was unconcealed boredom and a kind of irritated distaste capable of being ousted now and again by the pricking of desire. Probably—Kit did not trust his judgment in such matters—Rosetta had considerable sex appeal and Jamie was susceptible to it. Once it had been an overwhelming appeal, and at that time Rosetta had been shrewd, or careful or merely prim enough to demand marriage as the price of surrender, and so she had annihilated her own chance of happi-

ness. For the marriage was a failure, a poor posturing imitation
now and likely to deteriorate steadily with the passage of time.
And while Jamie was rendered irritable and impatient by it, as a
man might be by an ill-fitting garment, Rosetta was bitterly unhappy. She obviously adored Jamie and had not yet learned that
to adore is not to possess a valid claim to the right to be adored.
She resented her own bondage; she was puzzled by the change in
Jamie; she was slavish, aggressive, plaintive and shrewish in turn.

On the whole, because she was the more pitiable of the pair,
Kit sided with her. But even he could not deny that she was in-
credibly stupid, bone idle, both in mind and body, and curiously
irritating in a way that was difficult to define. Kit told himself
that she was "half-baked," and the slang turn did catch something of the incompleteness of her personality, the lack of ideas,
the formlessness, the facile transition of mood and temper. And
of course Jamie was the last person whom she should have married; he was too selfish, unreliable and changeable himself to be
capable of providing any bedrock or ballast in this or any other
human relationship; he was not the person to conceal contempt
or impatience, to compromise and so make the best of a bad job.
Kit, looking at the matter squarely, was forced to admit that he
could see no prospect of happiness for them; and in the face of
that realisation his endeavour to give them a happy Christmas
seemed rather fatuous. But he did his best.

On Boxing night they drove into Welford and went to the cinema. Kit had tried to exclude himself from the party. He liked
going to the cinema by himself and could not imagine enjoying it
in company, and he thought that Rosetta and Jamie ought to
make the modest jaunt alone. Rosetta obviously thought so too;
but Jamie would not be refused. Brandishing the Christmas issue
of the *Welford Weekly Press*, he announced, "There's a picture
about Rhodes and South Africa. Just your cup of tea, Uncle Kit.
If you don't come you'll sit here and read about Africa. Where's
the difference?"

"Perhaps he'd rather stay at home and read," interrupted
Rosetta.

"As a fellow bookworm you should know," snapped Jamie.

"No, seriously, if you don't care about it we won't go," he added, turning to Kit.

Rosetta's face fell instantly. Better a trio out than another evening spent at home. Kit succumbed, only making one last effort.

"I'd thought of staying and having supper ready when you came back."

"Oh damn supper. We've done nothing but eat for three days. We'll be like Strassburg geese."

"What on earth are they?" asked Rosetta.

Jamie said, "Oh . . ." with a glance and a grimace that finished the sentence with My God the ignorance! but did not offer any explanation. Instead he looked again at Kit with a peculiar expression and said, "At least drive in with us. Don't stay here alone. You needn't come to the flicks if there's anything you'd sooner do."

"There's nothing else to do in Welford," said Kit innocently.

The film entranced him. Borne away in time and distance he forgot his company and was oblivious to Rosetta, fidgeting, yawning, sighing with boredom by his side. When, at the end of the programme they emerged into the brightly lighted foyer he was startled, and a little shocked, to hear her say, "What a lousy film. Why did you pick it, Jamie? I never saw anything so dull. And *Stolen Moments* was on at the other place."

"I liked it," said Jamie shortly. "What about you, Uncle Kit?"

"Oh, I thoroughly enjoyed it. Perhaps it was a man's film. We ought to have thought of that."

"Rubbish," snapped Jamie.

Rosetta, who had complained about the film in the voice of a woman with a real and justifiable grievance, now went through one of her disconcerting changes of technique. Slipping an arm through Jamie's she said in a coaxing, kittenish way, "Take ickle Rosie for ickle drink to cheer her up."

"You can have a drink when you get home." Jamie's tone was almost cruel in its refusal to play.

"Only beer and whisky," said Rosetta in her own voice. "I'd like some gin for a change."

"Oh dear," said Kit humbly, accepting this reflection on his hospitality. "I didn't think of gin. That must be set right at once. Of course you shall have some gin."

"Spoilt to death, that's what you are." Jamie's tone lacked the teasing quality that alone would have made the remark accepta- ble. "Only beer and whisky," he mocked her. "What in God's name do you expect?"

"Not to be sworn at." That was her prim, rebuking voice.

"Come on," said Kit. "No more argument. We're going to the Magpie."

Jamie suddenly stood still. "Isn't there anywhere else? There's a—a dance at the Magpie. It'll be horribly crowded."

Normally the idea would have repulsed Kit, but tonight, out to be convivial, anxious to pander to his dissatisfied guest, he was undeterred.

"There's nowhere else," he said firmly and led the way towards the front of the inn.

Women drinkers had not yet attained the freedom of the Mag- pie bar; but, about five years before, when their influence began to be felt, the front part of the old tavern had been altered for their convenience. A wall had been taken down and the entry made one with the old coffee-room; the new apartment, called The Lounge, had been brightened by cream paint, madly pat- terned carpet, palms, pot-plants and little chairs painted green and gold.

Tonight the place was crowded; the wireless blared; a haze of blue smoke hung from the ceiling; a big tinselly Christmas tree stood in the centre of the space and conventional wreaths of holly and bunches of mistletoe paid formal tribute to the season.

At the doorway Jamie suddenly took the lead, pushed in first and after an uneasy glance which swept every corner of the uneven-shaped room, pounced upon a table which was just being vacated. A large palm and a high-backed sofa gave a spurious air of privacy to his choice.

Besides a number of people, like themselves, in street clothes, there were several men and women in evening dress who stood about or perched on the arms of chairs in a manner that implied transcience. Suddenly, from somewhere on an upper floor to the rear of the building, came the strains of a dance band striking up anew and most of the people in evening dress swallowed their drinks hastily, sorted themselves out and wandered from the lounge. Rosetta's eyes followed them, shining, animated, envious.

"Oh, Jamie, there *was* a dance. You might have told me. I could have brought my dress and we could have gone."

"I didn't know in time," said Jamie crossly. "Here, waiter!"

The harassed, flatfooted serving man hurried up in obedience to the testy call and took the order for two double Haigs and a pink Plymouth.

"Well, you might have found out," said Rosetta—not querulously, Kit noticed, but rather with childish persistence. "I haven't been to a dance since I don't know how long. These days you can't unless you have a settled partner. I did once try with Maisie and the gang; but it was awful. I sat out most of the time. Never again, I said."

"You should get a partner then," said Jamie, absently, getting out the money to pay for the drinks. Kit saw Rosetta's face tighten. She snatched up her glass and half emptied it at a gulp.

Jamie drank quickly too, and as soon as Kit, the last to finish, set his glass down empty, half rose and said, "Well, you've had your drink, will you come home now?" There was uneasiness in his manner. Kit attributed it to his fear of spending money on anyone but himself and he experienced one of his stabs of hatred for him. Damn him, he thought, it's not as though he hadn't the money, he has, I saw it. He bought nothing in preparation for Rosetta, his keep hasn't cost him a penny since September; if there is one thing I loathe it is that petty close-fistedness, you can't call it thrift. Aloud he said, "Here, what's the hurry? Why can't I have a turn. It isn't often that I have the privilege of buying a lady a drink."

He beckoned the waiter and re-ordered, putting his hand on his pipe as he spoke. Then he thought better of it and added a request for twenty Players. ". . . unless there's any kind you prefer," he said to Rosetta. She assured him, with her funny little smile, that there was nothing she liked better.

The drinks arrived and the cigarettes were lighted when the band stopped again and the wave of dancers began to creep back into the lounge.

"Why must they come down here? I suppose there's a bar up there," remarked Jamie peevishly.

"It's nice to see them," protested Rosetta. "Ooh, that's a pretty frock. That'd suit me."

A bunch of people came through the wide archway and then separated. Towards the back of it, revealed suddenly by the dispersal, was a tall, white-haired woman with a certain stateliness about her, a boy, too thin for his height, evidently in his first tails, and a girl who arrested the eye instantly. She was not as tall as her mother or brother (the relationship was obvious to the most casual glance) but she was straight and held her head with a promise of that same stateliness; and she was very pretty. Her hair was dark and glossy, her eyes very bright and black-lashed, her skin had a golden glow brushed with carnation on the cheeks and lips. A white dress, plain almost to severity, enhanced her colouring and emphasised her slender straightness.

There were two empty chairs half-way down the room between the archway and the table where Kit and his party were seated and the tall woman bore down upon them. Just before she reached them she looked ahead, seemed to recognise someone and smiled. The girl, following her mother, looked in the same direction and smiled too, a vivid, warm smile that lit her eyes and curved her mouth delightfully. At the same time the colour deepened on her cheeks a little. Kit, who had his good ear turned towards Jamie at the moment, heard the harsh intake of his breath.

"Excuse me a moment," Jamie said, and jumped up, hurrying towards the little group.

Both the woman and the girl greeted him warmly. The gangling boy who had dragged up another chair, pushed it towards Jamie who, at the obvious invitation, hesitated a second and then sat down. The boy found a cane stool, set it in position and then went off again in search of the waiter.

Kit, who had watched all this, now turned his glance upon Rosetta. She was slewed round in her chair staring openly and unashamedly at Jamie, and the expression on her face was anxious, pitiable and ugly. Perhaps luckily Jamie had sat down with his back towards the corner; but the girl in the white dress was facing their way and after a moment or two she shot a surreptitious but curious glance in the direction of the table where Kit and Rosetta sat. Her eyes must have met those of Jamie's wife, for her face changed and she looked away again quickly. But curiosity overcame her and in a very short time she took another peep. Rosetta's stricken face was still turned towards the group and the dark girl once more hastily veiled her stare.

"I don't think," said Kit quietly, "that I'd look that way if I were you. I wouldn't let that wench know that you minded."

Rosetta's head jerked back to a normal position as though a string had pulled it.

"Maybe you're right," she said a little breathlessly. "But I do mind. He's always doing it. If they're friends of his he should introduce me, shouldn't he?"

"They probably aren't friends. More likely somebody he's met in the course of business."

"It looked like that, didn't it?" Rosetta inquired with bitter sarcasm. "Besides, if *I* met someone in business and then ran into them when I was with Jamie I'd be pleased and proud to introduce my husband. Why shouldn't he feel the same?"

Knowing the answer Kit felt his pity quicken, but he only said, "Men like to keep things separate. Come on now, finish that drink and have another while the man is handy. We can't let Jamie get one up on us." For the tall boy had effusively pressed a glass upon Jamie and now the four had settled down to bright banter, punctuated by laughter.

"I think I'll have port," said Rosetta. "Maisie always said gin made you feel low."

The port came. It, or emotion, made Rosetta suddenly vocal and confidential. She loosened her coat and threw it back so that the lining, cheap, sleazy, artificial, betrayed it for the pretentious affair that it was, and leaned towards Kit.

"You'd hardly think, would you, that he used to be charming like that to me?" There was a new change in her voice: the real bred-in-the-bone Cockney coming into its own at last. "He did, honestly. You never saw anybody sweeter." She sighed. "Of course, I know I'm not quite his class; but Mother's awfully respectable and brought us girls up very strict. She never let us hang about on the edges of pavements. Both my sisters married very well; their husbands are in good steady jobs." She lifted her glass and almost emptied it. Her face flushed a little, relaxed, grew more defenceless. "I don't mind that about Jamie—that he isn't steady I mean—Mother's got her hands full, often as many as eight in the house, she's glad to have me at home. So I can always earn my keep, thank God. But I do mind his carrying on and the way he behaves as if being married didn't mean anything. Would you believe, from May last year till the middle of October I didn't know whether he was dead or alive. That's the kind of thing that makes a girl look a fool. I mean what can you say to people? Especially when you've always been respectable."

This time she drained the glass, but still holding it in her hand worked its base about on the table, making patterns in the dampness of the glass top.

"Of course, I knew he was in some sort of trouble. He'd got in with a bad gang, rotten shady fellows in the car trade, half of them stolen, I'll be bound. I'd warned him more'n once. Still, he *was* my husband when all was said and done, for better and worse as they say, and I'd have stuck by him. But all he could do was walk out on me and stay away without a word, till he writes, if you please, and says he's all right, he's with his uncle. I didn't half believe that for a tale, I may tell you. That was why I was so crazy to come and see for myself. I quite thought he'd dug himself in with some old dame or something and spun me that yarn about you and the farm at the back of nowhere just to put me off. I was dumbstruck when he brought you to the station. Maybe you noticed."

She stilled her hands suddenly, took a cigarette from the packet on the table and leaned forward to the match that Kit held out. The little flame cast the shadow of her lashes upon her rather full upper lids, fluttery, fleeting, strangely touching. Kit was conscious of a stab at the heart. Someone who genuinely loved her, who had patience and steadiness and a little generosity, might have made something of her. He shut the thought away and sought wildly in his mind for something to say that would change the trend of Rosetta's thoughts. While he was still seeking she leaned forward again and said confidentially,

"That girl he's with is pretty, isn't she?"

"Is she?" asked Kit. "I didn't notice much."

"Well, she is. And what's more she's got nice things. Trust Jamie to go for that sort. But I'm pretty too. If I had the money I could look as good as that, every bit. P'raps you doubt it."

"No, indeed I don't," said Kit warmly. "I think you're very pretty indeed."

A warm delighted look swept over Rosetta's face. Kit caught a glimpse of the vivacious, rather gamin charm that had been hers before something (was it Jamie?) had struck at the roots of her self-esteem.

"Do you really? It's nice to hear it said, though ackcherly, of course, I did know I was. And I haven't let myself go like some girls do direckly they're married. And as for the rest of it . . . God, you can't say I haven't tried. I've nearly killed myself trying to do and say things properly. You know, I thought I was all right until we'd been married a month or two. He'd never found fault before. Then he started to. And he never helped me a bit. He could say what was wrong but he couldn't tell me what to do instead. But I did try, honest." Her face sank into lines of disillusionment as though she contemplated long hours of wasted labour.

"You know," Kit ventured, "if I were you I should forget all that. All newly married couples have to make these—adjustments."

"We've been married rather more than two years," countered Rosetta. Kit smiled to think of the youthfulness which found two years so long a time.

"That's isn't long, really. And I think your case is rather more difficult than most. Jamie is a highly peculiar person."

Her eyes widened in surprise. "So you've noticed that too! How funny. Of course, Maisie says he's mad, but she thinks everybody except her and her Bert are mad."

"I don't think he's mad. But I do think he's moody and very difficult to understand. I should think being married to him calls for all the tact and patience any woman could possess."

"That's just what makes him so fascinating." Rosetta spoke earnestly. "Both my sisters' husbands, well, you know beforehand just exactly what they'll say and do. And they'll never amount to anything *really*, I mean they'll get on and all that, but Bert'll always just be an electrician and Tim'll live and die doing his insurance round. Jamie is different. You know, it is funny. When he wrote and said about his uncle and the farm I didn't really believe it and yet it seemed possible. And when I did believe it, just at odd moments, I thought it'd be a big place like you see on the pictures. I say, I hope you don't mind my saying that because it's ever so easy to see that you're good class though you do your own work and live in the kitchen. . . ." She faltered and stopped, finally bogged. Kit laughed, a hearty unrestricted bellow that rang out queerly in that room of semi-confidential mutterings or little titters of mirth.

"I've no claims to any class as you call it. I'm a farmer in a very small way. My father was a farmer and my mother was a farmer's daughter. And Jamie's mother was my sister. The Liddells were—well, a bit different. They thought a vast deal of themselves." His voice hardened with sudden passion. "I hate all that kind of thing. It makes for a lot of unhappiness. It spoilt the life of the person I liked better than anybody else. You take my advice and don't let that idea of Jamie affect you."

Rosetta naturally ignored the sound sense of these remarks and seized upon the non-essential. "That accounts for Jamie being so different," she said dreamily. She slewed round in the chair and stared at the back of his head, hungrily. Kit sighed with impatience. Really, talking did no good at all. He had no knowledge of psychological terms, and though he had been the victim of an escape complex for the greater part of his life he would not have understood the term. But he could see that Rosetta had, during the whole of her acquaintanceship with Jamie, comforted herself for his faults and failings by dwelling upon his difference from the rest of the men she met. She could not bear to think of him as he was, unreliable, unkind, critical, neglectful, shifty, so out of her own wishes and her experience of the cinema she had built up an idea of him which, if not perfect was at least interesting and not sordid. Poor little girl!

Across the room the tall woman rose with an air of decision. The pretty girl and the gangly boy got to their feet more reluctantly, leaning back towards Jamie as he finished something he was saying. He strolled with them as far as the archway and there took a smiling leave.

He was still smiling when he reached the table.

"Well, how about one for the road?" he asked, dropping into his chair and looking round for the waiter.

"Not for me," said Rosetta tartly. "This is a nice way to bring me out, I must say."

Jamie's affability vanished completely. He shot her a look of admonitory hatred. The look said what Kit was thinking—Careful now, careful. But Rosetta was not going to be careful; she had forgotten all about Jamie's interesting personality. She was a wife with a grievance and a little mixed drink working in her.

"Going off like that to flirt with your girl friend and leaving me alone."

"Allow me to point out that you were not alone; also that that is not my girl friend as you so elegantly term it. That was Mrs. Winchely who is a good customer, and her daughter whom I am teaching to drive the new car which was her birthday present. Does that satisfy you?"

Rosetta's capitulation was as sudden and ill-judged as her attack had been.

"I'm sorry, Jamie. I'm silly, I know."

"You're a jealous, stupid, narrow-minded little cat!" said Jamie dispassionately. "And if tonight is a sample of your behaviour it's a damn good thing that you're going back to your proper environment tomorrow."

Rosetta's big eyes swam in tears, her chin began to quiver. At the sight of her distress Kit became aware of a peculiar sensation in his chest wall, as though a butterfly were trapped there and madly fluttering. It was not a novel sensation though it was some time since he had felt it last, it was his natural nervous reaction to the sight of naked ugly passions in other people. He had felt it first when, as a small boy, he had witnessed quarrels among the members of his family and he had never outgrown it.

He now said "Jamie" very sharply, like one calling a small erring boy to order. Jamie, after an obvious swallowing of rage, responded with, "Well, what about you, Uncle Kit? You'll have a drink."

Two tears had escaped from Rosetta's lashes and travelled slowly over her cheeks, leaving tracks in the powder.

"We'd better get back, I think," said Kit. "Thanks all the same." It irked him that Jamie should, without saying anything, manage to imply that they were two sensible fellows whose evening was being wrecked, and who were in combination against this silly female.

The journey home was accomplished in silence, only broken when Rosetta's sobs became audible and Jamie said savagely, "Oh, stop snivelling." Kit consoled himself as he drove with his old train of thought, planning the things he would say.

He would say that a young couple who could not come to terms had no right to inflict their company on other people. But that was a selfish and unhelpful thing to say.

He would say that they were both young and unless they wanted to ruin one another's lives entirely they must both exercise patience and a little humour. But that sounded pompous and didn't really mean much when you looked at it critically.

Damn it, what could anyone say except, "You're a pair of silly young fools and I wish you'd get out of my house?"

A little drearily Kit looked back to the time before Jamie's coming. What had occupied his thoughts then? It was difficult to remember—the day's work, the next job, the book he was reading —honestly in retrospect it seemed as though his mind had been almost a blank. But he had been happy; wrongly, selfishly perhaps, but indubitably happy.

And suddenly it occurred to him, in a flash of insight, that he had always been and would always be at the mercy of other people's moods and emotions because he had so few of his own. If when he had been a youngster he had had a love affair of his own he would not have had time or energy or interest to spare for Eva's. And if he had been having quarrels and bits of business and love affairs during his years at sea the other men's would not have irked him so much. And at this moment if he had a wife and a family the mere fact that a nephew of his had married unwisely and was behaving badly about it would be no more than a matter of passing interest. The thought sobered him. It was all a matter of proportion. He must be very careful that he did not permit his emptiness to warp his judgment, and even more careful that pity, which could become a mania didn't . . . But he hardly followed that thought to its conclusion.

When they reached the house Rosetta, refusing all material solace, even a cup of tea, went straight to bed. Jamie said he wanted no supper, but he stayed downstairs, smoking spasmodically while Kit, whom emotion always made hungry, cut himself a hunk of bread and cheese and poured a glass of beer.

"It's a nice mess, isn't it?" asked Jamie at last, defiantly.

"I don't notice any willingness on your part to put it right," said Kit bluntly.

"Oh, you blame me, do you?" Jamie's tone was truculent. "Trust the little woman to get all the sympathy on her side."

"I'm not taking any sides," Kit answered with sudden passion. "If there is one thing I hate more than another it is people quarrelling in public, saying things that shouldn't be said, exposing themselves and making other people uncomfortable. I know there are people who can look on that kind of thing quite calmly, but I don't happen to be one of them. I hate it. That's one reason why from choice I live alone. And I tell you quite frankly, Jamie, that I can't stand this sort of thing in my house. It's altogether too wearing."

He had never spoken so frankly or at such length to Jamie before and Jamie looked rather as though the dog Guess had turned and rebuked him.

"Don't imagine that I enjoy it," he said sullenly. "It's not a situation I should choose."

"But you made it," Kit persisted. "You were grown up, you knew what you were doing when you married her, I take it. She's amiable enough, and she's in love with you, which gives you a great advantage. In fact I'm sure if you were to sort of settle down and act as though you were fond of her, so that she wasn't always on edge and nervy, you'd be happy enough."

Smiling a not very amiable smile Jamie addressed a point on the kitchen ceiling. "Listen to that," he mocked, "matrimonial advice

while you wait, proffered by one most fitted to offer it, a cagey
old bachelor who has never had a woman in his house. Or am I
wrong? Is this the voice of experience speaking? I must say you
lay great stress on that quality, non-existent in Rosetta, amiability. Do I detect knowledge there?" He looked at Kit quizzically.
Then, deadly serious, he added, "Rosetta isn't amiable, she's stupid and malicious and narrow-minded like all her kind. She's
good in bed and ought to be kept for that one purpose. I've made
a lot of mistakes in my life and she's merely one of them. I don't
let the others haunt me. Why should she?"

"She's not just a mistake. She's a human being with ordinary
human feelings. I'm sorry for her."

"Naturally. She is not uncomely," said Jamie nastily. He fore-
stalled Kit's protest by rising and going towards the stairs.

"Well, it's no use arguing about it. Back she goes tomorrow to
her respectable mother who brought up her girls 'very strict' and
so got us in this jam, by the way; and then perhaps you and I can
resume our happy bachelor life. I hope so." His tone was completely altered, persuasive now and charming.

"The only thing is you're not a bachelor," said Kit, half capitu-
lating.

"No, worse luck," said Jamie, and smiled ruefully. "Well, good-
night, Uncle Kit. Sorry about the evening." It was so like Eva,
that light-hearted dismissal of unpleasantness.

But that was the last time that Jamie reminded Kit of Eva. In
less than an hour that spell was lifted for good. For Jamie either
found Rosetta awake or wakened her, and soon the noise of their
quarrelling reached Kit, even through the dividing wall, even
through the barrier of his deafness. Jamie shouted, Rosetta
screeched until she was hysterical, and finally there came the
sound of a single sharp smack of a hand on flesh. At that Kit
tumbled from the bed and smote on the wall and shouted. There
was sudden and complete silence upon the other side. Kit, tum-
bling back, with the mad butterfly beating at his chest wall knew
that his tardy allegiance had been won—by Rosetta. That was
probably how Ed Liddell had treated Eva, dear bright Eva who
had also been foolish and simple and exasperating. From that moment Jamie was merely his father's son, to be regarded unsen-

timentally, while Rosetta stepped into the place that Eva had held in Kit's heart.

During the night it began to snow and the flakes were descending, quiet and relentless, when Kit went down to light the kitchen fire. There were sounds of movement from the room above and presently Jamie, narrow-faced in the cold, appeared carrying Rosetta's suitcase which he placed near the door. Kit fried the rashers and eggs and made the coffee and when the meal was quite ready Jamie bellowed up the stairs.

Rosetta, wearing her fur coat and little hat, came down and took her place at the table. She looked ghastly in the snow-light that filled the kitchen; the side of her forehead that the tilted hat left bare was like a bleached bone, the colour, carefully applied to cheek and lip, stood out like a clown's paint, her eyes were swollen and red and one side of her jaw bulged unevenly. It hurt Kit to look at her. She drank two cups of coffee, but left her breakfast untouched.

Jamie ate hastily, with nervous impatience, drained his cup and pushed back his chair.

"Did you bring the hatbox down?" he asked.

"Yes." Her voice was thick, hoarse, undisguisedly Cockney.

Jamie went out to fetch the car and Rosetta, as soon as he had left the kitchen, began to cry, feebly, with an attempt at control that was very painful to watch.

"Must you go today?" Kit asked, almost despite himself. "You don't look very well, and it's a horrible day."

"Of course I must, you know that. You said I must go, Jamie told me so. And you seemed so kind. I really thought you were kind." Speech defeated the control and her voice rose in a wail. She dabbed at her face with a ludicrously inadequate handkerchief which carried lipstick to the tip of her nose and other parts of her face.

"I didn't mean it that way at all. Jamie knew that. I meant that we couldn't go on as we were last night. Look here, would you like to stay? Would it make you happy to stay?"

"Oh, it would, it would indeed. You see, if I stayed there'd be some hope of making it up. If I go away now he never will forgive me. He won't write or anything. I know it. I can't tell you what it'll be like. I don't think I can face it, I'll be so miserable."

"Very well, stay then. If you take my advice you'll go back to bed and have a good rest."

"Will you tell Jamie?"

"Of course."

"Then I think I'll go up so he can't argue with me. And thanks ever so much."

She made for the stairs with surprising sprightliness and the door had just swung behind her when Jamie came in and lifted the case and looked round.

"Rosetta isn't going today," said Kit. "I didn't think she was fit to travel, especially on a day like this. I've sent her back to bed."

"The devil you have! Why?"

"Because I've got eyes. I can see when a person is on the verge of collapse, if you can't. And no wonder, after last night. What's more, Jamie, if you can't keep your hands off her you'd better get out yourself. I won't have any wife-beating under my roof."

Again that abrupt change of manner. Gently teasing, Jamie said, "You chivalrous old Galahad! Wife-beating indeed. I merely took the traditional means to stop hysteria. Haven't you ever tried it? It's infallible. Oh well, have it your own way. I'll be back in good time. Anything you want?"

He smiled from the doorway and was gone.

Kit carried up the case and set it inside Rosetta's open door. "Would you try to eat some bread and milk if I made it?" he asked gently.

"I'd do anything for you. You're the nicest person I know," said Rosetta enthusiastically.

"I'm the biggest fool in Christendom," said Kit from the stairs.

He had taken a stand now, and whatever happened would be on his own head.

All that day it snowed without intermission, and since there was nothing, save feeding the beasts and milking the cow, to be done out-of-doors, Kit cleaned and tidied the kitchen thoroughly and scrubbed the floor, a thing it had been impossible to do while people were sitting by the fire. Then he cooked, and at one

o'clock tip-toed upstairs with a meal on a tray. Rosetta was awake
and called to him to come in. She sat up in bed to take the tray
and showed her thin white shoulders, bare save for the narrow
straps of her nightgown, a flimsy garment made of some flowered,
semi-transparent material. Her collar-bone and top two pairs of
ribs were painfully prominent, but she was not flat-chested; above
the edge of the sheet was the soft upward thrust of her breasts.
Tenderness, like a warm melting wave, went over Kit, softening
the very marrow of his bones. And while he stood there, unable
to move or breathe, Rosetta's eyes met his, held for a moment,
and then dropped. Wildly Kit stared around, searching for something, some wrap or scarf to put about her, but he could see nothing, nor did Rosetta, by offering any direction, help him. Almost
stumbling with confusion he went into his own room and
brought his heavy plaid dressing-gown. His hands shook as he put
it about her shoulders. She said, "Thank you," as though she too
were short of breath.

Back in the kitchen he dropped into a chair and sat for some
moments like a man recovering from the shock of some shattering
experience. His heart beat all over his body, even in his fingertips.
And his thoughts were more disorderly than his pulses. He was astonished at himself, and appalled. He reminded himself that
Rosetta was his guest, the wife of his nephew, that the disin-
genuous way in which she raised herself in the bed was sufficient
measure of her innocence, of her trust in him, but no amount of
thinking or self-reproach did any good; thought was of the mind,
and that was temporarily dethroned, flesh was master, even
though it were flesh racked by that terrible yearning tenderness
and a yet more terrible desire. . . . And constantly, like a chant,
there sounded in his ears Jamie's careless callous phrase, "She's
good in bed."

In the room above Rosetta was also mentally fingering a new
idea. Jamie had made her jealous often enough, no longer ago
than last night she had known the familiar pang. But she had
never made Jamie jealous; many things she had tried but not
that. And Jamie was almost red-headed, people of that colouring
had a great capacity for jealousy—or so it was reputed. It was a
pity that it was only Uncle Kit; but it might have been worse.

Jamie seemed to respect him, which was more than he did the general run of men who might have served the purpose if she had thought of it earlier. And really, although he was over forty, and shy and rather deaf, there were good points about Kit Shelfanger; he was big and well-made and not half bad-looking: he was already disposed in her favour; he was what she called a "nice" man, not likely to demand too much. And at that moment Rosetta intended to give very little. Thanks to her respectable mother and "very strict" upbringing, she was already sealing away in the dangerous house of the unconscious, the memory of that fiery locked stare, and the thrill that had gone through her when Kit's big unsteady hands had laid the dressing-gown over her shoulders. It was not of her own feelings, nor of Kit's that Rosetta was thinking, but of Jamie's.

("Oh, Mr. Liddell, I hardly hoped you'd be in Welford this dreadful day, but I thought I'd just telephone on the chance. Mummy's got a sherry party this evening. Do drop in if you've nothing more exciting to do. No, no, this isn't *exciting*. Mummy insists on saying 'sherry' but there *will* be cocktails. Oh lovely. Soon after six then. Good-bye."

"Good-bye, Amanda—or must I say Miss Winchely?"

"Of course not—Jamie. Looking forward . . .")

"Jamie's late."

"He is. But it's a shocking night. In fact, I think he'd be wise to stay in Welford. There must be nearly three feet of snow on the Heath road. Nothing to wear it down, you see."

"Might we be completely cut off?"

"Hardly likely. And anyway there's nothing to worry about if we are. I guess our food and fuel will outlast anything the English winter can do. The most you'd have to fear would be boredom."

"Oh, I can find something to do. I should think you and Jamie must have masses of mending between you."

"Jamie may have. I generally keep mine in hand. I have a sewing day about once a month."

"It does seem funny to me, to see a man so handy about everything. Where did you learn it all?"

"At sea mostly. Men have to do everything on a ship, you know."

"Oh, tell me about some of the places you've been to. I've always longed to travel. And I say—do you mind if I don't say 'Uncle Kit' any more? After all you're not my uncle, are you? And anyway nobody would dream of saying 'Nephew Jamie' or 'Niece Rosetta,' so why the other thing?"

"I'd be glad for you to call me Kit. I'm afraid I've always been informal with you."

"Informal, and kind, and most awfully sweet." Her eyelids fluttered.

It would be tonight, of all nights, thought Kit, that the weather kept Jamie in town. And she would begin to call me Kit and exercise all her pretty ways for me alone. And, my God, whoever first said "There's no fool like an old fool," knew what he was talking about. Old fool, deaf fool, who wanted to live alone; crazy fool who for countless years hasn't given any woman a second thought; ridiculous doddering old fool who can only think that on the other side of that wall she will drop her garments one by one until presently there will be only that wisp of flowered stuff between her and. . . . "She's good in bed." Lead us not into temptation, deliver us from evil; and what was the saying from that same source about the sin of adultery by thinking?

Next day brought a cold thaw. On one side of the grey house the poplar trees dripped and shivered, on the other the pond shivered and swelled. But the roaring fire in the stove kept the kitchen windows shining redly and within all was warm and comfortable though neither inhabitant was fully at ease. Kit innocently hoped that Jamie would make the journey today; he had yet to learn that his agony would increase, rather than lessen when Jamie climbed into the bed on the other side of the wall. Rosetta was also anxious for Jamie's return, for added to her usual reasons for wanting to see him was the new factor of curiosity to see how he reacted to her new manner to Kit. So both were delighted when at about eight o'clock in the evening there came the sound of tyres cutting through the slush and the tootle of the horn that told that Jamie had arrived in a good temper.

Jamie had enjoyed his hours of absence. The cocktail party had been a success and during it he had been drawn aside and asked to stay for dinner. After the meal, which had seemed very elaborate compared with Uncle Kit's simple fare, he had joined in the games which, even in the most sophisticated circles, seem to be part of the Christmas ritual. At twelve o'clock when he attempted to leave the snow was still falling and he had been easily persuaded to stay the night.

In the course of the evening there had come from Amanda directly, and from Amanda's mother indirectly, the question about Rosetta's identity and Jamie had managed, in his own inimitable fashion, to imply that she was Kit's affair, not his. He felt fully justified for what was rather a suppression and a distortion of truth than a direct lie. He was making a new life in Welford; the Winchely family, socially mediocre but financially secure, had for some reason taken an exceptionally favourable view of him; with luck many such successes would come his way. Why should he cramp himself by open confession to that two-year-old mistake? He cursed himself for ever letting Rosetta know his whereabouts, but that action had been prompted by a fear that she might take steps to find him and by the hope that she was as tired of him as he was of her, and by the certainty that he had painted such a picture of Uncle Kit and Heath End as would serve to keep her in London. The fact that she had, after all, forced herself upon him for a brief stay was not going to affect his behaviour. She was going back to London, to help her mother with the lodgers, and he was going to stay in the place where he had, as though by a miracle, gained a free home, the use of a car, a job absolutely to his taste, and the chance of making valuable contacts. Between times, during the day and night he had been away, he had done some constructive thinking. He saw that he had been wrong to try to drive Rosetta away by surly treatment; and he returned planning to delude her. If she could imagine that she was sure of him she would go more easily—Kit had given him the ghost of that thought. And twenty-four hours, or rather more, immured at Heath End, with only a middle-aged, deaf man for company would probably have had an effect upon her too. So Jamie decided that he would be calm and unemotional, he would put to Rosetta, very reasonably, that at the moment it was impossible for him to make a home for her in Welford, but that if she went back to London and so did not annoy Uncle Kit into turning them both out, he would be able to save money and he would send for her as soon as he could. As usual he could see no flaw in his plan, that was a weakness in him that had led him into trouble before.

He apologised for his absence, saying that he had spent the night with Gordon Tillingham, that the bed had been uncomfortable and the food surprisingly bad and that he was very glad to be home again. That was nicely calculated to put Kit in a good temper; but the effort was wasted. Kit was momentarily so pleased to see him that his temper needed no sweetening; Rosetta was also glad, for *her* own private reasons; and Jamie himself was acting on his thought-out plan. So the three sat down to supper in good humour, quite different people from the three who had returned from Welford just on forty-eight hours earlier.

Jamie was the first to assimilate, and measure against his own self-interest, the main factor in the changed atmosphere. Before the meal was over he saw that the main prop of his argument—that Rosetta should go away before Uncle Kit tired of them both and so ended the free board and lodging era—was no longer feasible. Not only was Rosetta flirting in her unsubtle fashion with Kit, but he, God help him, was obviously disturbed by her. Disturbed, but unresentful. Rosetta, the crafty little bitch, had taken pains to dig herself well in during Jamie's absence; there were other things than conventional hospitality and sentimental sympathy now in Kit's attitude towards her. Jamie, to whom Rosetta's actions had long been a matter of indifference, so long as they did not interfere with his, watched her performance with cynical amusement; and as soon as he was sure that Kit was really vulnerable, not just pretending, the sadism in his nature licked its chops.

He let the play go on for a little, and then he dragged Rosetta down on to his knees, put his arm round her waist so that his hand lay in her lap and ran his other hand through her hair. He covered the caress by saying teasingly, "Very curly tonight, did you spend the day in curlers?" But Rosetta knew, and Kit knew, that the gesture was more important than the words; and Rosetta thought that at last she had found the talisman; and Kit suffered another sharp pang of jealousy. Jamie noted both responses—the sensual relaxing of the girl's body, the tightening grip of the man's hand on the arm of his chair; and his malicious nature knew a moment of gloating.

With a snake-like twist of his nimble mind he reversed his argument. "It won't do, Rosetta. The old man's fallen for you and I'm not going to leave you in the house with him." That was an argument that she would understand, for with all her posturing and making eyes she was a prude at heart as who should know better than himself. And it would at the same time flatter her vanity and send her back to London in a good mood. Once she was back at her home he would take a weekend off and go to see her, say he had left Welford and taken a job in, say, Liverpool. If necessary he would get a letter posted to her from Liverpool. This time he would give her the slip properly. But she must be away from Heath End before New Year's Eve, because he had promised to join the Winchely's party for the Farmers' Benevolent Dance and if Rosetta knew she would make a scene. That, in itself, Jamie did not mind a bit, but it would, he knew, set Uncle Kit against him, and free board and lodging was not lightly to be jeopardised.

Rosetta, held in the circle of Jamie's arm, was happy and triumphant. It had worked better than she had dared to hope, and the future looked pretty good. Kit could be kept doting and useful, Jamie reclaimed and rechained all by the same process, the exercise of her natural talent for being gay and affectionate, an exercise that came easily enough when she was happy.

Jamie, with smothered impatience, let two days pass before again broaching the subject of Rosetta's return. The two days passed rapidly despite his impatience because the thirty-first of the month seemed to be rushing towards him. She must be out of the way by that date. Already Thompson's best cutter was executing a rush order for evening clothes and being much harassed by the new customer's harsh criticism and extreme pernicketiness. For Rosetta too, with her newly-found happiness, the days sped. For Kit they dragged on endlessly like days spent in a particularly

ingenious torture chamber. Desire, jealousy, self-contempt and
desire again had their will of him in turn.

Immediately after supper on the twenty-ninth of December, Jamie
went upstairs, and after a few moments called Rosetta to join
him. Kit cleared away and washed the dishes alone in the little
back scullery. He was rather surprised to find the kitchen empty
when he returned to it; but he threw fresh logs on the fire,
stroked Guess absentmindedly, lighted his pipe, reached for the
Farmer and Stockbreeder and tried to imagine that he was alone
in the house. He hated himself for thinking that the bedroom
was cold and that there was only one warm place in it. . . .

But presently he became aware of the sound of rising voices.
Jamie and Rosetta were quarrelling more bitterly than ever. Unable to keep still, with the old trembling beginning in his chest wall
as though a mad butterfly beat its wings against it, Kit got up and
went to the door of the stairs.

There was no mistake about it. Jamie was shouting and Rosetta
was screeching back at him, both of them carried beyond any
thought that they might be overheard. The listener felt the impact of their hatred, even though no words that they spoke were
distinguishable. What could have happened? For three days now
they had seemed on the best of terms; what new thing had occurred to cause this fury?

Stealthily, though there was little fear that they would hear a
footstep, so engrossed did they seem, Kit went up the stairs almost without volition. It was the only time, save one, that he had
not moved away from a quarrel when such retreat was possible.
The solitary exception had been in a dock at Port Elizabeth when
two lascar stokers had set about one another with knives. It is
doubtful whether either of the combatants knew what it was that
had suddenly fallen upon them, dragged them apart and sent one
crashing in a somersault on to the deck boards and whirled the
other over the side; for Kit, greatly ashamed of an action that he
could neither explain nor excuse, had disappeared as soon as he
saw the water-cooled fellow fished out by a handy boathook. The
incident had vanished from his memory and he did not recall it
as he now, for the second time in his life, moved nearer the vor-

tex of passion. Had he done so he might have been warned. But
as it was he reached the head of the stairs and instinctively
turned his good ear towards the closed door of the spare room.

Just at that moment Rosetta's voice changed, faltered, broke,
became charged with tears.

"I know what it is. I know why you want me to go. To leave
you a clear field with that little bitch in the white frock. You
don't fool me, Jamie Liddell, any more than you did with An-
nette and Freda. And tomorrow I shall go into Welford and I
shall tell everybody, and that girl and her mother, that you're
married to me, and just what sort of a husband you've been."

Jamie's voice dropped too, into a menacing monotone. He said,
with a deadly seriousness that robbed the words of their melo-
drama, "I'll wring your neck first, you little hell cat."

"Wring it," sobbed Rosetta. "Go on! Put me out of my misery.
I don't want to go on living this way."

"Will you go home tomorrow?"

"No."

"All right then." There was a second's ominous silence in the
room and then Rosetta began to scream, no words, just a shrill,
heart-shattering "A-A-A-Ah."

Kit opened the door. He saw, in a flash that took no time at
all, Jamie, with his hands on Rosetta's shoulders, shaking her
backwards and forwards until her head lolled and the screaming
issued from her grotesquely open mouth in jolts and waves, like
water from a shaken uncorked bottle. Then the weight that had
fallen upon the lascar stokers fell upon Jamie. His hands shot into
the air as Kit's fist hit him on the side of the head, he fell sideways over the end of the bed, landed heavily, kicked convulsively
once or twice and then lay still. Kit stood rigid for a moment
trembling. Rosetta, the tears arrested in her eyes, the screaming
dammed in her throat, scrambled like a cat from the tumbled bed
and knelt beside Jamie.

PART FOUR

KIT AND ROSETTA

"It was the drawer that did it," Rosetta said at last, as though a correct explanation could improve matters. "It was the drawer. I left it open when I got out my things."

She looked down at Kit, who, after drawing her gently away, had knelt down himself by Jamie's body and had—unless his imagination had tricked him—felt the last pulsation flicker and die in Jamie's breast. The thought of brandy came to him and simultaneously the knowledge that there was none in the house.

As though some secret means of communication had opened between them, Rosetta seemed to catch the thought and stooping she thrust her hands into the muddle of half-packed clothes that lay tumbled in the open suitcase. One hand came out clenched round a tiny glass flask set into a cheap tin cup.

"I always have it, for train sickness," she explained, wrenching off the top and passing it across to Kit.

The liquid gurgled as it met the air in Jamie's throat and for a moment Kit knew the recrudescence of hope. But nothing happened. The hand with which he was supporting Jamie's head came away with blood on the palms and fingers.

"Blood," said Rosetta in a terrible voice, "he's bleeding to death. We must get a doctor. Oh, why aren't you on the telephone? Where is the nearest doctor?"

Kit tried to speak. His lips moved and there was a convulsion in his throat, but no words came. He looked from Jamie to Rosetta and shook his head.

"But you must," she said, seizing him by the arm and trying to drag him from the room. "You needn't be afraid. Nobody'll know you hit him. We'll say . . . say that he came up in the dark and fell over the drawer. Only be quick, quick!"

Once more Kit attempted speech. A noise like a strangled sob broke from him. He choked and swallowed. Rosetta, like a little desperate cat, sprang at him again and shook his arm violently.

"Have you gone daft?" she demanded. "Do for God's sake pull yourself together. Oh, if only I could drive . . ."

At last the words came, hoarse and unwilling.

"The doctor couldn't do anything. Jamie's dead."

Once again Rosetta dropped to her knees and put her hand inside the shirt that Kit had loosened.

"Rubbish," she said robustly, "he's warm."

"He isn't breathing."

Rosetta stretched up an arm and reached down the tarnished metal-backed mirror that lay on the chest of drawers. She held it to Jamie's lips and then, with an expert air, examined it.

"No," she said slowly. "You're right. He isn't."

She rose to her feet and stood still, one hand to her mouth, the other pleating and unpleating a fold in her dress. Kit braced himself for an outburst of hysteria. But strangely enough none came. They stood for what seemed a long time, looking at one another with stricken faces and between them lay that grotesque and terrible thing, the lifeless body of a man who so few minutes ago had been moving and speaking. Then, carefully avoiding the body, Rosetta came round and sat down heavily on the bed.

"This is serious," she said in a quiet practical voice. "We've gotta think."

Kit tried, but his mind went blank, or wandered. Once he wondered if this was how idiots felt always and thought that people were not sympathetic enough; on the other hand idiots generally looked pretty happy. From useless reflections such as these his mind would be jerked back to the consciousness of Jamie lying there on the floor, the reek of the brandy in the room, and

Rosetta, with furrowed brow, crouched on the edge of the bed, also trying to think. She looked at him at last.

"I still think that the best thing to do would be to go for the doctor. He couldn't tell to a minute *when* he died, he might still have been alive when you started off. And while you're gone I'll straighten up a bit in here and we'll stick to it that he came up in the dark for something he thought he could put his hand on, tripped over the rug and hit his head on the drawer."

Kit looked at her sickly.

"It wouldn't do, Rosetta. There'll be a mark where I hit him. I hit him very hard, you know. For all we know it might have been that that killed him."

"You mustn't go thinking that. Do you hear me? It was the drawer did it; and I left the drawer open. I'm as much to blame as you are."

"That's a generous statement, but quite untrue. And I'd really rather you didn't feel that way about it." (For at the moment, numbed by shock, or supported by morbid excitement, Rosetta might be able to bear the notion that her carelessness had resulted in Jamie's death; but afterwards—why, it might cause her sorrow enough to spoil her life.) "No," he added heavily, "I did it. I didn't mean to kill him; but at that moment I wanted to."

Rosetta gave him a queer look; but the practical question was still uppermost in her mind.

"What are we going to do?" she repeated.

"I suppose go to the police and tell them the whole story, hoping and trusting that they will believe it."

"Oh no! Oh, Uncle Kit, absolutely not that. It'd be in all the papers, with photographs of us. And I'd have to say that Jamie was attacking me. And everybody at home would know. I couldn't bear it. Really I couldn't. Besides" (obvious afterthought) "they'd probably hang you whatever we said."

"More likely they'd call it manslaughter and give me about fifteen years. It'd depend."

"What on?"

"Partly on what we said and whether they believed us; and partly, I suppose, on the medical evidence. They might say he was dead before he hit the drawer."

"Then we can't do that," said Rosetta decidedly. "Besides I'm sure they'd call it a triangle and go poking about making out that you and me had been up to something. And we *were* alone here the other night. Mother wouldn't like that if she knew. No, Uncle Kit, he's dead and we're alive. We've got to do what we can for ourselves."

"But, child, what can we do?"

Rosetta's small white face bleached and contracted until it looked like a fantastic mask, a caricature of a face made in hard white stone, and out of it, from between lids reddened and swollen by her earlier tears, her blue eyes stared at Kit.

"Would you do it, if I told you?" she whispered.

"I must know, before I promise."

"All right then. We'll bury him. Nobody comes here. We'd have all the time in the world. We could bury him so deep that they'd never find him even if they looked. And they wouldn't look; not if we kept our heads. I read once that they wouldn't have looked in Crippen's cellar if he hadn't made them suspicious by running away. You see, you and me are the only people who would really wonder where Jamie was; nobody else is much interested in him. He was lost, as you might say, for six months this year, and I was the only person who noticed it. He's never stuck to anything very long, he's always been on this ramshackle kind of business, here today and gone tomorrow. Even if this hadn't happened he was just as likely to have left that garage place tomorrow as to have stuck to it. I guess it was only that girl, you know, the one he talked to the other night, that kept him here this long. And if it looks as if he's gone off without even leaving her a word she won't want to talk about him or look for him. We'd be absolutely safe." She leaned forward, staring at him as though trying to mesmerise him. "Absolutely safe," she repeated.

"All these things sound so, otherwise no one would ever try them," said Kit. "I've read cases too. An accident happens, the person concerned doesn't want to explain, or fears that the explanation won't be acceptable. The body is disposed of, and then found. Then, even if it is an accident, it looks black and the person usually hangs. There's a dozen cases in a year."

"A dozen cases that are found out, for some reason. But what of the others? There are hundreds of people who disappear every year, everybody knows that. People with homes and families. And they're never found. Anyway, glory to goodness, Kit Shelfanger, you don't *want* to go through a murder trial and maybe hang, do you, just because I left a drawer open? And I won't. I'd sooner put myself in that duck pond of yours. I'm serious, I'm not just talking. I've got my mother to think of, and my sisters. I'd rather die than bring such disgrace on them." She had argued her case in a low earnest voice, perfectly, almost unnaturally controlled. Now for the first time a note of hysteria crept in. "If you won't do what I say, I'll drown myself." She rose from the bed as though to put the threat into immediate action.

"Sit down," said Kit. "I haven't yet said I wouldn't."

"Then you will."

"Let me think."

(Let me think about losing Heath End and all the things I have loved about it. The solitude; the pink of the apple blossom in the orchard; the first young leaves on the poplars; the warmth of the cow's flank against my head on a cold morning as the milk froths into the pail; cosy evenings by the fire with my pipe and a glass of beer. All simple things that must be abandoned because two people came uninvited into my house and twisted my good life out of shape. Let me think of the publicity, the questions, the searching eyes and the scandal-seeking tongues; the prison life with never a moment unobserved; the possibility of hanging. This is not a decision to be taken lightly. Don't hurry me, Rosetta. Let me think.)

He looked up at last.

"You must have nothing to do with it, Rosetta, understand that. Go downstairs now, make up a good fire and sit by it. I'm going to clear up here."

"And afterwards?"

"I shall do what you suggested. God send that we aren't making a terrible mistake."

Rosetta drew in a breath, so long and deep that it might have been the gasp of resurrection. She went out quietly.

"Welford two eight?"

"Yes."

"I'd like to speak to Mr. Tillingham."

"Tillingham here."

"Oh, good morning. This is Kit Shelfanger. I've got a message for you from my nephew, you know, Jamie Liddell. He's had to go to London suddenly on some bit of business; he didn't seem sure when or even whether he'd be back. I promised to let you know."

A little pause and then, "Mr. Shelfanger . . ."

"Yes."

"I think I should tell you something."

"Well?"

"I don't *want* him back, ever. I made a mistake about him; I knew it at the end of the first week. He isn't any good, if you'll pardon me saying so. And there were lots of things I didn't care for. I was going to tell him so on Saturday. Still, we'll skip that. If you're in touch with him you might let him know. And tell him I don't owe him anything, the boot's on the other leg if you get my meaning. He'll understand."

"Very well. I'll see to it."

"Thanks. Good-bye."

Rosetta had said, "We ought to let that Tillingham have some sort of tale. He might come nosing round; and we don't want anybody here while . . . do we? You run down to the nearest telephone directly after breakfast. I'll stay here in case anyone should come."

"You're not frightened?"

"I'm only frightened of one thing," said Rosetta.

She had undergone a startling transformation; from being timid and inefficient she had become bold and capable. No better partner in a nefarious business could have been found. And often during the next days Kit found a welcome relief from the monotonous, gloomy and macabre trend of his thoughts in wondering about her. She had seemed almost morbidly attached to Jamie, yet his sudden and shocking end had merely roused her instinct for self-defence; she had seemed simple almost to imbecility, ignorant, easily pleased and easily annoyed, commonplace. Now she was none of those things. She had attained, in that hour spent beside Jamie's corpse, an ascendancy over Kit's mind, and she held

it easily. He was unlearned and inexperienced enough to be startled at this manifestation of an ancient truth—that at heart the
female is a single-minded, practical, predatory creature, capable,
once her self-interest is threatened, of showing all the qualities
which a long and useful tradition of feminine behaviour enables
most women to keep concealed throughout their lives.

"Now about the place," said Rosetta. "Mind you, I'm sure
there'll never be any digging done. But we've got to act as if we
thought it might. We're lucky, most people only have a garden.
It ought to be well away from the house. Not the orchard or yard,
right away in the middle of a field. And very deep down. Is there
a field that couldn't possibly be overlooked?"

"Top Field joins the heath; you can see for miles each way and
I've never seen anybody there. The fence is wire, nobody could
hide."

"That's the place then. Bang in the middle. Is there anything a
farmer could dig in the middle of a field for, at this time of
year?"

"Draining, I suppose," said Kit after a moment's thought.

"You'd better have some drain-pipes about them. Just in case."

That last day of the old year brought a knife-edged wind and
squalls of cutting sleet. It was unlikely that anyone would choose
it as an occasion for a stroll on the heath, five miles from the road.
Below the level reached each year by the innocent ploughshare
the ground was hard in the Top Field, but Kit welcomed the
hard labour. It gave him some relief from his crowding thoughts.

At midday he found that he was hungry enough to eat the
piece of bread and cheese which Rosetta, despite his protests, had
insisted upon placing in his pocket. Neither of them had thought
about supper on the night before, and though Rosetta had made
an unusually early appearance and cooked breakfast for them
both, the meal had been a pretence. Kit had begun to think that
he would never feel hungry again. But now, emerging from the
hole that was already deep enough to take his height, he crouched
on the lee side of the pile of earth which he had thrown up and
ate his snack meal with appetite.

Some detached part of his mind was directing the digging with
intelligence and precision, while the remainder of his mental, and

all his physical, force was engaged in the mere physical process. He had made the original excavation twice as large as it needed to be, so that now, as he began upon the actual grave, he had no longer to throw the loose earth to the field's surface. It could be cast on to the other end of the original hole, which, as the business end deepened, became merely a shelf for the receipt of soil.

When the new hole was some two feet below the level of the old one his hard-driven spade met with more resistance than it had yet encountered, and as he pressed against the obstacle and the soil gave way, stirring to the overthrow, its surface was broken by chunks and fragments of something that was neither soil nor stone. Kit bent and sifted the spadeful with his hands. The alien substance looked like—it was brick, or rather tile, thin, pinkish grey in colour, brittle in texture. There were other fragments too, pale curved pieces that looked like broken pottery, and bits of stuff that seemed to Kit's incredulous eyes like oyster shells. Wonderingly Kit stared at them, allowing his mind to contemplate the possibility that here, six feet beneath the soil of his Top Field, was evidence of some long-ago human occupation.

He was no scholar, he had never had any formal training in the understanding of history; but he had read his paper and could remember two cases of local interest—the discovery of a Viking ship near Woodbridge, and the uncovering of a Roman villa on a farm at Stanton Chair. Half incredulous, half believing that some similar secret lay beneath his feet, he drove in his spade again, pried up and examined its load. There were the same fragments of tile, pottery and oyster shell.

The part of his mind which was avid for relief from the memory of last night and the plans and plots of today, seized upon the blessed opportunity which the find offered; and within the next half-hour (during which the spade brought to light two coins and some bones) Kit Shelfanger indulged in more imaginative exercise than he had known since the days when he dreamed, first of lonely islands and then of isolated farms. But soon the thoughts about men dead and gone this thousand years, about hands that had laid the tiles, made the pottery and split apart the oyster shells, gave way before a sternly practical consideration. Digging into the remains of a bygone civilisation was not as easy as dig-

ging even the undisturbed subsoil; his progress was being im-
peded. And presently he came to a full stop. There beneath his
feet and his spade was at last laid bare a stretch of tessellated
pavement made of small pieces of stone, or marble, closely set into
a cement-like substance. It was as firm and whole as if it had been
laid yesterday; and the spade's edge struck it with a futile, baffled
ring.

Almost idly Kit rubbed his foot over the slightly ribbed surface,
pushing away the soil and the fragments. Under the movement of
his heavy boot colour sprang to life, colour that had been buried
all these centuries—the red of flowerpots, the cool bluish green of
young wheat, the dark blue of the night sky, all inlaid upon a
background of greyish cream that once might have been white.
The cleared space (the grave for a man which had been dug upon
the grave of a civilisation) was too small to reveal the pattern,
but pattern there was, and there shot through the mind of the
simple man whose life had gone awry, a sharp regret that he had
made this discovery at a time when he had neither the leisure nor
the peace of mind to take pleasure in it. He would have liked to
have removed the obscuring soil, foot by foot, patiently, carefully,
so that he missed nothing however small, broke nothing however
frail; he would have liked to brood, blindly and ignorantly, in solitude upon the things he found. Twenty-four hours ago that
would all have been possible. But last night he had killed a man.
Because of that he had dug so deep into the smooth-faced ordinary field; because of that he must not now halt his spade to
trace a pattern in ochre and blue and green. He must regard the
floor of this forgotten house, not as a treasure, but as an obstacle.

Lifting his face to the sky he saw that the daylight, obscured all
day by the sleet clouds, was fading towards night. Never mind, he
had a lantern and at nine the moon would rise.

The sleet, changing now and then to a flurry of snowflakes, continued all through New Year's Day, and Kit, having finished the
inevitable jobs in the yard, kept to the house. The afternoon he
devoted to cooking. Both he and Rosetta were quiet and sub-
dued, kindly to one another, eagerly pursuing any small topic of
conversation that did arise but without much to say for long in-

tervals. They were a little like people convalescing from a wearing illness, glad to have emerged from the threat of pain but not quite ready yet to take up the business of ordinary living.

At three o'clock Rosetta made one of her countless pots of tea and she and Kit were sitting, one on either side the table with steaming cups between their propped elbows when she straightened herself and turned her head sharply. Simultaneously Guess barked.

"I thought so! A car," said Rosetta. Her face went chalky and in trying to set down her cup she spilled a quantity of tea. Kit rose and went to the window.

"Don't upset yourself," he said. "It's probably something quite ordinary."

She leaned beside him at the window. The car came into view, a long, low, cream-coloured thing splashed by the sandy mud of the heath road. Rosetta drew a gasp of relief.

"It's that girl. You know, the one in the white dress. I guess he had a date with her and she's come to ask. . . . I'll tell her something I bet she didn't come to hear. Come away from the window, Kit. Let her knock properly."

They heard the dull, soft thud of the car door, the light step on the cobbles and a diffident tap on the door. Rosetta braced herself, drawing her shoulders very straight and setting a look of cool, almost contemptuous calm upon her face. She strolled to the door and opened it.

Today Amanda wore a long coat of glossy brown fur and a little cap that matched it was tilted forward on her curls. The pretty outline of her features was a trifle blurred, like a smudged pastel drawing; she had danced until four that morning, drinking rather heavily to drown her disappointment and had lain awake the remainder of the night wondering about Jamie.

They faced one another; Rosetta assured to the point of truculence, Amanda miserably uncertain of herself and of her position. But she had been driven by the interest and concern that Jamie had awakened in her, and was upheld by the belief engendered by her upbringing, that anything she chose to do was right, simply because she chose it. So now, although the smile she gave Rosetta was slightly placating, her voice had the confident, superior ring that is the legacy of a good school.

"Good afternoon. Is Mr. Liddell here?"

"No," said Rosetta wooden-faced.

"Oh . . . Well, perhaps you could tell me where he is."

"So far as I know he's in London."

"In London!" Amanda's narrow black brows came together in a puzzled scowl. "But, you see I . . . he . . . I mean, did he go very suddenly?"

"Very suddenly," said Rosetta, with a grim relish which Kit found amazing.

"I *see*." Amanda's confidence was shaken, and perhaps for that reason she embarked, with hasty lack of caution, upon an explanation. "You see, he was going to join our party for the Farmers' Dance. Mother had taken the tickets and everything. Then he just didn't come. I rang the garage this morning but Mr. Tillingham wasn't there and the boy didn't seem to know anything. So . . . as I wanted to try the car by myself . . . I thought I'd run out this way and see if he was . . . ill . . . or anything." Her voice more and more uncertain under the cold stare that Rosetta aimed at her.

(Mentally Kit pleaded with Rosetta—go on, carry it off properly, say you're sorry but he went so suddenly there wasn't time for a message or anything. She's so young, hardly more than a child, let her down lightly. In the face of what's happened, knowing what you know, be merciful.)

Rosetta stood quite silent, obviously just waiting to shut the door.

"I suppose you couldn't tell me when he will be back?" tentative, faltering question. (Young ladies don't obviously chase men.)

"I think I should know if anyone did." It was like the sudden flash of a razor blade in a street brawl. "I'm Mrs. Liddell."

Something, training, or common pride, or feminine instinct rallied to Amanda's aid.

"Well, of course, then you would know, naturally. I'm so sorry I bothered you. Thank you so much. Good afternoon."

Her voice was bright and social again, she mustered a smile;

but she knew that nothing could wipe out the shame of having asked that question, of having explained the broken engagement, of having come here at all. That dreadful girl with her face of hatred and her strangled, affected voice . . . Mrs. Liddell! My God, thought Amanda, let Jamie Liddell show his face in Welford again, I'll see he doesn't get asked anywhere. I'll make Mummy take her custom away from Tillingham's. I wish I hadn't had this car. I wish I were dead. Three times she killed the engine in trying to let in the gear and she turned the car clumsily, imagining a gloating face at the window all the time. But before she reached the main road youth and a sanguine nature came to her aid. Let that little brat have her Jamie, she didn't have much else by the look of things. . . .

Rosetta shut the door smartly and returned to the fire.

"That's settled her," she said to Kit in her normal voice.

"I think you were a bit brutal with her," said Kit mildly. "She's young, and it wasn't a pleasant position for her. I don't think she meant any harm."

"Harm!" exclaimed Rosetta, reaching for the tea-pot. "And brutal! Why, I could kill her. It's all her fault. But for her it wouldn't have happened. We were quarrelling about her." She set down the pot, stared at the window for a moment with a hard bitter face, and then, lips trembling, eyes filling, dropped her head upon her arms and began to sob. Instantly Kit reviled himself. He had accused her of being brutal to a chit of a girl who had suffered a mild disappointment—what about the sufferings of poor little Rosetta herself? The old painful pity had him by the throat as he bent to comfort her.

On the following morning Kit, still penitent, said, "Would you like to come to Welford? I think it would do us both good to get away from the place for a bit."

Rosetta's volatile spirits responded to the suggestion with alacrity and she rushed off to the little room into which she had moved on the night of the tragedy, to change her dress and improve her make-up while Kit did a few chores about the house.

At the last minute Kit reached down an old tweed jacket from behind the door. "I'll drop this in at Thompson's," he said, "and get him to put leather on the cuffs and elbows. It'll lengthen its life by years."

They parted company on the Market Square. Rosetta had volunteered to perform some of the errands and they had arranged to meet at the Magpie for lunch.

Thompson himself, a grey, cadaverous man with a tape measure draped perpetually about his neck, came forward and accepted Kit's coat and order. He made a few remarks about the weather, which, he opined, was seasonable for the time of year, and then, after a moment's obvious hesitation, said:

"We were a trifle concerned about Mr. Liddell, Mr. Shelfanger. In fact my cutter was quite disappointed. He had put in a good deal of extra time in order to have the job ready on time."

(Was there always going to be this lurch of the heart at the sound of Jamie's name? Part of the punishment?)

"Let's see—what job exactly was it?"

"Mr. Liddell's tails for the Farmers' Dance, Mr. Shelfanger. One of the quickest, and if I may say so, one of the prettiest jobs we have ever executed. And then not called for. Grayson was almost in tears when we closed that evening without having seen Mr. Liddell."

"He was called away to London, very unexpectedly, the day before. I'm afraid he forgot everything. If you care to let me have them, in a box, I'll send them to him. I suppose I'd better settle for them as well."

"That's very good of you, Mr. Shelfanger. Shall I include the other items?"

"Oh, yes, everything." (What else could there be?) "You know what young men are about tailor's bills; especially in towns that they have left."

Mr. Thompson laughed in what he took to be an understanding manner, saw Kit to the door in a more respectful fashion than usual and retired to have the dress suit packed and Mr. Liddell's bill made out. Kit emerged into the cold air of the High Street wondering how many other reminders of Eva's son were still concealed, waiting to pounce out upon him when he least expected them. He was practically, rather than emotionally, concerned with the idea; it was his conscience, not his heart, that responded when Jamie's name was inadvertently mentioned. It even worried him a little to realise that it was the possibility of discovery rather than the memory of his action which had power to tauten his nerves. Was that because he was without morals; or because, for quite a long time, he had disliked Jamie; or because this was Nature's method for preserving sanity? And did all men who murdered, or killed another, feel this way? It was strange to walk into his usual shops and give his ordinary mundane orders and think, "Ah, what a lot has happened since I was here last," and yet to feel himself unchanged.

Neither cinema offered anything to his taste, so after lunch he let Rosetta choose and sat through a film which dealt, incoherently and inconsequently, with a gay modern couple who took great pains to qualify for and gain a divorce only to discover that they loved one another all the time. He was mildly bored, but not intolerant, he had seen several of the sort before, and Rosetta sat entranced for the whole of the performance and chattered about the beauty of the dresses, the cuteness of the coiffures and the magnificence of the settings, all the way home.

They stopped at the post box and Kit took out the solitary envelope that lay within. He held it to the car's headlamp and as he took his seat again, put the letter into Rosetta's lap.

"For you," he said.

As soon as he had the fire started and the lamp alight he took the lantern and went into the yard. When he returned with the milk he found Rosetta, still in her hat and coat, crouching on the fender. Her attitude was tense and her face a mere sketch of harassed lines. Try as he would, Kit could not hold back the impatient thought, "What now?" but he spoke kindly, "Something wrong, Rosetta?"

"Oh, awful. It's from Mother. She wants to know what I'm going to do."

"I reckon we should have thought about that too," said Kit. "I'll just put this in the dairy. Turn down the lamp, it's smoking."

He came back and seated himself in his chair. "Well?" he opened the discussion. Rosetta laid the letter on his knee.

He recognised the thin blue paper and the thickish ink from the letter that Rosetta had written to Jamie. But the writing—if indeed writing can show character—told a very different tale. Uneducated and unbeautiful it somehow managed to convey the impression that the writer was a personality and a force. The heavy down-strokes were harsh, intolerant, the black underlinings sweeping and violent. Nor did phraseology contradict calligraphy.

My DEAR ROSETTA,

Maisie gave me your Xmas present and message, for which thank you, but what I must know is when, if ever, you are getting back. Cannot clean and cook for all this lot and shop as well. I have seen nothing of Mrs. C. all over the holiday, drunk I suppose, so no help from that quarter. But there is a girl, just left school, willing to come in as daily, cheap. She could do vegetables for dinner while I shopped, that being the part left to you. But I must say yes or not to her this week. So you must let me know.

"Who God has joined" I wouldn't be the one to divide, but can't forget when you put me in a muddle before saying you was staying with J. in Rugby and then come home after a fortnight. You mustn't do that this time. I shan't want you if I get this girl. Best to have things straight. If you're staying I can send your things on, all the same you ought to look about carefully and see if he can support you and not give up a good home for a mare's nest. You know what he is, none better, and I rue the day he ever come here, but that's an old story as you know. So now make up your mind and let me know right away because girl won't wait being very scarce these days. A Happy New Year from your loving mother.

S. PHILLIPS.

"Well?" asked Rosetta in her turn, watching as he folded the letter and returned it to its envelope. "What am I going to do?"

"I don't know," said Kit cautiously. "It's for you to say, isn't it?"

"I don't know either. You see, if I go back it's going to be

dreadful. Everybody will ask about Jamie. You've no idea how curious people are if people don't live together and so on. And I
shan't ever have a letter or anything. It'll look so bad. And I guess
Mother'd rather have that little skivvy. And there's Maisie and
Freda with their husbands home at night, they can't help showing how they're sorry for me, sort of sorry and gloating if you
know what I mean. I used to bear it and tell myself one day
Jamie'd do something big, and come back properly and then I'd
show them all. But now I know that won't ever happen. I'll just
go on and on, getting older and uglier. A widow that no one
knows about. Oh God, I wish I'd never come here. I thought it'd
make everything all right and instead it ruined everything."

Unhappily Kit watched her and when he said heavily, "I don't
know what to advise," he stated the literal truth. Since the night
of Jamie's death he had tried not to think about his own feelings
towards Rosetta because there was something fundamentally
repulsive in cherishing a desire for the wife of a man whom you
have killed. Conscience and shock combined had dulled the edge
of his yearning, but he knew that the dulling was only a tempo-
rary affair. He knew that on the afternoon when he stooped to
comfort her after Amanda Winchely's visit. He had put a fatherly
arm about her shoulders then, but his physical response to the
touch of her body had shattered him. If she had made move or
sign of recognition, if she had even looked at him he knew that
he would have been lost. Luckily she had sobbed on and presently
he had been able to withdraw his arm and move away under pretence of seeing to the oven. But the danger had only been
evaded.

So now, faced with the question of what Rosetta should do, he
faced something that concerned him far more nearly than Rosetta herself could possibly know. He longed to say, Stay here, I'll
take such care of you everything that I have shall be yours, I'll
work for you, serve you, give you a life's devotion. But the words,
like so many others, could not be said. It wasn't a fair offer. It
sounded high-falutin', but actually it was merely an invitation to
a young woman to put herself in a dubious position, to cut herself
off from her kindred and to remain as the source of a temptation
which could not be forever resisted. On the other hand——

He began cautiously, feeling his way.

"Is there anything you would like to do, Rosetta? Anything you'd like to take up?"

"There's nothing much I *can* do, only bits of housework and that I hate and aren't very good at."

(Jamie had said, "She's good in bed." Was that her destined sphere? And what became of girls like that, especially girls so oddly placed as Rosetta? Memories of girls in ports all over the world waiting for sailors going on shoreleave tormented Kit's brain.)

"You're young enough to train for anything else you choose. I do realise, Rosetta, that the . . . the accident was my fault, and that I brought you to this unhappy pass. So you could let me look after you while you trained without feeling any obligation."

"What could I train for?" she asked apathetically.

Kit hesitated and then said triumphantly, "Why, typewriting, like the girl at the pictures this afternoon."

"Right enough on the pictures. In real life it isn't so easy. Typists, good ones too, are ten a penny anyway. And you have to be good at figures. I'm rotten." She studied her nails for a moment, then added, "There's absolutely only one thing I've ever wanted to do or be."

"And that is?"

"A film star," said Rosetta with a pretty expression of offering a confidence.

"Well, that is out of the question I'm afraid."

"You don't think I'm pretty enough?"

It had come as a surprise to him to learn in these recent days that one can feel a wild impatience with the object of one's adoration. He felt it now.

"I thought we were discussing possibilities," he said in a voice that was harsher than he realised. Rosetta flung him a startled glance and said, with a hasty, pitiable assumption of dignity, "I guess I'd better go home."

"Even so, don't forget that I'm responsible for you. As you can see for yourself I'm not well-off in any sense of the word, but I've lived very cheaply and I've saved money lately. I could easily let you have two pounds a week. . . ."

It was the highest sum that his rapid mental arithmetic embold-ened him to offer, and Rosetta never knew the depths of the generosity behind the humble words. To divorce two pounds in cash each week from a farm of that size would mean scheming at least and very possibly real self-denial.

At the mention of the sum there went through Rosetta's mind, with the swiftness of a dream just before waking and with a dream's deliciousness, the vision of herself returning to her mother's house the indisputable mistress of two pounds a week. Instead of doing menial jobs for her keep she would pay in money and enjoy privileges. And she could have her hair done, and go to the cinema, and go to the Kopper Kettle for coffee every morning. Why, Bert only gave Maisie two pounds a week and she had to keep the house going and feed him as well. It would be wealth to a girl alone; and best of all she could pretend that Jamie sent it. It would look like some visible proof of Jamie's success and care for her.

She looked at Kit with glowing eyes. In a voice that was moved by genuine and powerful feeling she said, "Oh, you're so good. I couldn't take it, really," and yet, to show that she had already ac-cepted the offer she dashed across the kitchen, flung her arms round his neck and pressed her lips to his cheek.

And then suddenly it was as though two substances, harmless apart, violently explosive in contact, had been flung together. Kit, with his arms clasped round her so that the softness of her bosom pressed warmly against his ribs, with her mouth helpless and up-turned under his, could neither see nor hear. Thought itself was suspended. As for Rosetta she was caught and swept away by a flood-tide of physical passion such as she had never known. All her trivial and secondhand emotions, all the disturbance which Jamie, himself too easily satiated, had roused in her, all the repression of the strict upbringing, everything that she had ever been or known, melted and merged together into a force in whose grip she was helpless.

Neither spoke. They stood there in the centre of the kitchen, pressing closer and yet closer, as though some unseen, irresistible power outside themselves were closing in, determined to weld them together. Presently under its compulsion they moved towards the stairs.

After two days Rosetta steadied herself sufficiently to write to her mother.

DEAR MOTHER,

I have thought ever so carefully over your letter and I think it would be best for you to close with that girl and for me to stay here. This mightn't be everybody's pick—quite five miles off the main road and then ten into the town which is a one-eyed place, but it suits me and I like it. There's a car, so it isn't so bad.

As soon as the weather gets a bit better I'll run up for the day and see you all. I'd be glad if you'd send my things. The old brown suit and the putty jumper and the red dress with the braid Maisie can have for doing housework in, or you can give them to the girl, also the shoes with the buckles. Don't pay on the parcel, I'll pay this end.

I'll enclose the last instalment on my fur coat. Maisie would take it round to Madame Yvonne's one day when she looks in if you haven't time. Actually you were quite right, it was a bad buy, and if this weather goes on I shall try to get a long one. There are some decent shops in Welford despite its size because all the farmers' wives have a lot of money about here, sugar beet and things.

Well, old dear, take care of yourself and don't work too hard. Give my love to Maisie and Freda and the boys when you see them and tell them I'll see them soon. I'll write when I have any news. . . .

Rosetta halted her pen and read through her missive before bringing it to a close. A smile of intense, cat-like satisfaction broke over her face as she read; it was, she thought, a very clever letter. It told no lies; it did not mention Jamie; but it implied many things. The car was mentioned, so was the possibility of a new fur coat. The lighthearted disposal of part of her wardrobe spoke of newly found wealth; the enclosure of Madame Yvonne's final instalment (which had worried her considerably) proved

that she was not short of ready cash. The mention of Heath
End's remoteness would deter any impulse of "popping down"
that curiosity might inspire in Maisie. The whole thing was
damned crafty. She congratulated herself again as she set down
the platitudes that rounded it to a finish.

Self-congratulation was, indeed, Rosetta's main feeling in these
days. Never since the forgotten days of her infancy had she been
so cherished, so surrounded by care. For with that first sweet
night of surrender Kit had become entirely enslaved. He could no
longer see a fault in her. That her mind was shallow made her the
more endearing; that she was mercenary gave him the more op-
portunities of pleasing her with gifts; that she was bone idle enabled him to take more frequent pleasure in waiting on her. For
the first time in his life he was experiencing a close human relationship and he revelled in it. His former misogyny merely gave
zest in his infatuation, just as sinfulness precedes wholehearted
conversation. He was no longer sufficiently aware of himself to
call himself an old fool. He hardly had a thought apart from
Rosetta all through the day.

Inevitably Rosetta took advantage of the situation. As proof
after proof of her power was laid before her dazzled eyes she became intoxicated by her success, which, like Kit's enchantment,
was all the sweeter for what had gone before it. The long years of
poverty, of makeshift, of pretence; the disappointment over
Jamie; the shame of his treatment of her; the constant humilia-
tion and uncertainty that she had suffered—all these were, if not
forgotten, thrust away to make a background against which her
present good fortune shone the brighter.

At first she accepted it as good fortune, was grateful to Kit for
his presents, ecstatically enjoyed the treats which he with ignorance and difficulty planned for her; but his very lavishness in
those earliest, infatuated days gave Rosetta a false idea of his
monetary status and like all people who have handled only trivial
sums of ready money she was over-ready to assume that the possession of a bank balance and a cheque-book necessarily implied
solid wealth.

The more substantial coat was indeed Kit's own suggestion,
and Rosetta's tacit assumption that it should be a fur one was

difficult to gainsay. Dragged along unwillingly to help her to choose it at Welford's most important shop, he found it impossible, both from emotional and expedient standpoints, to suggest that fifty guineas was too much to pay. Emotionally impossible, because Rosetta with the soft grey fur turned up about her face, her colour heightened and her eyes bright with excitement and pleading, looked very sweet and adorable; expediently impossible because, as she herself had pointed out before entering the shop, it mustn't look as though he were paying for it.

"You see," she said, giving his arm swift pressure and then releasing it as they stood before the shop, "I'm still Mrs. Liddell and you're just my uncle by marriage. It wouldn't do for them to know that you were buying it, would it?"

"Maybe I'd better not come in at all in that case," said Kit, making a last bid for escape.

"Oh, but I want you to. And that doesn't matter a bit. You just nod at the one you think I should have. I want to feel that you chose it for me!"

After that could anything but churlishness incarnate have nodded at less than the best the shop offered? And Kit was a man in love. What, he asked himself, as Rosetta, wearing the coat, tripped beside him from the shop, could fifty guineas do for a man? Could it smile, cajole, tease and surrender? Could it make waking a joy and each day a holiday? Could it, by a flutter of eyelashes, a touch of fingertips set every pulse pounding? No. So there was only one use for money, spend it on the one who could do all these things.

Most of Rosetta's purchases betrayed a pitiable incongruity. A big radio-gramophone in a glistening walnut case went into a corner of the kitchen, sharing the whitewashed wall with the old battered oaken dresser. Aslant across the hearthrug before the black-polished cooking range stood a plumply upholstered chesterfield covered in green velvet and bearing two cyclamen-coloured cushions. Rosetta could pose very gracefully and seductively upon it. She would, naturally, have preferred to open and furnish the parlour; but to do so meant a good deal of trouble and might have involved Kit in more housework than he was willing to do alone.

A similar anomaly was to be seen above-stairs. The pink eiderdown and Kit's own chest of drawers had been brought away from the room in which Jamie had died. On Rosetta's side of the ugly brass bedstead in Kit's room there lay a sheepskin rug, very white and soft and ill-at-ease upon the worn, faded drugget. Between the windows stood Rosetta's dressing-table, the one thing of genuine beauty and value in the house. It was a Queen Anne table with a standing mirror and to Rosetta's eyes had not looked like a dressing-table at all; but it had been offered as such at the shop where she was searching and casual inquiry had revealed that it was far more expensive than any of the modern combinations of pale wood, sharp angles and mirror glass; and so, being in a perverse and difficult mood that day, she had insisted upon acquiring the treasure. The shopkeeper, who had bought both mirror and table as a speculation and since despaired of selling them again, was fervent in his congratulations of madam's taste; and before the deal was ten minutes old, Kit in his simplicity and Rosetta in her ignorance were both assured that they were connoisseurs. Already the shining surface of the table, result of two centuries of care, was dull and ringed by the marks of Rosetta's toilet bottles, now lavishly displayed.

Rosetta's day was an example of the masterly inactivity so much praised by statesmen. She slept on in the morning while Kit rose and got the fire going. She roused herself to receive a cup of tea and snuggled down again when he went out to his before breakfast tasks. Kit, without any sense of martyrdom, cooked the breakfast. He had done so for himself, and later for Jamie; how much more willingly should he do it for the warm drowsy creature who, at his call, came downstairs, her pale hair afloat, her face, unpainted, pale and childlike, her slim figure wrapped in a long house-coat of coral velveteen. Languorous memories of the night clung about her.

After breakfast Rosetta turned on the radio and fetched from her bedroom some clothes and toilet necessities. In the glow of the fire she made a leisurely and complicated business of dressing and beautifying herself, breaking off every now and then to smoke a cigarette or turn the knob of the radio in search of more stimulating music. By one o'clock she had managed to clear away the breakfast things and set a cold snack on the table. When Kit had gone out again she curled up on the green chesterfield, smoked a cigarette, ate a chocolate or two and drifted into peaceful sleep. At dusk Kit came in again and then she roused herself into some pretense of helping him prepare supper. When the meal was eaten, Rosetta, full of stored energy and bored by the kitchen which had held her all day, would begin to wheedle to be taken out, and since too frequent appearances in Welford were deemed unwise, often enough Kit would bully the old car farther afield, driving as far as Norwich or Ispwich in an evening after a heavy day's work. In those towns the more urban atmosphere, the crowds of unknown and unknowing people, the brighter lights, the bigger cinemas and pubs, worked on Rosetta like a charm. She flashed, she sparkled. Her attractiveness had markedly increased with the loss of her frightened, anxious air and with the acquisition of better clothes and cosmetics. Kit knew that men looked at her with interest, women with envy. Often he wondered at his own luck. And sometimes he thought of Jamie, rotting away far below the green surface of the earth. He had killed Jamie, and Jamie had bequeathed him this. It was a queer world.

It was too good to last, of course. Early in March Rosetta complained of feeling ill and refused to come down to breakfast. No, she didn't want anything to eat; the smell of coffee would make her sick; even tea sounded repulsive. Much concerned, Kit suggested going into Pickthall for the doctor.

"Oh no!" said Rosetta pettishly. "But if you're going anywhere you might get a bottle of gin and some quinine."

For weeks, ever since Rosetta's complaint that she did not like beer, there had been gin and vermouth in the house and now Kit said, "There's the best part of a bottle of gin in the cupboard. But you don't want that *now*, do you?"

"There isn't a drop left," Rosetta said impatiently. "I drank it yesterday if you must know."

"I'm sorry. I didn't know. But—all that gin in a day, mightn't that be why you feel wrong this morning?"

For answer she tossed over in the bed, drew the pink eiderdown about her ears and ignored him. Kit hovered, helplessly.

"Of course I'll get you what you want, honey. I'm sorry. I don't understand these things. Will after dinner do?"

"Uh huh."

He tiptoed away to his cooling breakfast.

Like the abrupt bursting of a rainbow-coloured bubble the brief happiness that they had known disintegrated and shredded away. Despite the nostrums, simple and homely, professional and expensive, which Rosetta swallowed in the next few weeks, the fact remained that she was pregnant and no disease, however malignant, could have brought in its earliest stages such a complete destruction of happiness. She wept until her whole face was swollen and oddly transparent-looking; she was sick and would accept neither sympathy nor suggestions for alleviation; she was hysterical, and then said terrible things which afterwards Kit tried loyally to forget, but which remained, festering, all the same.

His involuntary question, the inevitable question of any man in his position, "Is it mine or Jamie's?" resulted in a passion of vituperation.

"I don't know. How should I? I never was that regular. I'm not a cow." Then that pause for reflection with which he had become familiar and which meant that what served Rosetta for a brain was busy working in her self-interest. "It's yours, of course. Fancy asking. Jamie was December; this is March. It wouldn't have happened with *him*. We'd been married two years. Two years without a scare; two months and then this. I won't go through with it. I can't. It isn't fair. Wallowing about like a great sow; and being sick and then *that* at the end. I can't face it. I'm highly strung. I shall go mad." Another pause. Then, "And I've thought of another thing. It'll be a bastard. That's a pretty thought, isn't it? A bastard. It's a judgment on us, that's what it is, only it's all on me. Oh, it's so unfair. *You* did it. You knocked Jamie down and you brought this on me and there you sit, getting off scot-free. You aren't going to get shapeless and hideous and sick and then be tortured. Oh . . ."

"But I'm with you, Rosetta. I'm as much concerned with it as a man *can* be. I'd get you out of it if I could. And I'd marry you, but you know that's impossible. We can't even pretend to be married here, you've called yourself Mrs. Liddell and you told that girl that Jamie was your husband. But you know I'll stand by you just the same as if . . ."

"Stand by, say you're sorry, and look at me like an old sheep. What use is that? God! how I wish I'd never set eyes on this place, or on you. You've brought me ill-luck all along."

"I loved you," said Kit gravely, using the past tense without realising it. Rosetta too missed the implication.

"Love," she said scornfully. "I've done with that mush. This is what love brings you to!"

Kit shifted his ground and asked diffidently, "Would it be any good your going to London and seeing your sister? Or mother? Might they be of help?"

Rosetta brightened slightly. "Not mother! But Maisie might. Yes, I'll do that. I'll go tomorrow. You'll take me to the station and give me some money, won't you? I might want rather a lot."

(This is what love brings you to.)

Once more he was alone in the sanctuary that he had desired and chosen; but this time loneliness brought no relief and the lost peace did not return. Rosetta had taken practically all her belongings and fifty pounds in notes, and there had been in her leave-taking the faint suggestion that if all went well she might not come back. Jamie had gone for ever. But even in this solitude Heath End was not, could never be, the same. And dimly Kit realised with a kind of mystic insight that his desire for solitude had been, in reality, a natural and necessary hankering for the only element in which he could live. For some reason any contact with his fellows was fatal to him—and to them. Within five months, without any intention to harm, he had killed a man and ruined a woman. That was more damage than many men wrought in a lifetime spent in crowded places of competitive living. For the first time he gave himself to remorseful thoughts about Jamie. Immediately after the catastrophe he had been stunned and too busy concealing his guilt to assess it rightly; and then there had been the mad, halcyon days of his love for Jamie's wife. Now, in the solitary evenings of Rosetta's absence he repeatedly asked himself:

"Why did I have to hit him? It would have served if I had

spoken. He laughed at me, but he always minded." And some-how, by the very subtlest degrees, there arose in Kit's mind the idea that perhaps even Jamie's manhandling of Rosetta was not so very blameworthy after all. Whether it was the inevitable human tendency not to think ill of the dead, or whether the thought had another, rather darker significance, he did not ask himself. But he began to think morbidly of Jamie, to remember his youth, and the times when he was in good spirits and told amusing stories about the day's encounters. He was male, and he was of his own blood. Ought they to have combined against Rosetta . . . ?

Ah, and that brought him back to Rosetta, and he stirred in his chair so that Guess looked at him uneasily, sensing his lack of repose. He traced his reactions to her. First interested in-difference; that is, interest of the eye and mind, indifference of feeling; then pity and that queer association of her with Eva, so that in saving her from Jamie he had really been saving Eva from Ed Liddell. Then the period of obedience, when in all things but one they had been partners in a conspiracy, with Rosetta's mind in the ascendant; and after that the brief impatient spell when her mopy indecision had irked him. And then the mighty on-slaught of passion and tenderness and carefulness, of doting and yearning and desire that could surely only be called love. And now? Could love indeed have been so easily destroyed, even by the loved one? That hard, irreconcilable, accusatory face that she turned towards him, the rejection of his sympathy, her lack of in-terest in anything save his money, would these have mattered if he had loved her? Truly loved? Well, he was an inexperienced, ig-norant man; he lacked the power of comparison. He only knew that if Rosetta had stayed sweet and kind to him, as in those early days, he would have gone through torture for her; but now enchantment had departed; she had herself destroyed it. He might remind himself that she was suffering both in mind and body, that she was not herself, but it did no good. The feeling he had had was gone, and neither self-reproach nor deliberate invoca-tion could recall it.

And so, for the third time in his life, he fingered the notion of escaping. The sea had failed, the farm had failed, but the human frame was chained neither to water nor to soil. It could depart, carrying its curse with it. He would transfer his bank balance to Rosetta's name and arrange for the sale of Heath End, the proceeds of which could be added. It would be enough to see Rosetta through this business and give her a start in anything she might fancy, though it would not make her a film star. And he would go back to Cumberland, probably under another name, and take a job as shepherd. Resurgent the vision rose, loneliness, no company save the sheep, a little hut tucked away in the fells, a fire to himself, escape. Escape now, not only from people but from the land where he had buried Jamie, from the house where Rosetta had abandoned herself to his embraces.

After toying with the idea for several days he spent an evening with pen and paper, outlining his plan to Rosetta. He took pains to emphasise that it would be to her financial advantage, and at the same time to avoid any hint of benevolence. So it was not an easy letter to write and he had to make more than one attempt at it.

She replied by return of post: "So that's your idea of standing by, is it? I am coming *home* tomorrow (Friday). Please meet the four fifteen train."

Escape, he realised as he read the brief message, was for boy alone, man alone as he had been on previous occasions. Man encumbered by past ill-doing and future responsibility might dream of escape, but could never achieve it. And Rosetta, on that first evening after her return, emphasised the lesson.

Maisie had proved knowledgeable and helpful. She had been impressed to find that Rosetta had fifty pounds in hand and undertook to make all arrangements for her. But at the last moment an incautious word of sympathy had betrayed to Rosetta the meaning of what she was about to face and she had retreated, hysterical, reproachful and horrified.

And by that time her brief stay in her mother's house and in Maisie's little villa had brought home to her a sharp sense of the advantages that she had enjoyed under Kit's roof. Provided she could pay (and Kit would see to that) she was very welcome to stay with either her mother or Maisie, but there would be no waiting upon, and precious little pampering in either establishment. Nor, in either house, was there a room so uniformly warm and comfortable as the shabby kitchen at Heath End. And the food, tempered in her mother's house to the necessity of making a profit from the boarders, and in Maisie's to the prior needs of smart clothing and frequent amusements, was sorely inferior to the sound country fare which Kit spread lavishly and thoughtlessly upon his table.

Kit's letter, coming hard on the heels of these realisations, threw Rosetta into a panic. She could see herself, with a little money it was true, but homeless, alternating between her mother's house and Maisie's, neither guest nor boarder, growing each day less able to share in the urban pleasures that were the only consolation which that form of life offered, and equally severed from the lazy, warm comfort that she had known in Kit's house. Her decision to return was instant, cat-like, the automatic reaction of her strong sense of self-preservation.

She was so much at the mercy of her latest emotion, so unable to take either a retrospective or far-seeing view, that the notion of returning to Heath End upon yet another footing caused her no perturbation at all. For Kit himself she had no feeling left. Her recoil from him was as instinctive and complete as her response had been. Without consciously summing up the position in words or thoughts she felt that she had been trapped by her body, and since Kit had helped with the trapping he must stand by and help her through the resultant imprisonment. And this, to her relief, she found that Kit, prey to remorse and pity, was quite prepared to do.

The cold spring dragged on into May of that year and then gave way with dramatic suddenness to summer. The cold-loving petals of the winter blackthorn had hardly faded from the orchard hedge before the apple trees broke in a smother of pink blossoms. The short-stemmed sturdy daffodils ran like flame through the rough grass and beneath the kitchen window the dark velvet clusters of the wallflowers yielded their scent to the sun. All day the air was loud with cuckoo cries.

The swiftly-changing procession of the seasons made little difference to Rosetta. She still spent hours listening to the radio, playing her favourite records, brooding over the love stories in the magazines with which Kit kept her supplied, or toying, in her more serious moments, with some ineffectual attempts at knitting or sewing.

She grew more peevish as her discomfort increased and had wild fits of crying, sometimes declaring that she still would not go through with it, that she would swallow a hundred aspirin, or put herself into the pond beside the house. But Kit, with daily evidence of her care for her physical well-being before his eyes, was less worried by such threats than he might otherwise have been. He bore with her patiently and constantly exercised his mind to find ways of amusing or relieving her, but he did it all with the deadly knowledge that his heart was not in the task. This was not the Rosetta who had known his brief, belated love. This was the woman with whom he shared two heavy burdens, the secret of a crime and the responsibility of a new life.

The year passed quickly; each day, in its monotonous leisurely progress, might seem long enough, but the sum of them mounted rapidly. Great white ox-eye daisies tossed beside the rusty-red sorrel in the hay that filled the meadows; soon the scented stacks of it awaited the thatcher in the rickyards. In the Top Field the barley ripened, and there came the burning blue August day when Kit fetched in from Pickthall the two gnarled, surly, arbitrary old men who each year helped him with the gathering of the corn. Their regular working days were done and they both drew pensions, but at harvest and sugar-beet time they were still capable of performing a full day's work, and they liked working for Kit because he fed them well and didn't talk to them much, and never suggested that they should stay at the farm overnight. Without question he fetched them each morning and returned them each night, an action which subtly flattered the old fellows' vanity.

As soon as harvest was done Rosetta began to show signs of anxiety. "These things have to be fixed up well ahead," she told Kit.

"All right. You tell me what to do and I'll fix it."

"But I don't know exactly what to do. I don't know whether it

would be better to go away into a Nursing Home or to have it
here."

"That would mean a nurse in the place, wouldn't it; and
they're terribly fussy and want a lot of waiting on."

(Odd to reflect later that the words which cast so stern a die
should sound so very unmomentous!)

"Yes, I suppose a Nursing Home would be best. Not that I
care where I go. I shall probably die anyway. I do think that
when you have such a dread of a thing it means it'll get you in
the end. I know a woman who won't have gas laid on in her
house; she's scared of it. One day I bet she'll go and stay somewhere where there is gas and it'll do her in. I always did mean not
to have a baby. But there you are."

She stared at the newly lighted fire with the dull resignation
which lately had alternated with her rebellious fits.

"I'll see about it when I go into Welford next. It's December,
isn't it?"

Rosetta cast him that odd, assessing look and evading the question said, "I'd better see a doctor, I should think. You can't really
tell with these things yourself."

Her report from the doctor was both sullen and succinct.

"He says it'll be early. October."

And now it was September again; and the green of the poplar
leaves was mellowing into gold. On an evening which had in it a
premonitory sense of autumn's chillness Kit sat in his kitchen,
once again alone. He wore his dark market suit, for he had returned from a visit to the Nursing Home and had not troubled to
change. A fire was roaring in the big belly of the stove and a kettle steamed on the top; but Kit's supper was already on the table,
a pallid, unappetising-looking pie from the cooked-meat shop. In
these last days he had troubled to cook hardly at all, his appetite
had gone; the stiff dark suit hung loosely about his leaner frame.
He had aged more than a year in the twelve months that had
flown so fast; there was more grey in his hair, new and harsher
lines in his weatherbeaten face.

He noticed the steam belching from the kettle and rising heavily poured the water into the teapot. He looked at the pie and

then at the collie dog. "Here you are, Guess," he said, and the
dog, with eagerness tinged with suspicion at the unusual nature of
the offering, bore it away to the doormat. Kit poured out a cup of
tea, settled back in his chair and lighted his pipe. Rosetta's green-
covered chesterfield was pushed away by the farther wall. The ra-
diogram had been silent for ten days.

Ten days before—and Kit could still quiver at the memory—he
had driven a gibbering half-crazy Rosetta into Welford and delivered her at the Home. She had certainly not exaggerated the extent of her terror. Never in all his life had Kit witnessed such
naked, mind-shattering fear. The Matron of the Home had taken
charge with her customary quiet efficiency and had at last got
Rosetta away to some upper region of the house. But returning
she had said, "Really, Mr. Shelfanger, I've had dozens of first babies and dozens of frightened young girls, but such complete collapse I never did see. I don't think such a neurotic young person
ought to have a baby at all."

Kit, perhaps wrongly, sensed a certain reproach in the statement and said hastily, "Well, these things happen, don't they.
And Rosetta is unfortunate in that her husband hasn't been able
to be with her for a long time. I've done my best, but it isn't the
same, you know."

(Ah, what did those words, with their diffident, avuncular
flavour, deny? Could this calm-eyed, capped woman see beyond
them, to the unlawful joys of early winter days, how then would
she look, speak, act?)

"Of course," she said soothingly, "It does make a difference.
But she'll be all right. Don't you worry."

He had called next day, rather ostentatiously laden with flowers
and fruit; but he had chosen his moment badly and there was no
news.

"You're not on the telephone, are you?"

"No. How soon will it be over?"

"Almost any time now."

"Then I'll wait at the Magpie till closing time. Would you telephone there?"

"Certainly."

Late in the afternoon the impersonal message, "Mrs. Liddell has a son."

On his next visit to the place he was aware of something queer in the atmosphere. The Matron herself received him and there were signs of curiosity, doubt and a kind of unwilling sympathy in her clear eyes.

"Oh dear, Dr. Baxter has just left, and he would have liked to see you, I know, Mr. Shelfanger. What a pity!" She hesitated and then decided to speak. "To tell you the truth we are just a mite concerned about your niece. Physically everything seems as it should be . . . of course she had rather a rough time . . . but that's over now. But she seems a trifle, shall we say, deranged?"

"She was never a very stable person," said Kit cautiously.

"No? Well, that may account for it. But Doctor and I did wonder whether she had had news of her husband which she had—not—shared—with—you—" She drew out the last words and then ended the sentence in the air.

"Such as?"

"Oh, nothing definite, you know, but just ill news. She seems to be very much concerned about him in a curious kind of way. She seems positive that he has had, or is about to have, a serious accident. Of course it is all delusion, but Doctor and I wondered whether you could throw any light on the matter, because, you see, the more we know the more easily we can deal with that kind of thing."

He was aware of a difficulty in breathing, as though his chest wall were of iron and would not expand to accommodate the labouring lungs. And those clear eyes, trained to observe, were watching him closely.

"I haven't heard anything," he managed to say in a surprisingly normal voice. "Of course, between ourselves, he is most intensely unsatisfactory as a husband. That may have preyed on her mind . . . and have taken this form at a critical time . . ." That sentence, too, was left in the air.

"Very possibly," her voice was brisk again, but doubt still clouded the depths of her eyes. "Well, I hope to have better news for you next time, Mr. Shelfanger." She moved towards the door. Kit said suddenly, awkwardly, "I'd like to see the baby."

"Oh, but certainly. He's a grand little chap. I'll have him brought down."

A young nurse with an air of grave responsibility entered the room after a few moments, bearing a bundle in a shawl. She pushed the wrap aside so that Kit could see the child's face.

Afterwards she reported that the man looked as if the baby had been a ghost. Nor indeed would Kit have denied it; for lying there against the background of the white shawl was no pudgy anonymous baby face but a tiny smoothed and softened replica of Jamie. Even the smear of down upon the little pink skull was unmistakably chestnut in colour.

This face, thought Kit wildly, worn and scored by a quarter century of living, lay just as still and peaceful against the white of the sheet as I wrapped it. . . .

His breathing was harsher now and his voice unsteady as he said, "Thank you," to the young nurse and then made blindly for the door.

It was two days before he felt he could face the place again; and it was from that last visit that he had just returned. He recalled each moment of it as he sipped his hot tea, trying to make the memory of it seem real, less like something from a crazy dream. He had been obliged to wait for some time in the bright flower-filled sitting-room, and although he thought the house more silent than usual it was a muffled silence, as though people were moving about secretly, whispering, listening at doors, making signs to one another. At last the door had opened with a startling suddenness and the Matron had entered hurriedly, as if she had stood outside the door bracing herself to enter and then decided to do it and get it over. Her fresh-coloured face was paler than usual and her expression was anxious. At first Kit thought that she had bad news of Rosetta.

"Is she worse?"

"Not in health. Do sit down, Mr. Shelfanger." Kit obeyed what was indubitably an order, but the Matron walked to the window, looked out, fiddled with the head of a heavy whitish-green chrysanthemum and then wheeled round to face him accusingly.

"This is a very peculiar case; and I'm afraid I must say that you were not frank with me when you came to make arrangements. . . ."

"In what way, not frank?" asked Kit, finding words with difficulty.

"Many ways. I take on what seems—apart from an undue but comprehensible nervousness a perfectly straightforward case. The husband certainly is out of the picture but there is a respectable, responsible relative apparently in charge—you. Then suddenly the patient, in the midst of what appears to be a prolonged delusion, demands her mother who turns up in person—no delusion there —swearing that not only did she not know that her daughter was about to have a baby, but that she had heard nothing of the husband's disappearance. Moreover, the mere sight of the baby throws the patient into the strangest state, so much so that it has to be kept away from her and artificially fed. It may sound a small thing but it is disorganising the whole place and the whole staff. I tell you frankly that I should not have taken the case had I known that there was this mystery." She paused again, eyeing him thoughtfully. Then, in a significant voice she added, "At first, of course, we attributed everything to Mrs. Liddell's state of mind, hysteria and delusion are not unusual. We even hesitated to send to the address she gave as her mother's, thinking that too might be delusory. But the mother's arrival has put a different complexion on the matter. It makes other things seem . . . possible."

("What things? What are you trying to tell me? What has the girl been saying?")

"I suppose Rosetta wouldn't see me?"

"I'll ask again. I have before. In any case I doubt the wisdom."

"Leave it then."

"I think that would be best. To tell you the truth she seems to have taken against you very strongly." She looked at Kit again, meditatively this time, noting the worn planes of his face, the air of rather wistful attention that his deafness had given, the kindly curves of his mouth, the serious grey eyes with the network of pale wrinkles scored in the harvest-tan of his skin. She contrasted what she saw, and what her lifelong experience seemed to read into his appearance, with the wild stories that she had heard herself from Rosetta's babbling writhing lips and what she had heard reported from others. She gave a sharp sigh, a blend of bewilderment and exasperation. One couldn't assess a man from his looks and it was dangerous to try; and it was even more dangerous to interfere. And yet at that moment something human and feminine and kindly in the woman gave rise to the impulse to tell him everything, to issue an urgent warning. But she beat it back. It was not her business; indeed her part was to resent the fact that he had brought their troublesome business within her respectable doors. With a resumption of her bright, impersonal professional manner she said, "Ah well, I suppose it will all right itself. And the mother's arrival relieves us of a good deal of responsibility, doesn't it? Good day, Mr. Shelfanger."

He had left the Nursing Home in a stunned and puzzled frame of mind, had remained puzzled during the rest of his time in Welford and during the drive home; but now, sitting alone by his fire while the wind rose steadily outside and sudden gusts drew the flames roaring into the chimney and then released them again with a puff of smoke, he knew in his inmost mind that he had only been puzzled because he had refused to believe the implications of the Matron's words and manner. Once he accepted the possibility of complete perfidy, either voluntary or involuntary upon the part of Rosetta, everything became perfectly clear. And with perfect clarity he could trace, mood by mood, action by action, the whole of Rosetta's outward and inward life since her arrival at Heath End.

First, she had adored Jamie with an adoration composed of physical attraction, snobbery, jealousy, uncertainty and that queer masochism which had its place in so many women's natures. His violent death had shocked her so profoundly that it had anaesthetised all that part of her nature, leaving the practical self-preservative instincts in charge. Under their direction she had sought to avoid scandal, had plotted with Kit, had carried on an appearance of normal living.

Of the second stage, that brief interlude of stolen bliss, it was more difficult to think calmly. Proximity had doubtless had a large share in it, lust a little, and cupidity, and a desire to fill the gap that Jamie's going had left in her life. That it had ended quickly was not remarkable; after all he had loved her more passionately and with greater tenderness, but nothing except pity and a sense of responsibility had survived even in his mind.

And thirdly had been the long ordeal, with its accompanying mental and physical changes of that unwanted pregnancy. The child, so obviously by timing and appearance, Jamie's child, had been born. That part of Rosetta's disorganised mind which had lain numb for so long had wakened again, the more vigorous for its months of inactivity. That was why she had not been able to look at the baby, or to see Kit himself. The baby was too poignant a reminder; and Kit had killed Jamie.

Was that what she was saying? Had she dissociated herself from her part in the affair? Yes, there were signs that pointed that way. Sending for her mother, for instance. It might look normal enough; a mother was the natural person to have with one at such a moment. But Rosetta had very carefully concealed her state from her mother; had sworn Maisie to silence; had written nothing but brief, unaffectionate notes to her mother at long intervals. Why send for her now? Because Mrs. Phillips, who had brought up her daughters strictly, who would have been shocked to know that Rosetta had spent one night with Kit alone at Heath End, represented Rosetta's conscience. To send for her mother and make a full confession would be her first action in this new phase of her bemused mind.

Oh yes, if you knew Rosetta and mingled your knowledge with a little observation, a little reason and a little imagination, it was not hard to understand what lay behind the Matron's silences and cautious words. Rosetta, deranged by fear and pain and hysteria, newly awakened conscience, latent passion for Jamie and remorse, had, no doubt, told a story well worth listening to.

A few days later came proof that somebody had taken the story seriously.

It was eleven o'clock in the morning when Kit was ploughing out sugar beet while Guess chased the rabbit scent in and out of the glossy turgid foliage. Suddenly she halted, stiffened, pricked her ears and then, with a glance from Kit to the house, stood barking loudly to arrest his attention.

There was no mistaking the big dark car; six of its kind had recently come into the possession of the Welford police. Under Kit's gaze it came to a gentle bouncing standstill on the cobbles, and from the driver's seat a uniformed policeman climbed and beat upon the house door. The sound came clearly through the still morning air.

The front of Kit's blue flannel shirt moved with the bumping of his heart; but, without hesitation as without haste he drove on to the end of the row; hitched the horse's nosebag into place and threw a sack over its back. Taking his own coat from the plough handles he began to push his arms into the sleeves as he walked towards the house. He was quite calm by the time he had reached the car.

He recognised Superintendent Maddox, and the young constable who had driven the car and knocked at the door; the third man was a stranger, young, blunt-featured, who managed, in some curious fashion to deprecate, almost to deny, his own physical presence. Introduced by Maddox in a voice which did not penetrate Kit's deafness the young man's shallow brown eyes slid over him, vague, uninterested, polite, and then resumed their look of contemplation upon some vision unseen by the others. The constable climbed back into the driving seat. Kit opened the kitchen door and invited the two men inside.

The Superintendent, square, cheerful and brisk, usually radiated an aura of commonsense and efficiency, but this morning it was faintly obscured by doubt and lack of ease. The young man, who was, Kit learned, Detective Gregory, looked once round the kitchen, and selected, with his unfailing instinct for comfort, Rosetta's abandoned chesterfield, upon which he seated himself with an air of retiring from the whole affair. Maddox stared for a moment at Kit, who, standing there in the middle of the clean bare kitchen, his head a little on one side with an inquiring and attentive look on his face, waited, as though to hear the reason for this disturbance in his morning's routine.

Maddox cleared his throat. "We've been asked to make some inquiries regarding a young man lately residing with you, Mr. Shelfanger. Your nephew, I understand."

"Jamie? In trouble, is he?" asked Kit.

"Not to our knowledge. The people in trouble are his wife and his mother-in-law who are very anxious to trace his whereabouts."

"Rosetta—that is Mrs. Liddell, his wife, knows as much about that matter as I do," said Kit gently.

"All the same, perhaps you wouldn't mind telling us your version . . . the time of his leaving, anything relevant that he may have said, and so on."

A sudden craving for tobacco came upon Kit. The words, "Do you mind if I smoke?" almost formed on his lips. Reflecting that he was in his own house, he did not utter them. Instead he took out his pipe, reached down his tobacco jar and filled and lighted his pipe as he said:

"I'm afraid I didn't take much notice because I didn't attach any importance to his going. It was either the last day of December or the last but one. He came in at his usual time—about six— and we had our meal. Then he went upstairs with his wife, and I reckon he told her then that he intended going to London. They had a bit of an argument. Either she didn't want to go, or else wanted to go with him. I didn't inquire. It'd be about seven, or a little after when he came down, in a bad temper and said that he would be too late to catch a train. I drove him as far as the main road where he said he could pick up a motorist and get a lift to Ipswich. That is all I know."

"It was a sudden decision?"

"So far as I know. He may have contemplated leaving. I don't think he had said anything."

"Did he take any luggage?"

"A small case. Most of his things, including some new clothes, are still upstairs. Not hearing from him we were unable to send them on."

"You weren't worried at not hearing?"

"I wasn't. Rosetta may have been. Though from what she said I gathered that the same thing had happened once or twice before. He was a peculiar, erratic kind of fellow."

"Would you say his absence preyed on his wife's mind?"

"It may have done. She said little about it."

"She decided to remain with you?"

"I think perhaps circumstances decided for her. From one or

two things I gathered I reckon that she was not over happy at home and rather shrank from letting her family know about Jamie's casual treatment of her. And since he was my nephew I had a certain feeling of responsibility towards her."

"Naturally. There's just one more thing. Have you, in the time that Mrs. Liddell spent with you, ever had cause to suspect that her mind was a little unstable?"

"Rosetta? Why, no. I never regarded her as particularly intelligent; but she was level-headed enough."

"Not a victim of delusions?"

"I should say not. Now, may I ask a question?"

"Certainly."

"What then, exactly, is the meaning of this visit and this sudden interest in Jamie?"

The Superintendent's uneasiness of manner increased visibly. It was with obvious relief that he turned towards the green chesterfield as the young man's quiet voice said distinctly:

"I think Mr. Shelfanger ought to know the allegation which has been made, sir."

"Well, then, to put it quite bluntly, Shelfanger, Mrs. Liddell declares that her husband never left this house; that you had a quarrel and knocked him down, that he struck his head and died of the blow and that you buried his body in a position which she described minutely."

"It seems I was wrong about the delusions!"

"We hope it is delusion." Maddox's manner had resumed its old imperturbable efficiency. He drew out and flattened on the table a map of Heath End.

Placing a blunt finger upon a patch washed in in pale brown colour, he said:

"That is known as the Top Field, I believe."

"That's right. And does the little red cross mark the supposed spot?"

Maddox nodded. Kit went to the dresser drawer, the one on the left which he kept for his orderly assortment of papers, and, with his customary deft gracelessness drew out his own map. Unfolding it he thrust it towards the Superintendent. In the Top

Field, in almost identical position, he had made a dot with the point of a pencil.

"D'you know what that marks?" he asked. "In sober fact, I mean."

"No."

"An interesting find, which I made early this year. Bones and bricks and oyster shells and a wonderful piece of coloured pavement. The remains of a Roman house, I should say."

"Is that so?" Gregory had left the chesterfield and now bent over the two maps. When he raised his head his eyes, alight with interest almost amounting to excitement, dwelt on Kit's face.

"*When* did you make this discovery, Mr. Shelfanger?"

"Oh, some time very early in the year. It might have been New Year's Day, even."

"Would you mind telling me how?"

"Well, once or twice, you know, ploughing, I turned out a coin just about there. But I'd never had time to investigate properly. I'd always promised myself that one day, in the winter slack I would. So this year I managed it; and I was lucky, I hit the right spot. Or maybe the whole field is the same."

"Are the remains visible now?" The young man's voice was eager.

"Oh no. I covered them again as soon as I had satisfied my curiosity."

"Oh dear. Why?"

"To plough over, I suppose. It's a good field and I didn't want a hole in the middle of it."

"Did you mention your find?"

"No. I didn't think Rosetta was interested in that kind of thing. And if I'd told anyone else there'd have been sightseers and arche . . . you know, those digging fellows, over-running the place."

"Mrs. Liddell was interested enough to watch your exertions from the landing window and to remember the spot pretty exactly," said Maddox sharply.

"So I reckon," said Kit ruminatively. "But how the two matters got mixed in her mind and why she waited until now to say such a thing passes my understanding. I suppose you gentlemen would like to dig there, just to be on the safe side."

"It might be as well," said Maddox, almost apologetically. And, "Oh, but, of course, we must," cried Gregory with enthusiasm, "I wouldn't miss such a chance for worlds."

"I'll send Blake back for the men and the shovels," said the Superintendent.

"And I'll get back to my sugar beet," said Kit. "If you really want to see that pavement go by my map; I paced it out to scale. But don't be influenced by me. I mean dig where you like. I'd wish that story exploded . . ."

Outside on the cobbles, after the constable had driven away, the Superintendent and the detective looked at one another.

"Well?" asked Maddox, with a note of satisfaction in his voice. "Do you see now what I meant?"

"About the unlikelihood? I see what led to your conclusions . . . but I don't agree with you. Though I admit that appearances . . . and that calm laconic manner . . . excellent cover. All the same I think the explanation is as simple as Mr. Shelfanger pretends he is."

"Simple enough. The girl is demented," said Maddox shortly. "I've known newly-calved heifers to go the same way."

Penn Gregory's eyes lost their inward-staring look and flashed round at his companion, full of delighted mirth. "Oh, you rural philosophers!" he cried on a gust of laughter. "How you love to reduce everything to farmyard terms."

"There are worse standards," said Maddox with unruffled amiability. "And if Kit Shelfanger turns out to be a murderer and a digger-in of corpses, there's a farmyard term that will describe me."

"'Call me horse,'" Gregory quoted, "And worse than that if the Top Field doesn't yield a crop of surprises."

But it was, in fact, Gregory who was surprised and Maddox who was triumphant when the men and the shovels had completed their activities in the Top Field. It was easy enough to see where the subsoil, turned by Kit's labours, differed from that in the rest of the field. And below lay the ancient pavement, ochre and green and blue, a great painted peacock with its tail outspread taking shape from the myriad pieces, cunningly laid. Penn Gregory stared at it, his academic and aesthetic nature satisfied by its beauty and associations, his professional mind dismally disappointed. It was plain that no clumsy shovel had pried up a section of that floor. No modern murderer had laid a secret beneath it, ignorantly reassembled the pieces, stamped them into place and gone away full of foolish and ill-founded confidence. And that was what he had expected. He had attributed Kit's calm of manner to the idea that the Roman pavement lay like a barrier between his secret and the world. But that pavement had not been disturbed in fifteen hundred years. The cement-like substance in which the pieces lay embedded had never been assaulted by any tool. Kit had, to all appearances, done exactly what he had said, dug until his own curiosity was satisfied and then filled in the hole.

"All right, say it," said Gregory to Maddox. "The girl is mad, or spiteful, and she saw Shelfanger digging and so invented the story. And you're a sound psychologist with 'He couldn't do it,' and I'm just a fool."

"I wouldn't go as far as that."

"As a conclusion it leaves so much unexplained. Why should no one remember giving the fellow a lift, for instance?"

"It's a long time ago, ten months. I'd distrust, personally, any motorist who could claim to remember one casual passenger at that distance. Or the motorist may be dead, or gone abroad. Come to that we have no grounds for saying that he did get a lift. Shelfanger said that he set off, walking, hoping to get one."

"That's true," Gregory admitted reluctantly.

"Moreover," said Maddox, taking advantage of his colleague's chastened mood, "I, for one, see no mystery in this Liddell's sudden bolting. *She'd* followed him down here and established herself against his wishes. He'd cheated Tillingham and must have realised that their association was bound to end soon; and he'd been playing around with Miss Winchely who admits that she didn't know he was married until she heard it from the wife herself. Wouldn't you feel like running, in the circumstances?"

"I might. But I doubt whether I'd make such a clean job of it. In fact I doubt whether anyone could. And there are three things that stick in my mind. The question of what the girl has to gain by spreading this story; the fact that in that first interview Shelfanger spoke of his nephew in the past tense—I noticed it specially, 'He *was* a peculiar, erratic kind of fellow,' he said; and the loose earth in that Top Field was in a hole just the size that a man would dig for a grave."

"Rubbish," said Maddox. "The girl is demented as I've said before. The tense means nothing. If I said tonight, 'Gregory was disappointed this afternoon,' would that imply that I had killed you? And the hole was twice as large as a grave at the top, and then got smaller. He got tired of digging, in my opinion."

Penn Gregory smiled. "He's innocent in your opinion, that's the trouble."

"The trouble. Why the trouble? Don't you think this is one occasion when a fair, open mind is an advantage?" For the first time in the course of their arguments on the subject, the Superintendent's voice betrayed a ruffling of temper. Penn, who liked and admired the older man, hastened to say:

"Oh well, let's hope you're right."

"You don't hope anything of the kind," retorted Maddox, refusing to be mollified. "What you hope is that something will happen to prove *you* right in the face of all evidence to the contrary."

"But naturally. Who wouldn't? And we might get something if we could get Shelfanger and the girl together. . . ."

"Well, there again," said Maddox triumphantly, "which of them behaves like a liar?"

"The girl," Penn admitted reluctantly. For Kit, with every appearance of calm, had professed himself willing to meet Rosetta and give her the lie to her face. It was Rosetta who had baulked the interview, pleading that she felt too ill, felt too frightened, could never set eyes on Kit again.

"Which," Maddox pointed out, "is highly peculiar considering that she had managed to live with him, apparently quite happily, from the night of the supposed crime until she went into the Home, nine months or thereabouts."

"Still, I'll suggest it again," said Penn.

But by that time Rosetta's mind had regained some of its balance. Already she was regretting the mad impulses which had inspired the denunciation. Mrs. Phillips, present in the flesh, inquisitive, censorious, declamatory, no longer seemed a desirable confidante. Her daughter's old fear of her scathing tongue revived and grew stronger every day. Suppose she should ever hear the truth about that long interlude between Jamie's death and the child's birth?

Urged by Penn Gregory to take part in a framed-up interview with Kit, Rosetta could only imagine—in terms of the motion picture version of reproach—the big man saying, "After all that we were to one another . . . after all that I did for you . . ." To her mother's questions, "Why have you held your tongue so long?" and "What on earth did you mean by staying with a man you knew to be a criminal?" she had been able to oppose the argument that she had been stunned, too miserable to think, too frightened to act. But if Kit now betrayed the secret of those few happy weeks, Rosetta knew only too well that no excuse would serve her. So she lay on her bed, limp, pale and pitiable, while her shrewdly self-preservative brain began to work again, and her answers to questions grew vaguer and more disjointed. "Did I say that? I don't remember." "Oh no. I must have been crazy." Finally, to Penn Gregory's inexpressible chagrin and Maddox's ill-concealed triumph, there came the day when even Mrs. Phillips said bluntly, "I think my daughter was out of her mind. I guess Jamie's desertion addled her brain so that when she was a little upset she was likely to say anything."

"So now we've got nothing," said Penn bitterly. "No corpse, no evidence, no story. I suppose this is where we go home."

"I, personally, have never given up an inquiry more gladly," said Maddox. "Poor old Shelfanger. I reckon somebody owes him an apology."

PART FIVE

KIT ALONE

He had not troubled to light the fire though the evening was chilly; desolate, as only a cold unlighted hearth can be, the stove stood empty, dull-barred beneath a smother of grey ash. At intervals the draught from the chimney sucked up a feathery spiral, held it suspended, let it fall again. Another draught from beneath the outer door lifted the corner of the rug. The old collie shivered, edged forward on her belly, seeking the evening comfort of the stove, and, not finding it, turned reproachful eyes on Kit.

The boldly-checked tablecloth, in need of washing, lay wrinkled upon the end of the table, and among the crumbs and the creases stood a number of used cups and plates, dumbly eloquent of the change that had come upon the master of the house. On the other end of the table were laid out, very neatly, a new pad of lined white writing paper, a packet of envelopes, a bottle of ink, a new steel-nibbed pen. A little apart from these was a bottle of whisky, practically full and a small cardboard box.

Moving in the fashion which looked so ungainly and was in truth so neat and dexterous, Kit brought a tumbler from the dresser, set it beside the bottle and seated himself in his chair. His face had a curious withdrawn look, and this, with the automatic manner in which he performed the next actions, gave the impression of sleep-walking, or of behaviour under hypnosis. The pallor that lay beneath the tan of his face gave it a dirty look against which his untanned forehead stood out bleached and bony.

He licked, with the gesture of a schoolboy anxious to postpone a task, the nib of the new pen. Then he dipped it in the ink and made a few experimental scrawls on the top sheet of the paper. As though satisfied by the feel of it, he laid it down carefully, reached for the bottle and poured out half a tumblerful of whisky.

He drank in the same abstracted way, without haste, without pleasure until the glass was empty. Then he took up the pen and the lines of firm, plain lettering strung out below his slowly-moving, clumsy-looking hand. It was evident that all that he wrote had been prepared beforehand; he never paused or looked up, even when figures mixed themselves with the words. Almost at the end of the page he signed his name and pushed the sheet away without reading it through. He knew that it was clear and plain. It might be disputed, but there was hardly anyone in a position to take action about it, and the sum involved was not large enough to invite attention. Rosetta had already had most of what he owned, she could take possession of the rest without much bother, he reckoned.

He poured another half tumblerful of whisky. Guess, on the cold hearth, stirred uneasily and sighed. Reminded of her existence Kit rose and opened the oven. A rabbit, neatly jointed, cooked and set in its own jelly, lay there in a brown pie-dish. He set it down before the dog, and she, forgetting her grievance over the lack of warmth, wagged her plume of tail and crouched over the dish. Kit watched her for a moment and some emotion seemed to be trying to break through the impassivity of his sleep-walker's face; then he turned and went back to the table. When the glass was almost empty again he set it down. Mustn't risk being the least bit muzzy; must keep very cool and clear-headed.

Once more the lines started to string out, going over on to a second page and a third, telling the story as Kit wished the world to know it, the story of Jamie's coming and going, the peculiar story, half truthful, half lying, yet seemingly frank enough.

". . . the girl had nothing to do with it. We had had violent quarrels before she came. We had rows about money. He took it from my room; he borrowed and didn't pay back. He took my car. He was impertinent when I complained. He pushed my dog around and made life unbearable. One day I lost my temper and hit him. . . ." On and on, the short, simple sentence, oddly convincing.

". . . the girl was right in most that she said, but she didn't know about the change of burial place. I couldn't spare time to dig under the pavement in Top Field. The body is in the Middle Meadow, the one where the water is. I make it by pacing twelve yards from the lower gate and twenty from the hedge. The ground was soft there and I got along well. I think that is all, except that the girl hadn't anything to do with it. She knew, of course, but I scared her into keeping her mouth shut."

That had better be signed too. He chose two envelopes and addressed them.

There, now they could stop their questions. And the puppy-profiled young man could turn to Maddox and say, "I told you so." Maddox would be sorry, but in future he wouldn't be above suspecting anyone and maybe that would be a good thing. Anyway, Kit hadn't to worry about Maddox's feelings, nor anyone else's. Other people's feelings, other people's thoughts, he hadn't to bother about them any more.

He realised that this, his final attempt at escape, was foolproof. Tomorrow, or the next day at latest, the crafty, worming, ferreting young man called Gregory would turn up at the farm, and he would be in time to see that Kit's animals did not suffer want. The mangers were filled and the water buckets wedged beyond all possibility of overturning. There remained only the dog, which, because of its age and its nature, would not happily endure a change of mastership.

He rose from the table and opened the little brown box. Within, neatly rowed, the agencies of death lay waiting.

The first shot shattered the quiet of the kitchen. Guess, with the last fragment of rabbit bone clenched in her blunt old teeth, heeled over on the hearth rug. Absolutely alone at last the master of Heath End laid his chin on the barrel, his finger on the trigger and set out on his last search for quietude.

F
LOF

Lofts, Norah

Requiem for idols

DATE			

C. l